A Cat on the Case

A Witch Cats of Cambridge Mystery

A Cat on the Case

A Witch Cats of Cambridge Mystery

Clea Simon

Copyright © 2021 by Clea Simon
Cover and jacket design by Mimi Bark

ISBN: 978-1-951709-26-6
eISBN: 978-1-951709-42-6
Library of Congress Control Number: available upon request

First hardcover edition January 2021 by Polis Books, LLC
44 Brookview Lane
Aberdeen, NJ 07747
www.PolisBooks.com

POLIS BOOKS

Witch Cats of Cambridge books by Clea Simon

A Spell of Murder
An Incantation of Cats
A Cat on the Case

For Jon

Chapter 1

"Oh, no, kitties! What did you do this time?"

Becca Colwin stood in the doorway, staring at the chaos within. Granted, her apartment had never been particularly neat. But even the most casual visitor would be taken aback by the potted plant that now lay prone on the floor, the sofa's pillows—all except one—scattered in its soil. The potpourri looked to be mixed in with that dirt, the small ceramic bowl that usually held it now face down and miraculously unbroken on the rug, next to a silver picture frame that had previously held pride of place on the bookshelf. Even the placemats had been pushed off the table, two of them draping the overturned chair.

Only the three cats who sat facing her seemed upright, clean, and in their customary positions as the welcoming committee at the door.

"Don't say anything," Laurel, the sleekest of the three, murmured to her sisters, too softly for human ears to hear. She lashed her café au lait tail for emphasis before coiling it once more around her dark chocolate booties. *"Let her take it all in."*

"But she's upset!" Clara, the youngest, longed to go to their human and twine around her calves, butting her parti-colored head—or at least her wet nose—against her in affection.

"She should be," Harriet, a marmalade longhair and the oldest and

largest of the three littermates, growled in response. *"She should be paying more attention."*

That growl caused Clara's black ear to twitch. A calico, whose orange and black markings met on top of her head, she had found that her black ear was slightly more sensitive to her big sisters' threats, while her orange one was better at picking up Becca's quietest musings. The harlequin-like markings might have been behind her siblings' usual taunt—*"Clara the Clown,"* they called her—but right now she felt like she'd risk any abuse to wipe that horrible shocked look off Becca's face.

"Maybe it's my fault." Becca dropped her bag and reached to pull off one heavy winter boot, hopping on one foot as she did so and veering dangerously to the left as the cats took cover. "No, it definitely is." Switching feet, she hopped to the right as she worked the other boot off, sending her pets scurrying again until, red-faced from the cold, she righted herself and walked into the living room to look around. Spying the frame, she picked that up first, dusting it off with a sigh. "I guess you're not used to being left alone."

Laurel shot a glance over at Clara, a feline smirk lighting up her blue eyes, as the youngest cat watched their person return the picture—a copy of a print—to the shelf and head into the kitchen. Clara didn't dare respond to Laurel's teasing glance. She might have her suspicions, but Laurel was her elder, if only by a few minutes, and, like Harriet, demanded respect.

"Don't worry, kitties. I'll feed you before I clean the rest of this up." Aware of the feline hierarchy, Becca first filled Harriet's special dish, covering its bright orange sunburst with the wet food she liked best. Laurel was next, getting her own small can of tuna and cheese. The slender sister might pretend she was a more finicky eater, but her sleek build was more a product of her Siamese heritage than of portion control. She buried her brown snout in the dish the moment it was on the mat.

"Are you feeling okay, Clara?" Clara's portion, in her own orange-and-black dish, was placed beside her sister's. Chicken bites, the kind with the good gravy, but the calico cat remained seated, looking up at her person with concern. "You should eat, you know, before Harriet finishes her dinner."

"*Unless you don't want it.*" Harriet's interjection, muffled as she lapped up her food, caused Clara's black ear to twitch again. Harriet much preferred her salmon to Clara's chicken, but she wasn't one to make fine distinctions. "*You are smaller, after all.*"

With a barely perceptible feline sigh, Clara turned to her own dinner. She was hungry, after the day's activities. More to the point, she didn't want Becca to worry.

Sure enough, once Becca saw the three eating, she fetched a dustpan and returned to the living room, not noticing when Clara left off and followed.

"*You didn't have to knock the picture over.*" Clara knew she shouldn't talk back to her sisters, but the thought eked out as she watched Becca sweep up the potting soil.

Laurel, who had come up alongside her, huffed with displeasure, a low barking sound that bordered on a growl. Too late, Clara remembered: the idea of a picture would mean nothing to Laurel. Both her sisters had difficulty understanding a static two-dimensional image. Even Clara had taken quite a while to learn to "see" such pictures as representative of three-dimensional objects, and of the three, she was the cat who spent the most time with their human, staring over her shoulder at such images for hours.

"*It shows another person,*" she tried to explain. "*It's important to her.*"

"*She hasn't picked it up in ages.*" Laurel dismissed Clara's concern and began to groom. "*And for the record, I know more about what that image of the old lady means than you.*"

9

Clara glanced over at her sister, intrigued, but in the name of peace decided to let her have the last word. Besides, what she said had some truth to it. Even now, once the framed print was back on its shelf, Becca had moved on without looking back. Instead, she focused on gathering the cushions that had been scattered throughout the room. Or appeared to focus. If she noticed that Harriet's special cushion— gold, with tassels—was the only throw pillow that remained on the sofa, she didn't comment. To Clara, the young woman with the sweet face seemed distracted, her thoughts as scattered as her brown curls. Clara didn't know if one of her sisters, Laurel most likely, had managed to block any more productive thoughts—say, about that pillow or what her cats had gotten up to—from her head. It might simply be that their human was tired from being at her new job all day.

Becca had only recently started work at Charm and Cherish, a New Age magic shop right in Cambridge's Central Square. She had been a regular even before she landed the position, and, with her own interest and experience in all things Wiccan, took her role as a sales clerk seriously. Her one concern about the job, Clara knew, had been about the long hours it kept her from her three cats, who had all come to expect twenty-four-hour service during Becca's months of unemployment.

This didn't bother Clara, who knew how much the job meant to Becca. That didn't mean she didn't have her own concerns about the little shop. Becca had landed the position following her involvement with the owner, the irritable Margaret Cross, in the wake of a complicated crime that had nearly taken her own life. For Harriet and Laurel, though, the time their person spent away amounted to a personal affront. That, Harriet had decreed, was reason enough to lay waste to the apartment—all of it except Harriet's special pillow, of course. But to Clara, who understood something of the conflict raging in Becca, such petty retribution was only adding to the problems facing the young woman who cared for them all.

"There we go." Becca, sounding relieved if still somewhat tired, returned the broom and dustpan to the closet. "Now what can I do to keep you three entertained tomorrow?"

"*Tomorrow?*" Laurel's voice rose in its distinctive Siamese howl. "*She's going out again tomorrow?*"

It was all Clara could do to keep her claws sheathed. She knew better than to escalate, though. Especially because she, like her sisters, could pick up the vibrations already coming down the hall. Harriet, always quite sure of her appeal, was already trotting, plumed tail high, toward the front door.

"*Tomorrow?*" Laurel, however, kept on wailing. Her sister was really overdoing it, Clara thought, but Becca, her pale face increasingly pinched, appeared to accept the scolding as her due and was in the process of scooping up the yowling beast when a sharp rap sounded on the door.

"Already?" Becca glanced up at the clock and then went to answer, still holding the cat. Laurel, her blue eyes crossed, appeared to be enjoying the treat, even as her legs stuck out from beneath Becca's arm in the most undignified manner.

"*You look like a chicken.*" Harriet appraised her sister with her own cool yellow eyes. "*That is not effective.*" Poised for compliments, if not treats, the big marmalade made a few quick adjustments to her thick ruff. Clara, suspecting an ongoing squabble, chose not to get involved. Better to focus on Becca, especially since she sensed that her person was in for a surprise. Sure enough, Becca's face fell and her grip on the cat in her arms tightened as she opened the door. Clara couldn't tell for sure whom she had expected, and Laurel wasn't sharing. But it certainly wasn't the tall, dark-haired woman standing in the doorway.

Becca recoiled as if startled. Peeking up from her feet, Clara saw why. With her full lips and wide-set eyes, the woman—a stranger to the calico—should have been pretty, her rosy sweater playing up the unseasonably warm glow of those prominent cheekbones. Despite the softness of that sweater, however, to the cat she appeared hard, as if the glossy fall of her chestnut hair had been lacquered into place. Or maybe, the cat decided, it was the sour look on her face.

"Hello." Becca, still clutching Laurel, put on her best smile. "May I help you?"

The woman must not have heard. "So that's the creature." Her dark eyes flicked from Becca down to the cat in her arms, her cool appraisal striking them both momentarily dumb.

"Excuse me?" Becca rallied first, although Laurel soon followed, wiggling to be let down, where she immediately began to groom.

"The animal that makes that ungodly racket." The newcomer pursed her dark red lips. "Your cat—oh my!"

That was to Harriet, who had seized the opportunity to rub against the visitor's legs, so sure of being admired and petted that she glanced up in surprise as the tall woman danced back, flicking a long white hair from her black wool trousers.

"Harriet." Becca, exasperated, looked like she was about to grab the stout feline, but Harriet had already sat back on her wide haunches, affronted eyes wide. "Yes, these are two of my cats. I'm Becca Colwin, and you are?"

"*Two* cats?" The visitor, a good head taller than Becca, peered over her shoulder into the apartment, perfect brows arching. "How many do you have here?"

"Three. They're littermates." Becca caught herself. Her tone grew frosty to match the stranger's, but, as always, she remained scrupulously polite. "I'm sorry, may I help you with something?"

"You've already done enough." The brunette drew back, her lips spreading in a closed-mouth smile as if she'd scored a triumph. "I knew there was something going on here, from the ruckus and, frankly, the

12

smell." She wrinkled her pert nose up in disgust, seemingly unaware of how this accentuated the lines around her mouth. "Now that I know there's an animal control issue here, I can go directly to the authorities."

"What are you talking about?" Very few things could aggravate Becca like an insult to her pets. "My cats are healthy and well cared for. I've never had any complaints."

The brunette showed her teeth. "That was clearly before the building began to transition, I'm sure. Not that, as a renter, you'd understand." Those teeth, Clara thought, looked ready to bite. "Now that I own the unit beneath yours, I can assure you, I will not put up with this crazy cat lady nonsense."

With that, she turned on her heel and stepped back out into the hall, leaving Becca gasping for a response. Clara looked around for her sisters. Surely, such an assault merited a counterattack. Becca seemed to think so too, following her out the door. But whatever rebuttal Becca had been considering seemed to evaporate just as quickly. A tall, lean man was leaning out of the apartment next door. Clad in a Hempfest T-shirt and jeans despite the January cold, his shaggy blond mop fell free to expose eyes wide behind wire-rimmed glasses, a wispy goatee framing a surprised "oh" of a mouth.

Seeing her startled neighbor, Becca swallowed whatever retort she had been planning, smiling at him instead in wordless apology. Clara could almost feel her embarrassment. That woman had been scolding Becca as if she'd jumped up on the counter, all because of Clara and her sisters. Although the little cat had her doubts about how much noise her sisters could make, none of that was Becca's fault. But the man who now stared, wide-eyed, at Becca hadn't had a chance yet to learn what a wonderful person she truly was.

They'd all heard the movers, only a few weeks before, thumping and cursing as they carried that sleek leather sofa and all those boxes up the stairs. But, busy with her new job, Becca hadn't had a chance to pop over and properly introduce herself to her new neighbor, the young tech investor who'd bought grumpy Tony's place. It was Tony who'd told her that the buyer was a venture capitalist, or, as he called it, an "adventure capitalist." Becca's longtime neighbor had been grumbling about "some kid with a so-called career," although as a tenant he'd had the option of buying the apartment where he'd lived for longer than Becca knew, a two-bedroom with a view of the street and a bigger-than-average fire escape.

If Tony hadn't said anything, Becca might have thought the newcomer a displaced surfer boy, with that shaggy hair and his torn jeans. As it was, she seemed pleasantly surprised, her flush of embarrassment fading as her smile relaxed into something real. But as she opened her mouth to comment—a greeting, perhaps, or a quip about surfing on the Charles—the woman from downstairs turned, as if to deliver one last parting shot, and the shaggy blond man ducked back in, like a frightened turtle, closing the door behind him and leaving Becca alone with the sound of heels click-clicking down the stairs.

Chapter 2

When the doorbell rang not ten minutes later, Becca flinched. Laurel had already taken to her usual safe place on top of the bookshelf, and Harriet had not emerged from the bedroom, where she had retreated in the wake of the previous visitor's insult. But Clara, who had remained staunchly by her person's side, could have told Becca that she needn't have worried. Although her cats might not have liked the idea, these new visitors would please Becca. Her so-called coven was assembling, and the first of the would-be witches was at the door.

"Hey, Marcia." Becca's shoulders sagged with relief when she saw her friend. "Come in out of the cold. I mean, blessed be."

"Blessed be." The shorter woman pulled Becca into a hug, not noticing that her friend snuck a peek over her shoulder and down the hall. Harriet, meanwhile, had emerged.

"Have they served the cookies yet?" The bigger cat nudged her little sister aside.

"Look, your cats are talking to each other." Marcia pointed as she unzipped her coat. Bundled into a puffy purple parka with a knit mohair cap of the same shade pulled low over her dark bob, she looked a bit like an upholstered grape. "Hey, who's selling?"

"Excuse me?" Becca closed the door, turning once more toward her friend. "Selling what?"

"The sign out front." Marcia pulled the hat off next and bent to stroke Harriet's broad back, oblivious to how the cat's golden eyes narrowed as they focused on her dangling cap. "Someone in the building is selling their unit."

"Not someone. Something." Becca scooped up the big marmalade before the claws in her mitt-like paw could snag the soft purple wool. "The management company is selling. I've got to find a new apartment."

"No!" Marcia stood, aghast. "They can't kick you out, can they?"

Becca shrugged and held the fluffy feline closer. "Not exactly. But they're breaking up the building, selling it off as condos. If someone buys my unit as an investment, the new owner could keep renting to me—if he or she wants to. And if the condo association says it's okay. Some of these condo buildings don't allow renters at all."

"You don't get any say?" Marcia sounded suitably horrified.

"I get first dibs on buying it. But I can't afford a place like this." Becca looked around, as if already saying goodbye. Harriet, aware that this conversation wasn't leading to food, squirmed to be put down.

"I'm sorry, Becca." Marcia's natural ebullience faded as she hung her coat on the coat tree. "Is the slick guy next door one of the new owners?"

"Slick?" Becca gave her friend a quizzical look, even as a light tap announced another visitor. "You saw him?"

"He was coming down the hall as I came up. Gave me a look." She frowned, miming a glower that rumpled her cold-reddened face.

"Oh my, if he's talking with the woman downstairs…" Becca's fretful frown faded as she opened the door to a willowy woman whose layers made her appear almost bulky. "Hey, Ande. Blessed be!"

"Merry meet, Becca." With the grace of a model, rather than the accountant she was, the new arrival glided into the apartment, shedding her long wool coat, scarf, and gloves in one fluid motion. Pulling a felt cap off her short, tight curls, she bent to kiss Becca's cheek.

"You're half frozen." Becca took her friend's garments. "I was just about to make the tea."

"I'll get it." Ande hurried toward the kitchen. "I need the warmth. It's nice and toasty in here."

"We'll see how long that lasts." Becca turned to hang the coat, draping the scarf over it. "I think they want me out."

Ande leaned back out, kettle in hand, a puzzled frown creasing her brow.

"The building's going condo." Marcia looked up from petting Harriet. "Becca might have to move."

"Don't you have the option of buying?"

Becca shook her head. "I can't even talk about it."

"We should, though." Ande looked down at the kettle as if it held the answers then returned to her task. "I can run the numbers."

"We'll do a circle too," Marcia called after her. "Generate some good will."

"*Generate some cookies would be more like it,*" Harriet said, waiting till the feet were safely past before following. Even Laurel had climbed down from her perch by then. Although Becca's original group of Wiccan devotees had shrunk over the last few months, the ritual remained the same. The three would talk and then try their hand at various incantations, oblivious to the fact that their human mouths were unable to form the necessary sounds for any spell. Then, to close, they'd join hands and close their eyes to make the circle Marcia had mentioned. That, as the cats knew, was often their best opportunity for stealing cookies off the plate, though in truth the soft-hearted Marcia was prone to sneaking broken pieces to Harriet, having a fondness for the big orange-and-white cat.

She looked down at Harriet now, and for a moment, Clara wondered if the two were having a silent conversation. Silent, that is, until Harriet coughed.

"Uh-oh," Marcia called. "Becca, is your cat okay?"

"Maybe a hairball?" Ande emerged with three mugs, which she set on the table.

"I don't know, Becca." Marcia, who had no felines of her own, appeared unduly concerned. "You think you should call your vet?"

"Marcia, no." Becca was blushing. "It's nothing."

"Wait, what am I missing?" Ande looked from one woman to the other.

"The new vet at Cambridge Cat is something of a hero." Marcia followed the tall woman back into the kitchen. "He and Becca met last fall, and I gather they have quite the rapport."

"He likes my cats." Becca said with an emphasis that had her two friends exchanging a smile, even as Ande counted spoons of mint into the pot. "And I'm sure it's nothing. Harriet does have a lot of fur."

"*He admired my lush coat.*" Harriet, eagerly awaiting the cookies, was not immune to a compliment. "*A man of taste.*"

"*Indeed,*" Laurel purred, peering up at Ande as she rubbed against her fleece-covered shins. With the black leggings and matching socks, the accountant's coloring almost resembled the sealpoint's, which Laurel understood as a compliment. "*And Becca should remember it's always good to have options.*" But if she wanted to keep the conversation about the new vet going, she was out of luck. Becca's friends were more attuned to her mood than her cats—her two older cats, anyway—and had already moved the conversation, along with the tea, to their weekly ritual.

With no new magic to report—"But we did get some interesting new books in," Becca chimed in—that meant it was time for the circle.

"Maybe we should call it a triangle," Marcia joked as the three leaned over the table to join hands.

"We're still acknowledging the four points of the compass and the elements," their host pointed out.

"And a circle gives us equality too," Ande added, with a meaningful glance at the gold ring on Marcia's left hand. The short Sox fan had married her longtime partner Luz the previous spring. "No sides, no race or gender distinctions."

"Fair enough." Marcia agreed, squeezing her friends' hands. The three women closed their eyes then and began to chant.

This was the "gathering of energy," as Becca had called it when she had tried to explain the weekly gatherings to Maddy, her skeptical best friend. A colleague from her days as a researcher, Maddy's open, round face had twisted into a dubious frown at that, and Becca had tried another tack, talking about ecology rather than mysticism, describing the Wiccan focus on balance and nature. That was embodied by Mother Earth, she had explained—although as the chanting continued, invoking the ultimate goddess, Harriet, listening from her pillow, began to purr, her body vibrating in response to what she considered her due.

"Has anybody heard from Larissa?" After a moment of silence, Ande looked around at the half-empty table. Larissa, one of the coven's original witches, hadn't shown up at the weekly meetings for months now, but Becca always made a point of inviting her.

"I think she's in Boca for the winter. With Trent," Becca added. The romance between the older witch and her protégé had outlasted anyone's expectations. "She says they might attend again when the weather warms up, but I'm not holding my breath."

"Good riddance." Marcia held a grudge. "Sorry," she added, without conviction, as Becca suppressed a smile. It was hard at times to follow the Wiccan rule of only sending out positive energy.

"Maybe we should make sure she—they—know they're still welcome." Ande tilted her head, her voice growing thoughtful. "Larissa has money, Becca. And she owes you."

"No." Becca shook the idea off. "I'm sorry. She's welcome, of course she is, but I don't want charity, and I certainly don't want to be in her debt. Look how she treats Trent."

Neither of the other witches had an answer to that. Although Trent had been an original member of the coven, his lover acted as if he were more a pet than a peer.

"Besides," Becca continued, determined to find a positive spin. "I like that it's the three of us. We actually get along."

"If we were a bigger coven, we might have more power," Ande tried again. "There were seven of when you managed your successful summoning."

Clara looked up in alarm. That summoning, which had produced the tasseled pillow, had been Harriet's work. It had been purely bad timing that the big marmalade had conjured the cushion for her own comfort just as Becca was trying out a spell.

But Becca only laughed. "Honestly, Ande? I don't know what was up with that. It was just one spell, that one time. These days, I'm not even sure I have any power. It all just seems kind of hopeless."

"Enough," Marcia spoke up. "Becca's right, Ande, but not just because we get along. Three is a powerful number. Think about *Macbeth*, and look at, well, look at your cats."

The young women turned to stare, startling the felines. Harriet, perched on the back of Becca's big armchair, froze, caught just as she had been about to attempt a leap to the tabletop. Laurel, bathing, looked up, wide-eyed, one brown paw raised in midair, while Clara, who had begun to relax, simply sat there, willing her anxious tail not to lash.

"Do they know? I think they know." Harriet's urgency carried to her sisters, though whether she was anxious or proud, Clara couldn't tell. *"If they didn't gather to pay homage to us, then why the cookies?"*

"Hush!" Laurel lowered her leg, ever so slowly. *"They can't know. At least, I don't think they can."*

"I don't think so either." Clara blinked at her person, willing Becca

20

to understand the love and loyalty this implied. *"But I'm not sure."* The calico had had some odd experiences recently, the kind that almost made her doubt the feline prerogative in all matters of magic. She was on the verge of explaining these, when Marcia burst out laughing.

"Dear Goddess," she said, wiping tears from her eyes. "Look at those three! It's almost like they know what we're saying. But I'm telling you, Becca, something is going to come through for you. I feel it."

Ande jumped in before their host could comment. "What's going to happen is some good financial planning," she said. "But for now, is there any more of that tea?"

By the time her friends left, Becca sounded relaxed and happy. Almost, Clara thought, as if her fur had been stroked smooth by a loving hand.

It couldn't last, and as Clara watched her person bid her friends farewell, she felt her heart sink. While Harriet and, truth be told, Laurel busied themselves hoovering up crumbs, Clara had seen the signs.

"Bye!" Marcia had called as she followed Ande down the stairs. And although the short brunette's sneakers, her year-round footwear, didn't make much sound on the steps—for a human, anyway—Clara could feel as much as see how Becca winced. The way she ducked back inside once her friends had passed out of sight made her loyal pet hang her head. Becca deserved better.

An hour later, no angry neighbor had come pounding on the door. But Becca couldn't seem to relax. Instead of cuddling on the sofa surrounded by her cats, or in bed as she should be if the day had been as tiring as her person's deep sighs intimated, Becca was sitting hunched over the table once again.

Silent as a cat can be, Clara watched her from a perch on the back of the room's big, stuffed chair. Despite the evening's activities, her person had none of the magic books open, not even the latest that she'd brought home from the shop. Instead, she had a small ledger on which she had scrawled symbols that may as well have been ancient Egyptian, for all her youngest pet could read them. Except that, of course, the little calico would have had a fighting chance with hieroglyphics. And Becca wouldn't have her hands knotted in her own short, curly hair. Although she was staring with brown eyes wide open, Becca doubted she saw anything beyond those scribbles—not her devoted pet on her perch, nor the squat candle before her.

"If I could buy this unit…" Her words made little sense to the calico, who jumped to the tabletop to better assess the situation. Her person was tense, and so proceeding silently to her side, Clara leaned against her arm, adding the low vibration of a purr in her bid to will away the tension. Physical contact always aided the connection, but Becca didn't seem to notice. "It's not like I can afford to move," she said.

Clara closed her eyes, concentrating on her person, only to feel Becca shift away as she reached for that candle. Set on a brass base, it was a heavy thing, smelling pleasantly of beeswax, so honey sweet that Harriet had licked it when Becca brought it home from Charm and Cherish a few weeks before. Clara remembered her sister recoiling at the waxy taste, and the cats had left it alone after that. That coven had lit it earlier that night, cooing over its aroma, and what Ande had called its essence.

"Maybe I should have brought her a welcome gift?" Becca stared at the candle. "Maybe I shouldn't have kept this for myself?"

The candle, Clara knew, had never been meant for the foul-tempered woman downstairs. It had originally been intended as a housewarming present for the man next door, and Clara knew Becca well enough to sense that this was the at the root of her person's unease. As a gift, the slight splurge had seemed justified, as a personal indulgence, less so. If only the new neighbor hadn't been so elusive.

Despite Laurel's silent urging, Becca hadn't been spying out the new neighbor as a potential boyfriend. She was still cautious after a bad breakup the year before and a series of near disastrous flirtations. Although she did pink up at any mention of the cat hospital's new feline specialist, Clara believed her person was being wise. Now that the neighbor had a face, the sleek Siamese was sure to start urging Becca to drop by, using her powers of suggestion to encourage a flirtation with the newcomer, but the initial impulse had simply been friendly. Neighborly, in the best sense. For Becca, whose Wiccan understanding of balance meshed well with a basic sense of fair play, a candle like this one would have been a way of sweetening a stranger's new home.

If only he had appeared a little sooner. Over the course of a week, Becca and her cats had watched with interest as movers had brought in furniture and boxes labeled "kitchen" and "bath." Not long after that, Becca had knocked on the door. And knocked again, trying at different times of the day three days running, before giving up. That brief sighting today was the most she had seen of the man next door since he'd taken over the unit from Tony Rogers four weeks earlier. "Maybe I shouldn't have given up."

"What's she doing?" Laurel landed beside her soundlessly. *"Is she going to light that stinky thing again?"*

When Laurel sniffed, revealing her fangs, she looked a little like a bat, Clara thought. Now did not seem the time to mention this.

"I think she's regretting keeping it." Clara was parroting words she'd heard Becca use, but she managed to signal the feelings of sadness tinged with guilt.

"I don't blame her." Laurel drew her apple-shaped head into her ruff, which gave her a bit of a double chin. *"It stinks."*

Clara knew better than to comment, but her sister must have picked up the vibrations of her emotion. Or simply observed her whiskers twitching. *"What?"*

"She's thinking of visiting the stranger next door." Clara felt that was

23

likely. At any rate, it served to distract Laurel.

"*Good!*" The Siamese closed her eyes in satisfaction. "*A man, so close by, and with whiskers, too.*"

Clara didn't argue. Instead, she did the little shimmy cats do when they're about to jump and, shading herself into invisibility, followed Becca into the hall.

"Hello?" Becca knocked, leaning in to address the door. "Becca from unit six here. Do you have a moment?"

Sitting at her feet, Clara could hear the tightness in Becca's voice. Between that and the way she bit down on her lower lip as she waited in silence for a response, she could tell her person was nervous. Partly, she knew, that was because she had shown up empty-handed. Partly, Clara suspected, that was because the new neighbor hadn't bothered to say hi.

"We met on the landing earlier." Clara could hear the movement within, but Becca appeared about to give up when the latch clicked and the door opened, revealing the same sandy hair that had poked out before. Seeing Becca, he opened the door wider and blinked down at her, eyes wide behind those big lenses. Easily a head taller than Becca, the slim man was still casually dressed, this time in an MIT sweatshirt. Although the wispy goatee had initially made him look younger, Becca figured him for his late twenties.

"Hi." Becca smiled up at him. "I wanted to introduce myself properly. I'm Becca Colwin. I live next door." She laughed, a bit awkwardly. "I guess that's obvious. You must be the new owner?"

"Yes. Yes, that's me," he said, sounding distracted. His gray eyes, owl-round behind the glasses, looked past Becca to peer down the hall. "That other woman…"

"She's gone." Becca dropped into a conspiratorial whisper. "I think she just wanted to vent. At least, I hope so."

The neighbor didn't respond. From the way he kept staring past

24

her, Becca wondered if he'd had his own run-in with the flashy brunette.

"She was complaining about my cats." She looked up at the tall man, noting his pursed mouth, the anxious blinking, and fear crept into her own voice. "You don't mind them. Do you?"

"Your cats?" He looked down then, as if seeing her for the first time, and a broad grin lit up his face, taking years off it. "Why would I? This is a pet-friendly building, isn't it?"

"It always has been." Becca's grin wavered a bit. "I mean, as an owner you make your own rules, but the previous tenant in your unit, Tony, had a retriever."

"Never met him." He shrugged, looking even more boyish. "I'm sorry. I'm not around much. I've been letting some friends stay here."

"Oh, that's fine. I'm just glad we met." Becca's relief was palpable. "And that my pets haven't bothered you, or your friends."

"Not at all." His hand still on the doorframe, he stepped back. "Now, if you'll excuse me."

"Of course. Bye." But the door had already closed.

Laurel and Harriet were waiting inside the apartment as Becca let herself—and Clara—back in. But despite their twining around her ankles, she barely seemed to aware of them.

"*I knew it!*" Laurel was practically purring as she sniffed Becca's jeans for clues. "*He's tall and right next door.*"

"*That could work.*" Harriet sat and began to wash. "*Becca would still be able to spend most of her time with us.*"

"*Our Becca deserves better.*" Clara's interjection earned a wide-eyed stare from her sisters. "*I mean, she deserves someone who cares—who pursues her. Besides, that's not what she was thinking about.*" Clara cast about for a way to explain their predicament to her sisters. Neither was likely to understand how their presence could be a negative. Finally, she settled on what seemed like a simple answer. "*He's not interested.*"

"*You shouldn't have let her go over there looking like that.*" Laurel

25

sniffed. She might be the sister who had the most power inserting suggestions into Becca's mind, but Clara was the one who accompanied her everywhere, which made the little calico easy to blame. *"Did she note how that other girl was dressed? Becca would look great in a sweater like that, all that soft wool. In fact, I think I'll—"*

"No, please, Laurel." Clara turned toward her older sister with a plaintive mew. Laurel could easily implant thoughts of fashion and makeup, and maybe that would distract Becca. But Clara had the impression that her person needed to think. She had been drawn to the new neighbor. That much was obvious. But her feelings were more complicated, and more than romance was on her mind.

"Maybe I should have stayed in school," Becca was saying, as she pecked away at her computer. "He can't be that much older than I am, and he's bought that place."

"See?" Laurel purred. *"He's got money, too!"*

Clara wasn't in the mood to argue. *"Maybe you could suggest to that other woman that she should stay away?"*

"Nonsense." Laurel extended one hind leg balletically and began to give her toes a thorough bath. *"Becca needs to spend more time with women like that. You don't have to trust someone to learn from them."*

"But if she can't trust a person, why should she get close to her?" As soon as the question was formed, Clara regretted it. There was no reasoning with Laurel when she was in certain moods, but at least she was loyal. And so Clara hunkered down by Becca's elbow and watched as images of buildings with strange symbols attached began to appear. As a cat, Clara might not have a fine grasp on real estate, but she knew one thing. Her person needed to find a place to live, even more than she needed male companionship, and although Clara was a cat of many powers, both of these were beyond her capabilities. If she couldn't offer any actual help, though, at least she could provide company, a soft, comforting presence in an increasingly difficult world.

Chapter 3

"Do we have any spells for ridding a home of an, uh, negative influence?"

The string of brass bells that hung from the little shop's front door were still jangling as Becca burst into Charm and Cherish the next morning, still red-faced from the cold. The January day had broken bright and clear, the sky so blue it made the looming forecast of snow laughable. Cheered, perhaps, by the winter sun, Becca served the cats' breakfast with less than her usual ceremony and had almost jogged to the store, the carefully shaded Clara trotting at her heels. Although she lacked Laurel's facility, the calico was learning to listen to her person's thoughts, and so was able to pick up on her eagerness to peruse the store's well-stocked bookshelves. But seeing Elizabeth, the owner's older sister, there ahead of her, she changed tactics. Clara could feel, as well as hear, the shift as she addressed the older woman, who despite being well into her seventies, was sitting cross-legged on the floor. "You know, something that could do a purge?"

"Good morning to you too." The gray-haired woman looked up from the opened cardboard box before her, her bushy eyebrows rising comically. Rising without apparent effort to her considerable height, which was increased by a halo of gray hair as wild as Laurel's was smooth, she examined Becca over a nose best described as Roman. Only then, after brushing down the purple corduroy tunic she wore over green velour pants, did she speak again. "You're in early."

"I know," Becca acknowledged, looking down sheepishly. "I didn't sleep well. I'm sorry if I was brusque, but I've got a problem."

"And you're wondering if the craft can help you get rid of it." For all her outlandish attire, the older woman had a way of focusing that made Becca take her seriously. Clara, too, if her person had only known it.

"Yes." Clara waited for her person to elaborate, looking from one human to the other, but Becca said no more. She was being careful, Clara sensed, for which her pet was grateful. Shaded as she was, Clara knew neither woman could see her, exactly, but Becca had been growing increasingly sensitive to her cats in recent months, and the older woman had made several uncanny remarks in the past, which hinted that she might have some awareness of the little calico's powers.

Clara needn't have worried. This morning, Elizabeth had eyes only for Becca.

"You want to do someone harm?" Although she spoke so softly the little cat could barely hear her, there was an edge to the older woman's voice Clara couldn't identify.

"I've thought about it." Becca seemed to be speaking to the box on the floor. "I don't know what else to do."

"There's always another option," said the older woman, hefting the box to her hip as she turned to go. "Let me look into dispelling negative energy, for starters. I've got some books upstairs. And you, my dear, should open the shop."

Becca nodded, as if released from an examination, and got to work, starting with a quick check of the Charm and Cherish's more in-demand stock. After topping off the pyramids of incense—the patchouli always went fast—she replenished the colorful polished stones for offer in their shallow brass bowl by the register. Pouring them out from the box they kept in the back, she ran her hands through the supply, fishing out a few of the brighter ones, a rose quartz and a tiger eye, to top off the mix, making sure that the card listing their qualities—"jade for healing, quartz for clarity"—was in place.

As she paused to admire her work, Clara jumped soundlessly up on the counter to sniff at the stones, enjoying the mellow glow that came off the cinnabar and the garnet, even on such a frosty day. Becca, she knew, was growing skeptical about the craft, as the other woman had called it, as the months passed. She hadn't witnessed any magic—and certainly not done any—since the summer, and her pet could see how she considered the stones with longing.

"Even if they're just pretty, that's something," she said softly as she reached out to touch a glittering pyrite so full of energy Clara could feel the tingle in her skin. The sensation added to her decidedly un-feline jumble of emotions. Perhaps it was better if Becca gave up on the idea of magic. That would make it easier for Clara and her sisters to look after her as they should. But Becca would miss it, her pet knew, particularly the weekly meetings with her friends. Besides, Becca was special. Clara was convinced. Surely, her person could sense power, even if it was simply gemstone magic.

The power of the stones was fairly straightforward. The most basic humans could sense their appeal, she knew. After all, almost every customer who made it up to the register picked up at least one, and many of them ended up purchasing the smooth round stones. Over the four months since Charm and Cherish had been open, Becca had brought home six. Of course, her pets had knocked them off the shelf where she'd arranged them, and although Becca had only found two, Clara could have told her that the other two—a golden topaz and violet amethyst—were, in fact, now properly placed to provide maximum protection: one under the bookshelf, the other tucked beneath the rug.

Becca must have had some inkling of this. As she watered the plants in the front window, Clara realized that her person was thinking of those missing stones—and wondering if their disappearance just might be confirmation of their powers. For a moment, the little cat held her breath, waiting to see what would happen. Only just then her person caught sight of the clock behind the counter. All thoughts of magic were quashed as she did a quick check to see that she had small bills in the register—some people still liked to pay in cash—and Becca was ready. Ten on the dot. She turned the *Closed* sign over to *Open*, unlocked the front door, and returned to her station behind the counter, waiting for her day to begin.

One hour later, and she had nearly finished the third chapter in *Contemporary Witchcraft*. This was the second book she'd read while on duty. This wasn't slacking off, she had explained to Margaret, the store's owner, only a week before. Knowing the stock made her a better salesclerk, able to provide informed recommendations not only about the store's literary offerings but about the craft itself. In truth, Clara knew, Becca was looking for answers to her questions about what she considered her own powers.

Poor Becca. Like most cats, Clara considered books suitable for sitting on at best. But as Becca tried to work out the puzzle of her own situation, she had ended up reading passages aloud, and while Clara might not have any insight into the scrawl and scratching that made up human writing, she could easily interpret her person's thoughts once she voiced them aloud.

"I still don't understand." Becca stared down at the page, as if the black-and-white symbols could give her an answer. "I made that pillow appear out of nowhere. But since then…"

While Clara was grateful that her person had given up the idea of using magic against that nasty neighbor—at least for now—her relief was short-lived. Becca might be distracted, but the questions she now repeated were so familiar, her tone so wistful and confused, that her pet longed to rub up against her person. It would be a poor consolation, she knew. But while Laurel, with her powers of suggestion, might be able to redirect Becca's curiosity, Clara had no way to direct her person into a more profitable train of thought.

If only she could implant the truth in Becca's mind—that she had nothing to do with that one act of magic, so many months ago now, that had started Becca on her current path. True, Becca was already interested in witchcraft by then, her curiosity piqued by the discovery of an ancestor in an old and timeworn chronicle. But Harriet's shortsighted selfishness—summoning that tasseled cushion from the ether—had come at the most inopportune moment.

If only Harriet had been a little more careful, or less lazy, their person would not have gotten the idea that she had magical powers. That would not only have relieved her of her current frustration, Clara knew, it would have cleared the way for her cats to actually take care of her, as all the best cats do.

As it was, all Clara could do was watch as Becca slumped back against the wall behind the counter, book in hand, looking for answers she wouldn't find. Just as Clara was considering a distraction—maybe knocking over that candle would rouse her person—she picked up a change in the air. Not a scent, exactly. More of a vibration. Still, it sent the cat scurrying moments before the bells over the shop's front door alerted Becca as well.

"Welcome to Charm and Cherish." Becca's voice lifted with her smile as she greeted a young woman with dark shoulder-length hair and a pale heart-shaped face that appeared free of makeup. "Feel free to browse, but if I can help you find anything, please let me know."

"Thank you." The newcomer, who appeared to be Becca's age or possibly a little younger, returned her smile, a curious lilt to her words, but then she turned away. Her tan duffle coat and black tam, slightly old-fashioned, added to the hint of an accent to suggest she wasn't a local. An exchange student, perhaps, an impression made stronger by the violin case that hung over her shoulder. Clearly that case was made for traveling. Cambridge was full of students and tourists, and like any city attracted a cosmopolitan crowd. Could this woman be enrolled at one of the area music schools? Auditioning for the symphony perhaps? Although Becca found herself musing about the day's only customer—and Clara, picking up on the general direction of these thoughts, stood on her hind quarters to sniff at the instrument case with care—there was little else revealing anything about the new arrival. In fact, after a few minutes, Becca returned to her book, and Clara found herself distracted by a bug that had was climbing up the front window as if eager to return to the cold outside.

"Excuse me?" The visitor's accent softened the X to almost sound like the S. Becca looked up with a smile, to see the newcomer leaning over the counter. Although she couldn't have explained how exactly, Clara had the feeling that she'd been standing there for a few moments already, gathering the nerve to speak. "Can you tell me about this?"

She extended her hand, holding a small slip of paper, and Becca's polite smile widened into a grin.

"You're looking for a detective?" Becca answered the question with one of her own, which Clara heard her with a sinking feeling. Just when she was hoping that her person had given up on this. Seeing the other woman's hesitation, Becca caught herself. "I mean, you're interested in hiring a witch detective?"

"Well, I am not sure." The young woman searched Becca's face, her large, dark eyes ringed with fatigue. "I am hoping someone can help me, but I don't know..."

Her voice, already quiet, trailed off. Becca reached across the counter to lay her hand on the other woman's.

"I'm sorry," she said, matching her tone to the customer's. "I didn't mean to pry. I'm the witch detective, you see. And I have had some success in helping people solve some mysteries—or at least sort out some things in their lives."

She paused and bit her lip. A sure sign, Clara knew, that she was thinking something over.

"In all honesty, I'm not exactly sure if I have any powers. You know, magical ones." Becca leaned in, as she met the other woman's eyes. "But I have had a summoning spell work, and I do think that I've got some sensitivities that help me uncover that which is hidden."

The visitor took this all in and then nodded, her face thoughtful. "That might be what I need."

"Wonderful!" Becca brightened visibly and, despite her misgivings, Clara felt her own whiskers perk up. "Would you like to make an appointment? Of course, we could speak now." Her voice dropped down again. "I doubt we'll be disturbed."

The customer flashed a smile, even as her dark eyes darted once more toward the front of the store. "I am being silly, I know I am," she said, her phrasing oddly formal. "But I was coming from the conservatory, and I saw this shop…"

"I think you came in for a reason." Becca nodded as she spoke. "And, honestly? I'm grateful for the interruption. It's been so slow, I'm beginning to think nobody out there is interested in magic of any sort."

With a sigh, Becca turned to look out the window, and the newcomer followed her gaze through the store's colorful front window. Painted with bright zodiac signs and other mystical symbols, it offered a vibrant frame for the day outside. At some point in the morning, clouds had begun to roll in, crowding into the brilliant blue sky of the morning. They were carried along by a brisk wind off the river that appeared to be hurrying the pedestrians along as well. Bundled up, a variety of city types scurried by, oblivious of the shelter Charm and Cherish could provide. Following Becca's gaze, Clara watched them bending into that wind, tuned into their own thoughts, if not their ear buds. The only exception—a harried-looking young mother struggling to convince the child in her stroller that mittens needed to say on—was nearly run over by a wiry man in a leather jacket walking quickly by. Her squawk was audible, even inside the store, but the dance as the man backed up—hands raised in apology or excuse—was over so quickly the cat didn't have a chance to catch their scent.

"See?" Becca turned back to the other woman. "They're in their own worlds."

But something had changed for her potential client. Her smile was gone, replaced by an open-mouthed gasp.

"Are you all right?" Becca started toward the end of the counter, the better to aid the visitor if she had taken ill.

"No, no, I am fine." The other woman turned her wide eyes on Becca, raising her hands as if to ward her off. "It is just—I forgot an appointment. The time." She pointed up at the clock on the wall behind the counter. "I must leave now. Goodbye!"

And with that, she raced toward the door, pulling it open so roughly that the bells were still jangling as she disappeared into the crowd.

"How odd." Becca stood there, watching her go. Though whether it was concern for the departed visitor or disappointment over losing a potential client that made her sound so thoughtful, Clara couldn't tell. As it was, she spent several minutes staring out at the street. Only when she turned back to check the clock herself and then reach for her book again did she stop with a gasp and pull herself up short.

"Miss! Miss!" Dashing around the counter, Becca raced to the door, opening it to the gusting wind. The resulting cacophony of bells was so loud a few of the passersby stopped in their paces to peer into the colorful shop. Ignoring them, Becca stepped out onto the sidewalk, wrapping her arms around herself to ward off the chill as she pulled herself up to her full five-four and scanned the crowd. "Miss?" She called again, louder. "Miss? Hello?"

Nobody answered, and the two pedestrians who had stopped turned away before hurrying on. "Miss?" Becca called once more. Nothing. With a sigh, she went back inside, rubbing her hands up and down her arms for warmth, and looked down at the violin case that the visitor had left on the floor.

Chapter 4

"I don't know what to do." In desperation, Becca had rung Elizabeth, who lived with her sister in the building's penthouse apartment. "I called out, but she was gone," Becca explained when the older woman rushed in, a weathered book under one arm. "Then I figured, well, she'll realize, and she'll be back any second. But it's been almost a half hour and there's no sign of her. She's got to be frantic."

Elizabeth didn't respond immediately. Instead, she set the thick leather-bound volume down and turned her attention to the violin case. Covered in brown cloth, with a wide strap that had allowed the young woman to sling it over her back, it lay on the counter where Becca had placed it.

Becca snuck a glance at the book, the embossed lettering on its cover too worn to read, before turning to the case beside it.

"I thought of calling the conservatory, but I didn't even get her name, and I couldn't find a tag or any kind of identification on it."

"And inside?" Elizabeth reached for one of two metal catches.

"I didn't look." Becca's fingers stiffened on the counter, as if she were resisting the urge to pull the case toward her. "I didn't want to, well, intrude."

Elizabeth turned her attention to Becca, those bushy brows rising in surprise. Her tone, when she spoke again, was serious. "Are you picking up something about this case, Becca? Something, say, that your cats would notice?"

Becca looked up at her and took a breath, as if about to speak. But after a moment's pause, she shook her head. "Funny you should say that about my cats," she said, almost to herself. "But no, nothing really. Only, well, I wouldn't look in someone else's bag."

"You would if someone had left it, and you were trying to find the owner." Elizabeth sounded much more matter-of-fact as she popped first one catch and then the other. "And we have been talking about purging negative influences. But since I'm here." She lifted the lid, her eyes growing wide under those bushy brows. "Oh, my."

"What is it?" Pushing the book aside in her haste, Becca leaned forward, and Clara, still shaded, jumped up on the counter beside her. Inside the dull brown shell lay a time capsule. Blue velvet that must once have been lush was now stained and worn smooth. A satin pull on the rosin compartment was threadbare, the leather catches tattered, and the wooden spinners that held the bow in place showed wear from many hands. The violin itself, cradled like a jewel, had not fared much better, its rich red-brown finish was almost rubbed off in spots while in others it glowed with age.

"That's—I could be wrong." The older woman reached out to the instrument, her fingertips just grazing the wood, while Clara, unseen beside her, sniffed at a corner of the case, where the velvet had been torn and glued back on. "I think this may be a very old instrument."

"It doesn't look like it's in the best shape." Becca pointed to a rough oval near the instrument's curved bottom, where the pale wood showed through. Only after a moment of silence did she look up to see Elizabeth regarding her curiously.

"Didn't you have any kind of musical education growing up?" The

37

question sounded rhetorical, but Becca heard the reprimand in it.

"I took piano lessons for a while." She regarded the bare patch. "I just mean, well, it looks like the finish has been worn off. Surely, that can't be good."

"It means this violin has been played constantly. It's a sign of use, not mis-use." As she spoke, Clara dabbed at the velvet. It felt warm, somehow, as if all those hands had left their mark.

Becca nodded, accepting the older woman's correction. "Well, that means she's more likely to miss it, I guess," she said. "But that doesn't help us identify the owner."

Clara jumped out of the way as Becca pulled the case forward and closed it to examine the cloth traveling sleeve, her fingers resting on a concealed zipper along its edge. Making an excited, and rather cat-like sound, she unzipped what turned out to be a large pocket and pulled out the contents.

"Dvorak, Bach, and Telemann," she read, thumbing through the pages. Watching her, Clara had the distinct feeling that her person could make no more sense of the black marks on those pages than she or her sisters would have. Still, she seemed enthralled, taking in the dense cascades of rising and falling marks as well as the smudged pencil notations that ran between the lines. "This seems to be a counting exercise." She flipped over the lined sheet.

"Have you found something?" Elizabeth, who had been examining the case itself, asked.

"Just music." Placing the pages on the counter, Becca reached into the pocket once more. "Wait. There's something down on the bottom."

She pulled out a scrap of staff paper apparently torn from the same notebook as the rhythm exercise. The writing was in the same soft pencil that had marked up the music scores, a stub that now rolled out onto the counter. But while Clara eyed that pencil, resisting the urge to send it rolling with a swift swipe of her paw, Becca seemed captivated by the paper.

"I don't know what language this is." She raised it to show it to Elizabeth. "Those accents are all over the place. I'm guessing it's something from Eastern Europe?"

"I'm not sure." Elizabeth reached for it, lifting it closer to her face. And as she did, Becca gasped and grabbed it back.

"What?" Elizabeth looked on as Becca laid it flat on the counter, back side up.

"I don't know what the rest of it says." Becca was pointing at a set of symbols that appeared vaguely familiar. "But 13 Highland? That's where I live."

Chapter 5

"Go." Elizabeth was close to shoving Becca out the door. "If she had your address, it's likely she was looking for you. People don't often wander in here by accident, my dear."

"But…the shop." Becca hesitated, her eyes darting from the other woman's face to the leatherbound volume that still lay on the counter.

"I think I'll be able to handle things here." Elizabeth placed her hand on the weathered cover, though whether to shield it or draw strength from it, Clara couldn't tell. "And I'll put you down for the full shift. Don't worry."

"But if she comes back?" Becca's focus homed in on the book, and Elizabeth slid it back.

"This is a time for action." Elizabeth's eyes, under those brows, were hard.

And so Becca nodded and then grabbed a flier off the wall behind her that advertised a crystal therapy workshop, two weeks past. Flipping it over, Becca used the pencil and began to write.

"*Did you lose your…*" She paused, thinking. "I won't say 'violin.' We want to make sure only that girl or someone who knows her picks it up. *Did you lose your instrument? Please inquire inside.*"

"I'll hang it on the door." Elizabeth took it from her, as if to forestall any further questions. "You might be able to catch up with her if you go now. Hurry!"

Although she couldn't see the cat trotting alongside her, Becca did just that, slinging the case over her shoulder as the other woman had done, and racing through the square to make it back to her building in record time. Even from the street, Clara could hear her sisters prowling around the apartment as Becca raced up the stairs, unlocking the building's front door. As she trotted behind her, the shaded cat caught the soft thud as Laurel jumped down from the bookshelf. That was to be expected—Laurel and Harriet might not venture out as Clara did, but they would never admit that they were any less aware of happenings in the outside world. As she started up to the apartment in Becca's wake, the calico began to suspect that something more than the vibrations of their approach was stirring her sisters up. Yes, she decided as she heard a heavier tread. If even Harriet was pacing, something was up.

Clara knew that her person had no special powers. Still, she wondered if Becca was picking up some vibrations as she slowed on the stairs, making her way cautiously to the second floor.

Only when she paused on that floor to look down the hallway did Clara understand. Becca wasn't picking up her sisters' distress, she was anxious. That horrible newcomer lived down here, and from the slight movement of her door, it appeared the hard-looking woman had been peeking out, perhaps alerted by the sound of the front door swinging shut behind them.

Clara couldn't tell if Becca had seen it too, though from her hesitation she suspected her person had noticed something. But if Becca had thought about calling the other woman out, she quickly dismissed the idea and instead crept as quietly as possible up the remaining flight to her own floor. So quietly that she appeared to startle the dark-haired young woman in a duffel coat who stood outside the apartment next door.

"Oh, there you are!" Becca exclaimed, exhaling in relief. "I was hoping I'd be able to find you."

The woman in the duffel coat turned, one hand still on the knob. Her face was deathly pale.

"Are you staying here?" Becca paused to catch her breath.

Clara could see the key in the lock, but something in the way the other woman started made the ordinary act—the unlocking of a front door—seem furtive, as if she were a skittish cat. "Are you friends with my neighbor?" Becca asked again, confused.

"I—well, not exactly." The young woman looked down at the key as if it were foreign to her. As if her hand had not already turned the knob to open the door. "In fact, I was going to leave—"

"Leave! That's right." In her surprise at finding the young woman, Becca had almost forgotten the reason for her search. "You left your violin at the shop."

Without waiting for a response, Becca shrugged to lift the strap over her head. For a moment, there was silence. Becca extended her arm, holding the case out to its owner, whose pale face lit up with surprise and what Clara hoped was joy. And then, as the door swung open with a slight squeak, she turned—and began to scream.

"No!" she shrieked, and like that, Becca was at her side. Clara too, although neither woman knew it, staring into the apartment, where a skinny body lay face down on the floor, its straw-colored mop dark with blood. To Clara, the smell was overwhelming. Its metallic tang almost drowning out the stench of sweat and of fear.

Even to Becca the odor must have been obvious, but it didn't stop her. As Clara stared aghast, her person raced in to kneel by the prone man's side. With one hand she brushed back the blood-soaked hair, revealing the gray eyes, wide and sightless, the wire-rimmed glasses nowhere to be seen.

"What's all this noise?" Both women jumped at the sound behind them. The nasty neighbor, a scowl on her face, was mounting the last of the stairs. With one pointy toe she shoved the violin case abandoned on the landing. "If I hear any more of this, I swear I'm going to call the police—"

"Yes!" Becca, panting, jumped to right the case before it fell over. "Call 9-1-1. There's been—someone's hurt."

The newcomer craned around her to look before stumbling back. "What the? Who's that?" Her voice sounded more affronted than concerned.

"My roommate." The pale musician stammered out the words, her eyes fixed on the body on the floor. "I'm sorry, I mean, landlord? The English…"

"You know him?" The woman from downstairs had recovered quickly and was now punching numbers into her phone. "He's a friend of yours?" This was addressed to Becca, who made herself turn back to the body even as she put her arms around the young woman to draw her away.

"He—we had just met." Becca stammered as if she found it hard to speak, her mouth gone suddenly dry. "He is—was—my new neighbor."

"No, he's not." The brunette glowered, though whether at Becca or the blood that stained her hands, Clara couldn't tell. "Justin Neil owns this unit. I met Justin at the condo association's first meeting, and we've become friends. But I've never seen this man in my life."

Chapter 6

"*What's she saying?*" Laurel's voice reached Clara through the door, so loud and clear that even the cop interviewing Becca must have heard her yowl. "*What's happening?*"

"*The police are talking to Becca,*" Clara, still shaded, murmured to the closed apartment door. The calico understood her sisters' curiosity—the howl of sirens had only added to the cacophony of screams and sobs since that body had been found roughly a half hour before. "*Can't you hear them?*"

While Laurel did tend to brag about her ability to hear thoughts, she could also have joined Clara out on the landing. The calico knew her Siamese sister might not have quite her facility with shimmying through closed doors, but she had shown an amazing ability to get where she needed to be when she wanted. Laurel, Clara suspected, was hanging back out of deference to Harriet. While all three felines did share some powers, Clara was learning, travel of any kind was not the hefty marmalade's forte. Passing through a solid object like a door would be particularly uncomfortable for their older sister, especially if she had just eaten. The subject was understandably touchy.

"*Hold on,*" she mewed when Laurel didn't respond. "*I'm trying to find out more."*

Making her way carefully across the crowded landing, Clara found her person seated on the stairs, a balding, moon-faced policeman standing above her and the violin case by her side. A female officer had already escorted the dark-haired violinist down to the lower floor. Her sobbing had calmed somewhat, but Clara could tell from Becca's furrowed brow that her person was listening in on the other conversation with concern.

"No, I'm sorry." Becca looked up at the officer above her, her own face drawn. "I know what she—the other girl—said, but I don't know who that man was."

"You said he was your neighbor?"

"I thought he was." Becca shook her head slowly, as if trying to shake off a bad dream. "I thought he must be the new owner. What's his name? Justin Neil. I'd just met him yesterday. The man in the apartment, that is. Not Mr. Neil. But my other neighbor, the woman from downstairs, she says that's not him."

The officer frowned, lines appearing in high forehead, as he waited for her to go on.

"I saw him in the hall, and I guess I just assumed. There've been so many changes." Becca sighed, as if to shed the weight of the world. "I've been here for close to five years, and I knew the old tenant, Tony, pretty well. But he moved out. The building's going condo. There've been a lot of changes."

"Your friend referred to the deceased as her roommate and as her landlord."

"She's not my friend." Becca sounded exhausted. "I mean, I just met her."

"Your life is full of strangers, Miss Colwin." The statement came out like a judgment.

"I don't know what to tell you. I thought he was my neighbor. And

45

she, well, she came into my store, the shop where I work. I didn't know she was living here."

"According to the unit owner, she doesn't."

"What?" Becca perked up. "You've met the owner? Who is he?"

"Justin Neil." The cop eyed her curiously. "Just like you said, and like it says on the mailbox."

"What's going on here? Who's in charge?" Loud footsteps caused them both to turn as a man with dark, slicked-back hair and a face like a thundercloud came storming up the stairs, a chubby young cop hard on his heels.

"Sir, sir, you can't go up there!" the young officer called, her voice tight with strain. Despite the weather, her round face glowed from the effort.

Moving with all the authority of his pinstripe suit, not to mention the touch of gold at his wrists, the glowering man ignored her, the overhead light casting reflections like lightning as he barreled toward the apartment. If Zeus were a businessman, Clara thought, an old tale of Becca's taking shape in her brain, and she danced out of his way. The cop questioning Becca stood a good foot shorter than the newcomer. Still, he frowned and, raising one hand to pause Becca's recital, stepped sidewise to block him.

"I'm sorry, sir. You can't proceed further." He held his arms out, evidently unwilling to do any more to restrain a man of such obvious authority.

"But that's my apartment." The newcomer spoke as if that settled it. The cop didn't move, however, and the man relented, brushing at the sleeve of his jacket where the policeman's outstretched hand had touched it. As he did, he took in the scene, scanning the landing from the man in blue who had dared to stand in his way to the panting officer who had followed him up the stairs, passing over Becca along the way. "What's going on here?" It wasn't a question so much as a

46

demand.

"As I tried to tell you." The cop who'd chased him up the stairs took a deep breath, though whether that was because she'd run up the stairs or to help her control her temper, Clara couldn't tell. "There's been an incident."

Clara felt Becca flinch at the word. The man in the suit didn't seem to like it either. "An incident?" His glare turned on Becca, as if she might be responsible.

"I didn't—" She caught herself. "Wait, are you Justin Neil?"

"Did you have a tenant or a roommate, sir?" The chubby cop interrupted before he could answer Becca.

"A tenant?" The man looked back at the chubby cop, frowning in such confusion that Clara wondered if he didn't know the word. Within a moment, however, the light dawned. "You must mean my assistant." Another frown, though at the mistake or the mention of the man himself wasn't clear.

"Does this assistant have a name?" Now that she'd caught her breath, the young cop was all business.

"Why?" Another bark and a brief staring contest ensued. The stranger relented. "Yes, of course. Larry Rakov. What's happened?"

"Would you describe your assistant, please?" Swiping the back of her hand across her brow, she pulled a pad out of her back pocket.

"Rakov's more of a property manager." The man frowned. "He was someone I hired to set up the apartment, and to watch over it while I'm away on business. I travel frequently, you see."

The officer tried again. "Was he a younger man? Long hair?" With one hand, she stroked her own round chin, miming that scrawny beard.

Another frown. "Why?"

"I need you to describe this assistant, sir." The officer paused to usher the newcomer back toward the stair as two technicians emerged from the apartment.

47

"What's happened?" The suit pulled away. "Have I been robbed?"

"Please, sir." The balding cop who had been interviewing Becca stepped in front of him, blocking his way. His tone might be more deferential than it had been with Becca, but he was just as persistent.

"He clearly wasn't a genius." The man was still grumbling, even as the chubby officer ushered him back down the stairs. "But I thought he'd be sufficient for the job."

"He seemed nice enough to me." Becca responded under her breath as the two descended to the lower landing.

"He did?" The cop beside her had heard. "What else can you tell me about the man you thought was Justin Neil?"

"Not much." Becca shook her head, as if shaking loose the few memories. "I assumed he was the new owner, but I might have misunderstood him." She paused, the impact of what had happened weighing on her. "He did say something about having friends over. And that he didn't mind cats."

"Cats?" The balding cop's voice rose in an almost Laurel-like crescendo.

Becca nodded, a trace of a smile playing over her face. "Yeah, I'd worried that my cats were making too much noise, but he said they didn't bother him. He seemed nice."

"In what way?" Becca looked too preoccupied to notice how the cop's eyes narrowed.

Clara's ears pricked up at that. If only she had Laurel here beside her. *"Laurel, are you getting any of this?"* But although her sister could have spied on the officer's thoughts, she didn't seem to be in earshot. Pique, Clara thought, at being left out of the action.

"We didn't speak for long." Becca looked better, as if the effort to remember was a useful distraction. "Come to think of it, he didn't actually say he was living there. But since he was next door when we spoke, I assumed he was my new neighbor."

The cop answered with another question. "Do you know your other neighbors in the building?"

Clara picked up a sharpness in the cop's tone, but perhaps it was too subtle for human ears. Becca simply shook her head once more before responding. "No, there's been so much change."

"You've had no interaction with your other neighbors at all?"

Becca looked up at that. "Did the woman downstairs say something?"

When the cop didn't respond, Becca swallowed, realizing, perhaps, that she'd talked herself into a corner. "I did have an exchange with one of the new owners," she confessed. "Last night, after I got home from work. I gather my cats made some noise. They're not used to me working full time, and I think they get lonely."

She paused, but the officer stood there waiting.

"They knocked some things over. A potted plant and some books." Becca scanned the moon face, looking for sympathy or at least understanding. "Just the usual house pet mischief. Anyway, the woman on the second floor, the one with the big hair, she was really upset."

"She told you this?" A simple question, asked with no inflection.

Becca nodded. "She came up and knocked on my door. She—well, she threatened to call animal control on me."

The officer regarded Becca, his round face growing thoughtful. "That must have made you angry."

"Well, yes." Becca stopped herself. "I mean, I was upset, of course. But—she didn't say anything about me. Did she?"

"I'm really not at liberty to discuss that." With that, the officer closed his pad and stepped aside. Becca stood as well. To Clara, it looked like Becca was about to say something, maybe ask another question, but just then a deep voice interrupted.

"Excuse us. Coming through."

Becca stepped to the side, pushing the instrument case against the wall to make way as two EMTs, a covered stretcher between them, went past. Becca and the officer who was interviewing her watched them navigate the stairs' turn, but as they made their way across the landing below, Clara could hear the dark-haired young woman start to sob again, with a desperate gasping for breath.

"I should go to her." Becca reached for the railing.

"So she is a friend." The officer didn't block her, not exactly. However, it was clear that he suddenly had more questions for Becca.

"No, like I said, I only met her today at the shop." While Becca spoke, she kept her eyes on the woman below, who was once again seated on the step, curled forward like a scared hedgehog. "She came in looking for—well, never mind. But she left her violin."

"Wait, she left something with you?" The pen scratched across the paper.

Becca nodded, remembering. "She and I were chatting, when she saw someone pass by—we were in Central Square. She ran out suddenly, and then I realized she'd left her violin case. I ran out from behind the counter, but she was already gone. So I looked in the case and found a slip of paper with this address on it. My address, and so I left work and came home."

"Just in time to find a woman you'd never met before opening a door to an apartment that doesn't have her name on it and revealing a dead man who isn't the legal owner."

As Clara looked on, Becca turned white and sat down once more, hard.

"You think she's involved." Her voice was breathy, almost as if she were whispering to herself. "And that's why she was asking me for help."

"She was asking you for help?" The officer repeated Becca's words, as if making sure of them.

Becca nodded, a dazed look coming over her. "She didn't tell me the details, but it was easy enough to see that she was scared."

"Did she mention a roommate or a boyfriend to you?" He paused before that last option, and Clara felt the fur along her spine start to rise. The little cat wasn't sure what the balding cop was implying, but she could sense that he had chosen his words deliberately.

"No." Becca only looked thoughtful, and once again Clara wished her sister Laurel was there. Laurel could have implanted the idea that perhaps Becca should be careful. Something about this line of questioning felt like a trap to Clara. Almost as if the officer was waiting outside a small hole, hoping for a mouse to emerge. "I don't think she mentioned a boyfriend."

Good girl! Clara wasn't sure why this mattered, only she had the feeling the officer had dangled it, like a piece of string, hoping that Becca would go for it.

As it was, the cop simply nodded. "And yet you believed she felt threatened."

"Yes, she…" Becca bit her lip. "She was asking me for help before she ran out."

"In what way were you going to help her?" Clara bristled at the cop's question, her tail growing stiff, but Becca only shrugged, her face a blank of confusion.

"We didn't get to that." She had gone pale. "I'm sorry."

"What kind of help do you think she expected, seeing as how you were a total stranger?" The cop's question sounded routine, but Clara picked up on an undertone that set her ears back.

Becca, to her pet's dismay, didn't seem to notice.

"It's kind of hard to explain." Becca looked down the stairs, where the dark-haired girl had been. "Wait, where did she go?"

"I've just got a few more questions." The officer reached out, but Becca was already on the stairs. It didn't matter. The young woman, and the officer who had been interviewing her, had disappeared.

"Miss, please." Becca felt a hand on her arm and turned. Not soon

51

enough. On the landing below, a pile of dark hair turned up to reveal a familiar scowl outlined in dark red. The woman from the floor below was standing by another uniformed cop and had broken off to stare up at Becca. Dressed in a creamy blue angora cowl neck that set off her dark hair and lips, she was leaning on the arm of a tall man in a tweed blazer who looked up, his blue eyes following her gaze.

"There she is." The brunette's dark eyes flashed up at Becca, her shock turned to scorn. The man beside reacted as well, his smile settling into a grim line. "She's a troublemaker. I knew it from the start."

"Wait." Becca stepped back onto the landing, nearly stumbling over the case.

"And to top it all off, she thinks she's a witch!"

Chapter 7

"This is how it starts." Harriet sat, regal on her gold velvet pillow, fluffy tail curled around her feet as she glared at her youngest sister. *"You had one duty, to keep our person out of trouble, and now this."*

"I didn't know." Clara, on the floor, looked up at her sister on the couch. *"I've been trying."*

"She has been, you know." Laurel, unfazed, stretched out on the couch beside Harriet, bathing one chocolate-tipped leg. *"That's all she thinks about, Clara the Clown. She can't help it if she's clueless about what to do. Or why."*

"Why?" Clara looked from one sister to the other, her desperation growing. *"Please, would one of you explain? You must have heard something. What happened?"*

The two cats above her exchanged a glance. Although neither so much as mewed, Clara suspected they were communicating silently. She could try to join the unspoken conversation, she knew. While she might never have Laurel's facility with the reading or suggesting of thoughts, she had learned that all three of them shared some basic skills. However, even as she pleaded with her sisters, Clara was using all her energy to focus on her person.

The nasty neighbor had done Becca a small service, distracting the officer enough so that he nodded his assent when Becca asked if she could return to her own apartment—at least until she was needed for more questions.

Grabbing the violin, she'd retreated and, locking the door behind her, pulled out her phone. The first call she had made was to the shop. Clara could almost feel the calming tones the store's manager was using to reassure Becca.

"Thanks, Elizabeth." Becca was already breathing easier. "I think I will take the rest of the day. I'll be in tomorrow, though."

The next call, Clara suspected, was to Becca's friend Maddy. Even from the living room, the calico could hear her person relating the horror she had witnessed.

"He was just lying there, Maddy." Becca's voice had once again grown reedy with strain. "Call me?"

While Clara waited for a response, Laurel cleared her throat with a discreet feline cough. Having regained her sister's attention, the sealpoint announced in her most officious pitch, *"She's not there, silly. And, since you asked, we didn't tell you because there was no sense in it."* Even speaking softly, her characteristic Siamese yowl made her displeasure clear. *"As is so often the case, these humans argue about nothing—and then violence is done."*

"But you must have heard something." Clara strained to keep her own voice level and respectful.

"It was loud." Laurel recoiled in distaste at the memory, her final word stretching into a howl.

"Like when we broke that vase?" Clara was fishing. The "we" was a euphemism. The vase in question had been knocked over during one of Laurel's more acrobatic, but less well judged, leaps.

"No." Laurel was shutting down. Clara had chosen her example badly.

"*Was is it like the time that we upset the teapot?*" Desperate to keep her sister talking, the calico reached back to the days when Becca was still brewing Larissa's foul-smelling blend, which the cats had been eager to get rid of. Clara had not been entirely sure whether the incident had been as accidental as Laurel had implied. The sealpoint rarely angered Harriet enough that the big marmalade would chase her over a table, and Clara suspected that her sister had used her powers of suggestion to urge the clumsier cat to make the leap. The resulting spill had had the unfortunate effect of spreading the noxious brew all over. To the cats' dismay, the odor lingered for days. "*Everybody was in an uproar.*"

"*No, this was nothing at all like that.*" Laurel paused, apparently deep in thought. "*There was no...chasing. Just, 'That's not it.' 'Yes, it is.' 'No, it's not.' As I said, it was all nonsense.*"

"*There had to be some reason for what happened.*" Clara looked from Laurel to Harriet. But the older cat merely plumped herself up.

"*It was as your sister said: nonsense. A stranger came in from the cold, but rather than appreciating the warmth, he turned...*" A slight growl as Harriet shuddered at a memory. "*What happened next door was regrettable.*"

Clara got a sudden vision of two figures grappling. Faceless and indistinct, they appeared to be only vaguely human, and vaguely male. She waited, turning after a few moments to Laurel for clarification, but no further details were forthcoming from either of the two other cats and the mental image remained fuzzy. Her sisters, Clara realized, had heard the violence that had resulted in a man's death, but not what had led to it. Not even how the two men had ended up together in the apartment next door.

"*There must have been something, some reason.*"

"*It was as we said.*" Laurel's tail lashed defensively, whisking the tassels of Harriet's pillow. "*Loud.*"

A fight, but not a break-in. The thought flashed through Clara's mind, even as she did her best to banish her sudden awareness. Neither of her sisters liked to be thought of as inexperienced, simply because they were house cats. They certainly didn't want to be considered naive. Clara wasn't sure what her sudden insight meant, or how she could communicate it to Becca. If, that is, she was even interpreting her sisters' report correctly.

"*The loudness started when the two were in the apartment? They had a fight?*" Fishing, she did her best to visualize Becca in a rare moment of pique. For example, when she had arrived home to find the apartment wrecked.

"*No.*" Laurel drew out the word in a classic Siamese howl. While she liked to complicate every situation in this case, Clara suspected, her sister was telling the truth. "*You think we're too stupid to have heard something like that? Silly girl. Like I said, a lot of loud voices for no reason.*"

"*As your sister has already stated, the altercation was loud, but it made no scents. At least not initially.*" Clara couldn't tell if Harriet was intentionally mishearing Laurel's words. Questioning her oldest sister was never easy. "*Humans always think that they know everything and that they maintain control. As they are obviously mistaken, whatever they yelled about is inconsequential to our purposes. However, given the circumstances, we have reached a decision.*" Harriet shuffled on her pillow, more to recall Clara's full attention than to ease herself into a better position, the littlest cat realized. Harriet would never have settled anywhere that was less than comfortable in the first place, and so Clara sat up, ears alert.

"*It has become increasingly apparent that you are failing in your primary duty of watching over our person when she is outside.*" Harriet paused, but Clara had enough sense not to argue. If she dug her claws into the carpet a bit, it was only because she felt the need to flex her toes.

"Becca must be kept away from controversy, at all costs."

"But…" The slight peep escaped, and as Harriet's eyes widened, Clara risked the rest of her question. *"She was worried about that other girl, the one from the shop."*

Harriet appeared to consider her sister's outbursts, and Clara tilted her ears forward in what her older sister could only see as a respectful move. In truth, she was also anxious for Harriet's response.

"As I was saying." Harriet settled back, pulling her round face into her ruff for what she knew was a leonine effect. *"You are failing in your primary duty. However,"* the glare in those gold eyes warned Clara not to interrupt, *"your sister and I believe this may be due to ignorance on your part. Therefore, we have decided it is time for you to know more of our family history."*

That wasn't the tongue-lashing Clara had been expecting, and her ears pricked up in anticipation. Although she wasn't sure what their history would have to do with her own latest actions, or with Becca's recent adventures, she was always eager to hear more about their family and the mother she barely remembered. She'd had clues about their history, of course. There was that picture—Becca called it an engraving—of a cat who looked strikingly like her, seated on the lap of a strangely dressed woman, who resembled Becca with a less modish haircut. Becca had found it on her computer, the workings of which were strange even to her attentive pet, and had a copy made not long ago.

Becca had been entranced by the picture because of that woman, from what Clara could tell. She had commented on its connection to her own family, without even noting the resemblance between her great-great-great-grandmother's cat and the youngest of her three pets. That could have been because it was hard to tell in the black-and-white print if the cat depicted had an orange patch over one eye and a dark patch over the other, like Clara herself did, but she got a tingle in the end of her guard hairs when she looked at that print, almost as if someone had come up behind her. Someone she could neither see nor smell. It unnerved her, and yet at the same time, Clara couldn't deny its intrigue. Maybe, she thought, Becca had her own version of that strange tingling. No, she told herself. Humans could be adorable, but they simply weren't that sharp. If anything, it seemed that the ability to read the scrawled symbols that appeared on so many surfaces made her human blind to other things she should see.

"Tell her about the burnings." Laurel almost purred the word, but Harriet's ears went back, flat against her head.

"Do not lecture me." The marmalade was practically hissing. *"And it makes no sense to start with those…unfortunate times."*

This time it was Laurel whose ears flicked momentarily back. *"She needs to hear what can happen."*

"One time." A sweep of Laurel's brown-tipped tail, and Harriet paused. *"Well, a few times."*

Clara realized she was going to have to speak up. *"Please,"* she implored her sisters, doing her best to keep her tone respectful. *"Whatever you begin with, would you please tell me more?"*

Laurel shrugged and went back to washing, as if that one chocolate bootie were all that had ever concerned her.

"Properly, we should begin in the land of two rivers." Harriet tucked her front paws under her snowy breast, a sure sign that she was settling in for a long story. *"For it was there that our great mother first took pity on a hapless noblewoman—"*

"She wasn't a noble woman." Laurel was still staring at her toes, but Clara suspected that her nonchalance was faked. *"She was a slave, tasked with protecting the granary."*

"She was a woman of great discernment." Harriet's lip pulled back to reveal the edge of one fang, and Laurel wisely shut up. *"Who had been*

given an impossible responsibility for a human. Because even then, little sister, humans had the mistaken belief that they were much more capable than they really are."

"And our great mother?" Clara knew she shouldn't interrupt, but she had heard Becca end her call.

"Eight millennia and she wants to rush the story." Laurel was working on her front paws now—and playing up to Harriet.

"I'm sorry." Clara dipped her head. A wave of fatigue had come over her, and she felt her eyes closing. It must be the heat kicking in, the radiator warming her like the brightest of suns...

Chapter 8

"*Stop it!*" Clara shook herself awake to find Laurel staring at her, blue eyes unreadable. Harriet, meanwhile, had flopped over on her side, out cold. "*What was that?*"

Harriet's paw, beside her head, twitched as the big marmalade began to snore.

"*What do you think?*" Laurel turned to their sleeping sister and then opted for the brown tip of her own tail instead. "*You say you want to learn, but when we try to share the family memories...*"

"*Is that what that was?*" Clara, embarrassed, sat back down. Tucking her own paws beneath her breast, she studied Harriet, her green eyes growing wide. "*Is Harriet in a trance?*"

"*She's the oldest.*" Laurel shrugged as she continued to groom. It wasn't exactly an answer, but Clara hunkered down to consider.

"*I'm sorry,*" she said. "*You could have warned me.*"

"*Sometimes, you have to trust.*"

"*But you said that I* shouldn't...*" Clara was confused. "*How do I know who to trust?*"

"*We can't teach you* that.*" Laurel paused in her grooming to give her sister another inscrutable look, staring so hard her eyes crossed. She was about to say more, Clara was sure, when they felt it—the vibration that announced an imminent arrival. Laurel jumped off the sofa, while Harriet woke with a snort. Clara, after a moment of indecision, bowed once more to her eldest sister and trotted after Laurel to the apartment's front door, just as a sharp rap sounded.

"Hang on!" Becca must have been doing dishes. Clara could hear water running. "Maddy, you didn't have to—"

Becca opened the door, but if she expected her good friend, she was in for a rude surprise. The downstairs neighbor, a sneer contorting her pretty face, stepped past her into the apartment.

"So you knew her," she said, ostensibly to Becca, although the way she was staring at Laurel would have been considered intimidating to any other feline.

"Excuse me?" Becca scrambled after her as Clara made a strategic retreat.

"The illegal." The neighbor's eyes narrowed as Laurel stared back at her. Clara watched from beneath the sofa with growing alarm.

"I don't know who you're talking about." Becca stepped in front of the woman, blocking her from going any further, and prompting Laurel to duck around her to keep the woman in sight. "But that's a rude way to talk about anyone."

The woman sniffed. "I don't know how else to refer to someone who is where she has no right to be. In a luxury building, no less. Her and her friend, the squatter."

"I don't know what you're talking about." Clara felt Becca's confusion, though which part of the intruder's statement had spurred it was beyond her. "If you mean that poor man, he worked for Mr. Neil. He had every reason to be there."

"Right." The intruder sniffed. "Justin only said that because he was embarrassed, an employee taking advantage of his hospitality by camping out in his new home. I wonder if he slept in his bed." She recoiled, her face drawing up like Laurel's when she smelled something foul. "I only hope he doesn't reconsider his move. I'm sure a man like Justin Neil understands the risks of moving into a neighborhood in transition, but really, a murder? He might as well have been one of the homeless."

Becca only shook her head, the other woman's words clearly as incomprehensible to her as they were to her cat. "I don't understand how you can talk about that poor man like that. And, just for the record, I don't think he was here illegally."

"How would you know?" Her brusque tone caught Becca up short. As did her own second thoughts, Clara realized.

"He wasn't hiding," she responded, but Clara could see how uncertain she was. "He answered the door when I knocked." She paused, as if reviewing her memories. "He seemed shy, but he wasn't being weird about being there. He seemed nice."

Another huff from the glossy brunette only served to bring Becca back to the present.

"And that poor girl who found him? She had nothing to do with any of this. She's new to town."

"Really?" From those red lips, the word became an accusation.

Becca nodded. "She's a student. A musician. We talked because she came by my—my place of business this morning."

Good for you, Clara thought. The less this nasty person knew about Becca's life the better. Laurel, meanwhile, had begun to advance on the woman, stepping slowly and carefully, her blue eyes fixed.

"So you say, but I heard you call out to her. You were trying to get her attention." The woman leaned in, screwing up her eyes in a most unflattering manner. "You have something of hers."

Now it was Harriet's turn. Rising from her pillow, she slowly arched her back, her fur beginning to puff up.

"I don't know what you're talking about." Becca stepped sideways, confusing Clara until she realized that her person was moving to hide the violin case.

"Yes, you do. I heard you." The woman brushed her hair back from her ear, then paused to scratch at it.

"What are you doing?" Clara focused on her sisters, who were both staring at the intruder. *"And can I help?"*

"Remember the desert." The idea came with a wave of heat, as if the radiator had just gone into overdrive. Although her coat was short, it was thick, and Clara didn't suffer from the cold as Becca did. Still, after the morning's adventures, the warmth was welcome, and she purred, feeling herself adding to each rising wave.

The woman before her, however, didn't seem to find it quite as pleasant. Pushing her thick dark hair back from her forehead, she gasped slightly, and looked around. "What's with this place?"

"Sorry?" Becca didn't seem to feel the rising heat. At least, she wasn't pulling at her collar as the brunette was, drawing the lush blue wool away from her throat as if it were strangling her.

"You—this apartment." She wiped at her cheek, then looked down to see the mascara there. Another blink, and a clump of lashes went flying, leaving her eyes lopsided. "It's an abuse of our resources!" Clasping her hand to her eye, she turned and stormed out.

"How strange." Becca stood in the open doorway as the other woman clattered down the stairs. Beside her, Laurel began to purr.

"Don't all thank me at once." The sealpoint stretched out her dark paws, as if admiring her claws.

"How did you do that?" Clara yawned and stretched, the heat making her sleepy.

"Isn't it obvious?" Harriet lumbered over to the sofa, determined to insert herself into the conversation. The orange patch across her back heaved up and down with what might have been laughter or possibly a hairball.

"*There's so much warmth here. I built on that.*" Laurel must be feeling generous if she was willing to explain. "*And you remember more than you realize.*"

At that, Clara sat up straighter. This was what she wanted to learn about. Before she could inquire, a familiar buzz broke Becca's reverie.

"Maddy! Thank the goddess."

Becca took the phone into the kitchen, laying it on the counter as she fixed herself another cup of tea. Speaking softly, as if the departed woman might overhear, she filled her friend in on the events of the day.

"Poor dear, you've been through the mill." Maddy's soft voice came over the line as soothing as the smell of mint. "Tell me everything."

Becca did, running through the encounter at the shop and the horrible discovery of the body next door. By the time she had gotten up to the police interrogation, she had taken her mug to the sofa, where Clara joined her. Becca was shivering slightly, even as she cupped her tea in her hands. Shock, Clara realized as she leaned in, doing her best to provide solace. To her, the room still felt toasty, heat rising in waves as soft as velvet, and as Becca and Maddy chatted, the calico felt it enveloping her. Lulling her to sleep. Was this Laurel's doing? Harriet's? Moving cautiously, so as not to disturb Becca, the calico looked around, but her sisters were nowhere to be seen.

"It just gets worse." Becca was too caught up in her recollections to take much notice of her pet. With an anxious glance at the front door, Becca told her friend about the intrusive neighbor. "I'll tell you, Maddy. I was almost afraid to answer the door."

"That's horrible." Maddy sounded suitably appalled. "Didn't she even care that another tenant in your building had been killed?'

"Well, that's just it." Between the tea and the conversation with her friend, Becca sounded like she was recovering—and gathering her thoughts. Clara forced herself to focus. To stay awake. "The victim wasn't even my neighbor."

"Wait." Maddy stopped her. "You just said you—that girl—found that man, the one next door?"

"Yeah." Becca swallowed, turning deathly pale at the recollection. Watching her, Clara worried that her person was going to be ill. "And it—he—was the man I'd just met. Only it turns out he wasn't my neighbor."

Maddy waited while Becca took a few deep breaths. "So, I thought he was my new neighbor," she explained after a pause. "I swear, he said he was. Maybe he misunderstood what I was asking? Or maybe he was embarrassed to just be a caretaker."

"Becs, I don't care if he was the new janitor." Maddy's tone had changed from outrage to concern. "A man was killed in the apartment next to yours. This is bad."

"It's not his fault. He seemed nice." Becca was still pale, but her voice had grown more thoughtful. "Poor guy."

"Nice." Maddy sounded exasperated. "Becca, I don't want to sound like that harridan downstairs. Really, I don't. But she might have a point here. You'd just met the man. He led you to believe he was your neighbor. Who knows what else was going on with him?"

"What do you mean?" Becca sipped her tea.

"Sometimes people bring trouble on themselves, Becca. Maybe he was dealing drugs out of the apartment. Or…" She paused, searching for an alternative. "I don't know. Something else."

"You make it sound like he deserved to be killed." Becca's voice sounded as frayed as her temper. "It's true that the poor guy—whoever he was—said something about friends coming over. He asked if he'd been any bother. Oh, Maddy, if I'd been home earlier, or if that poor girl had opened the door only a little sooner…"

Becca shivered, and Clara stretched herself along her side, the better to comfort her.

"Do you want me to come over? As soon as I get off work, I can come over." Her friend clearly had the same instinct. "Even better, say the word, and I'll help you pack."

"You don't have to, honest. I'm so wiped out anyway, I'll probably sack out early." Becca had rarely sounded so downcast, even as she slumped on the couch. When Maddy began to protest, she cut her off. "And I don't want to move, Maddy. If I could, I'd buy this place, I would. But maybe all this…" she waved a hand in the general direction of the wall "…will mean I have more time. I've been meaning to make an appointment at Cambridge legal services. I think it's pretty hard to evict a long-time tenant."

"I don't know. I know you love Cambridge, but, Becca, it's not just that person downstairs. Whatever he was and whatever he was into, a man was killed right next door."

"I know." Becca looked around the apartment, tears glinting in her eyes. "But this is my home."

The phone fell silent then, until Maddy spoke up once again, her voice loud with forced cheer. "Well, maybe this will drive the price down. And if you can borrow enough for a down payment, I bet old Rogers would co-sign your mortgage." Maddy's boss owed Becca for helping him out of a jam. "And if you needed to show more of a steady income…"

"Thanks, Maddy, but no thanks." Becca seemed to be rousing, as she shook off her friend's half-spoken offer with a smile. "I know it's only retail, but I like working at Charm and Cherish. Besides, it gives me time to pursue detecting."

Maddy had no response to that, although both Becca and Clara could clearly hear her sharp intake of breath. They could also hear a male voice booming in the background.

"I'm sorry, Becca. Roberts is having his four o'clock crisis."

Becca chuckled. "And you really want me to come work with you?"

"Hey, old Roberts never killed—" She caught herself short. "Sorry."

"No apologies necessary, Maddy."

A soft thud broke the silence that followed, and Clara jumped down to investigate, following the sound to the front door, where Becca's parka lay puddled on the floor, right by the violin case that Becca had abandoned there. From the glint in Laurel's eye, Clara didn't think the coat had fallen of its own accord.

"What are you doing, kitty?" Becca clearly had similar suspicions. As she hung it back on the coat tree, she turned toward the sealpoint, who stretched to claw at the case's cloth covering.

"No, no, Laurel." Becca lifted the case away from her and brought it over to the kitchen table, where Harriet lay sprawled out sleeping.

"Excuse me, Harriet." The big marmalade blinked up as Becca switched on the overhead lights, the winter dusk having thrown the apartment in shadow. As those white mitts reached out in a yawn, Becca unzipped the outer covering and flicked the catches to open the case. "I almost forgot I still had this."

As Clara watched, Laurel approached, sniffing at the case and delicately pawed the corner of the velvet. "Be careful, Laurel." Becca gently removed her pet's paw. "This isn't ours, and, no, it isn't a cat toy."

As she lifted the slim cat, placing her on the ground, Clara decided to investigate. Laurel, she knew, was intrigued by pretty things and shiny things, and the old violin in its battered case was neither. Leaning forward, she took a sniff, taking in the sharp pine smells of rosin and old wood, warm and almost live. The result of centuries of human touch, she figured. Maybe this violin was as old as—

"Clara, not you too." The calico drew back, coiling her tail primly around her paws as Becca lifted the instrument, which seemed to hum as she moved it.

"It looks ancient, doesn't it?" Becca must have been talking to herself, rather than following up on Clara's musing, but her cat looked up as she spoke. "I wish I knew more about it. I wonder..."

"Quick, take a bite!" Harriet's hiss made Clara jump, and she looked over in time to see Laurel land silently back on the table. As she watched, her sister crept up on the case, fangs bared. *"See what you can—"*

"Laurel, no!" With her free hand, Becca did the unthinkable, pushing the slender sealpoint off the table, and nearly dropped the violin.

"I don't know what's gotten into you three." Becca tutted as she replaced the instrument and closed the case, flipping the catches closed and zipping the cloth covering for good measure. Clara hung her head. "It's almost like you don't like it. But it's not another cat. It's precious to someone, and for better or worse, I've got to take care of it until I can get it back to that poor girl. Speaking of…"

An hour later, calm had been restored. Becca had taken her laptop to the sofa, and with the silence of the careful feline, Laurel had jumped back up on the table to lie, stretched against the violin as if measuring herself against the case. Making the leap by way of a chair, Harriet landed with a huff beside her, stretching her furry back against the instrument's other side.

Clara, watching from the sofa, pondered her sisters' apparent attraction to the curved case and the instrument inside. It couldn't simply be that intriguing mix of odors—age and resin combining for a heady concoction—that made the thing appealing. Maybe, Clara thought, her own eyes growing heavy after the day's adventures, it was that the violin was roughly cat sized, and, even silent, seemed to glow like a living thing.

It made perfect sense for Becca to rescue it, Clara decided as she curled up beside Becca. After all, she believed she had rescued them. As her eyes closed, Clara found her mind drifting back to those early days. They'd been kittens when Becca had taken them home from the shelter, but even then she had understood that she had a mission. A mission she wanted to learn more about.

"If there's a message board…" Becca tapped away at the keyboard, pausing only once to glance over at the table where Laurel and Harriet lay sprawled on either side of the case, as if it, rather than Clara, were their third sister.

"Cats," Becca muttered to herself as she absently stroked Clara's orange-and-black back. Her hand was soothing, and so much more real than Laurel's odd conjuring, and Clara sighed, leaning her furry weight against Becca's thigh. This, the contented calico told herself, as her head drooped once more to rest on her white paws, was how Becca should spend her time. In that, Clara agreed with Maddy. Becca should avoid trouble, and anything involving dead bodies. Although her tutorial from Harriet had been interrupted, Clara didn't need a history lesson to understand that problems like this one were bad for Becca.

Still, as Clara drifted off, a contrary thought crept, almost mouse-like, into her consciousness, nibbling away at her conviction. That dark-haired girl in the duffel coat had seemed quite lost, and as a small creature in a big city, Clara knew she should feel sympathy with that. Plus, the fact that this girl had come to Becca for help endeared her further to the cat. If only Clara didn't already know as well as her sisters that their person didn't really possess any particular magical powers at all.

Chapter 9

Clara didn't know what time it was, in human terms, when Becca's voice woke her. She knew it had to be close to dinner, however. Not only from the rumbling in her belly but from the way her person was apologizing.

"I'm sorry to call after business hours. I appreciate you picking up. Could you tell me if the conservatory has a lost instrument department? Or maybe someone who can identify an instrument?" Becca paused, and Clara looked on as she tried to explain. "No, I didn't lose anything. But someone left an instrument, a violin, at the shop where I work, and I think she's a student."

Despite her acute hearing, Clara couldn't make sense out of the reply, despite concentrating like Laurel had instructed her. That focus paid off indirectly, though, as her middle sister leaped up and, yawning, settled beside her.

"I don't understand what she's thinking about. Something with numbers or registration?" She looked to Laurel for confirmation.

Her sister's dark ears twitched as she concentrated. *"Like those tags some cats wear, maybe."*

Laurel didn't like to admit when she didn't understand something, especially when it came to her ability to read their person's thoughts, and after their earlier tussle, Clara didn't press her. Besides, Becca had moved on, taking her phone over to where the violin lay in its case.

"Where did you say to look?" More noise as she lifted the violin by its neck and held it close to her face, one eye peeking through the curved f-hole in its curved surface. "No, I can't find any kind of mark. Is there any other way of identifying it?"

"Hang on." Reaching past the violin in its bed, Becca opened the pocket that held the rosin and released the bow from where it was held. "No," she added a moment later. "It's pretty beaten up. Wait, there is one mark." Becca kept talking, but to Clara what was more interesting was how she let her fingertips slide over the worn velvet and circle the glass dial inset into its surface. Inside the dial, a black needle bobbed slightly, pointing to a faint imprint in the velvet—a circle with two points. "Almost like a child's drawing of a cat."

"I'm not describing it well." Becca slumped, and then perked back up. "What if I send you a photo of the violin in the case? Maybe it's just a stain, but maybe someone will recognize it. Can I text one to you or do you have an email? Yes, tomorrow would be fine. Thank you."

Laying the violin back in its velvet bed, Becca grabbed a pencil and started to write. The sound of the pencil on paper, so reminiscent of tiny claws scrabbling across a wood floor, was awfully tempting. But Clara made herself focus. For the moment, the violin case was open, giving her a chance to investigate.

Rubbing the side of her face against the velvet, she felt the silky smoothness where the nap had worn down. Closing her eyes, she imagined how soft it must have once been and, picturing it as a sun-warmed grass of spring, felt an almost overwhelming urge to nibble on it. In one corner, a torn patch had begun to peel back up, tempting the curious kitty further. Stepping gingerly on the edge of the case, Clara lowered her moist nose to the curved body of the violin instead, moving from the deep-hued stain to that bare patch where the grain of the wood showed pale, and finally the black fingerboard.

Opening her mouth, she took in its scent, which recalled not so much the trees she had encountered on her outings with Becca as the incense they burned at Charm and Cherish. Over it all, a scent so subtle it was more like a memory, concentrated on the surface of the fingerboard, just below the four taut strings. Clara felt as if she were sniffing the fingers of all the people who had played it. And there were many, Clara thought, without really knowing why. Very many. In fact, if she closed her eyes and pitched her whiskers forward to catch all the vibrations, she thought she caught a vaguely familiar scent—

"No, kitty." Clara felt herself lifted by the middle, and the scent was lost as Becca lowered her to the floor. Undaunted, the agile calico leaped back up to the tabletop. This time, however, she was careful to keep her distance as Becca hovered over the instrument with her phone. If her person would only focus a little more on that phone…

It was not to be. Becca not only closed the lid, she buckled it as she turned away. "You just want your dinner, and I don't blame you."

"*What's going on?*" Laurel landed beside her, almost with a sound. "*Dinner, I think.*"

"*I know that!*" Laurel nodded in the direction of the kitchen, where Harriet was wrapping herself around Becca's legs, whining softly even as she hindered her progress. "*Look at our big sister. Doesn't she realize she's slowing her down?*"

Clara knew better than to let herself be drawn into that conversation and instead simply followed Laurel to join their oldest sister in the kitchen.

"*What's up with Becca?*" Laurel asked again, once the three had eaten. "*She should be asleep after a day like this. I can tell she's tired, and if she expects to keep up her looks…*"

"*She hasn't eaten.*" Harriet joined them, licking her chops. "*That can't be good. Just because she's seen a body is no reason not to feed oneself,"* she concluded, clearly pleased with the logic of her argument.

"I'm not sure," Clara confessed as her two sisters began their post-dinner toilette. *"She is trying not to think about the body, I believe. Instead, she's focusing on the violin. It's very old."*

"Not as old as we are." Laurel sniffed, and Clara's ears pricked up as she joined her on the table. *"And if you hadn't been so resistant..."*

"I'm sorry. Please tell me more." She didn't have to fake her eagerness. *"I want to hear about grandmama especially."*

A grunt—half growl, half cough—interrupted them. Harriet, on the sofa, was staring up at her two sisters, yellow eyes glowing.

"Harriet does know more of the story." Laurel dipped her head in acknowledgment, and Clara followed her to the table's edge, ready to jump down. Harriet was already plumping herself up in preparation, wiggling her large behind into her pillow and fluffing her ruff with her tongue. Clearly, the eldest of the three cats was readying herself for a performance.

"Come get comfortable, sisters." With one outstretched paw and the kind of feline smile that almost closes the eyes, the big marmalade invited Clara and Laurel to join her. *"Clara, you especially will want to hear about how we came to our present responsibilities."*

Eager as she was, Clara let Laurel jump first. This was no time to buck precedence. But as soon as her sealpoint sister had arranged herself along the sofa's back, the little calico prepared to jump. First to the floor, she thought. The sofa was within reach, but if she skidded and bumped into Harriet, it might be interpreted as disrespect. No, she decided, better to go for that blank spot of carpet, over by the coffee table—

Only just then she felt it. They all did, she saw as first Laurel and then finally Harriet turned toward the door, the eldest of the three with a particularly sour look on her flat Persian face.

73

"Not again!" Clara picked up her oldest sister's growl and realized why that particular vibration felt familiar. Just then Becca turned too, alerted by the footsteps in the hall a split second before a soft tap sounded on the door.

"Hello?" Becca called through the door, before opening it. Although Clara had recognized the visitor, she silently applauded the measure. Becca's friend Maddy was right. At times their person was a little too trusting. "Who's there?" Her voice shook ever so slightly.

"It is me." A female voice, speaking softly and with a light, lilting accent. "Ruby. Ruby Grozny. We met at Charm and Cherish."

"Ruby! I'm so glad it's you." Becca quickly unlatched the door and swung it open, revealing the slight, dark-haired young woman, still wearing the duffel coat and tam. If she appeared taken aback by Becca's exuberant greeting, she did her best to hide it, smiling shyly back. "I'm Becca. I was looking for you, you know, but you'd left."

"The police." Ruby's voice dropped and her eyes darted to the side. Toward the neighboring apartment, Clara realized. "They had questions."

"Of course they did." Becca must have recognized her visitor's distress, because she reached forward to usher her in, closing and latching the door behind her. "Finding him like that and having to talk to the police—that must have been upsetting."

"Thank you." Ruby managed a weak smile. "It was." The pale young woman bowed her head as if bashful. Or, thought Clara, as if she were concurring with Becca's insight in a particularly feline way.

"I am sorry." The visitor spoke so softly, Clara had to tilt her ears to hear. "But did you—do you have my violin?"

"Oh, yes! Of course. What was I thinking?" At Becca's urging, Ruby surrendered that coat and the cute hat, and let Becca lead her over into the apartment. Clara was staring at the hat—the pompom on top had a fascinating appeal—when she heard a quick intake of breath.

"That picture." Ruby stood frozen, facing the bookshelf. Wordlessly, Becca stepped back and let her pass, following her over to the shelf, where the stranger picked up the silver frame with both hands, examining the old-fashioned print of a seated woman and her pet. Clara knew the picture well. Not only was it one of Becca's favorites, but the cat on the woman's lap appeared, even in the grainy reproduction, to be a calico like Clara, with one ear lighter and one darker, and a gaze as direct as the woman's, staring out at the viewer.

"Do you know it?" Becca asked. "I found it online. I think—I'm not sure, but I think it may be my great-great-grandmother."

"A wise woman." Ruby nodded, as if in confirmation, before replacing the picture on its shelf.

For a moment, the two women stood in silence, and although Clara had the distinct impression that Becca was sizing up the other woman, she couldn't be sure what exactly she was weighing. She turned to Laurel, hoping her sister's ability to read thoughts might provide some insight. *Are you getting any of this?* But the sealpoint had stalked off, most likely in protest of the interruption.

"Anyway, there's your violin." Becca nodded toward the table, where Laurel had once again stretched out alongside the case. "I didn't think the conservatory would be able to identify it and get in touch so fast."

"The conservatory?" A pause and a quick puzzled glance, dark brows bunching in confusion.

"You mentioned the conservatory when we met, so I called them. You're a student there?"

"Yes. That is, I hope to be." The newcomer began to nod and then broke off, her pale face growing wistful. "What a pretty cat." She reached out just as Laurel yawned, showing her fangs.

"The conservatory is why I came to Boston," Ruby explained with a slight stammer as she drew her hand back. "I am still waiting to hear the result of my audition. There is a scholarship, and the panel was very encouraging. I know it is unusual to begin with the spring semester, but given my circumstances..."

"I bet you did great." Becca pulled the sealpoint toward her, ignoring her grumbling whine.

The visitor glanced up with shy smile. "They gave me a private practice room already. I know they are between semesters, but I believe that must bode well."

Becca returned her smile without comment as the musician opened the case to reveal the instrument inside. Laurel, also looking on, kept up a low feline grumble.

"Thank you." A mix of emotions played crossed Ruby's face, as Laurel, fed up, jumped to the ground with a grunt. "I was so worried."

"You're welcome. But..." Becca looked as quizzical as a cat. More quizzical, Clara thought, as she slipped by her peeved sister to watch the two humans. "Can you tell me why you ran out of the store so quickly? Does it have anything to do with the problem you started to tell me about?"

"Problem?" As Becca spoke, Ruby had been reaching for the violin's neck, as if to lift it. As she responded, she stopped herself, so that only the tips of her fingers touched the time-darkened wood.

"You were telling me that you needed the services of a witch detective."

"Yes, I do." Ruby was nodding even as she closed the case, flipping the latches shut with a sigh. "And, yes, it has to do with my violin."

"Is there something you'd like to tell me?" Becca paused, searching for the words. "Is there something wrong with the violin?"

"Yes, no. I am not sure." Her eyes darted around the apartment. But only the cats were listening, and although Clara sat there rapt, Laurel had begun bathing. She was acting as if she didn't care, but her baby sister could tell how irritated she was by the vigor with which she bit her toenails. "I am wondering if it is haunted."

"And that's why you left it with me?" Becca's voice dropped further, causing Clara to prick up her ears. Even Laurel stopped grooming. "Is it valuable? I can tell it's old."

"I value it, but no." Ruby smiled, as if at something the cats could not see. "It was my grandfather's and his father's before him. It has been in my family so long…"

She looked over at the print in its silver frame. "I cannot believe I was so careless, but yesterday was such a long day. I have been traveling, and I had the audition." She sighed. "I am so grateful you found it and that you kept it safe."

"Of course," said Becca. "But I'm concerned about this feeling you had. Like, maybe you were picking up on something." She chose her next phrase carefully, as if she could make the truth less hideous. "That perhaps there was a connection to what happened next door." She paused, but Ruby did not reply. "You were staying there. Weren't you?"

A flash of distress crossed the other girl's face. "Yes, I arrived late the night before. Everything took so much longer than I expected, and then today I had my appointment at the conservatory." She hung her head but couldn't hide the single tear that ran down her cheek. "That poor man…"

"Oh, dear." Becca nearly pushed her into a chair. "I'm sorry. You must be wiped out." Another tear. "Do you have a place to stay tonight?"

A sniffle, as the other woman shook her head. As if on cue, the wind howled, shaking the panes of the kitchen window, and the old radiator started to clank as the heat came on.

"That's it," Becca said. "You're staying here."

"No, I cannot." Ruby shook her head. "Really."

The window rattled again, as if to chime in. The sky outside was already dark, but Clara could smell the clouds gathering.

"I won't hear otherwise," Becca insisted as she began to gather up the sofa cushions, waking Harriet, who had settled in for a nap. "Do you have a bag? Or are your things next door?"

"No, I brought my bag to my new practice space."

"Great." Becca exhaled, her relief apparent. "Shall we go get it?"

"I-I can do that." That slight stammer, though this time with a hint of a shy smile. "I will have to show an ID, but they gave me a temporary card. Almost like I am already accepted."

"I bet that's a good sign." Becca piled the cushions on the chair, further discomfiting Harriet, who fled the room. "And I'll make up the couch in the meantime."

She was rewarded by a beaming version of that smile. "Thank you."

"I may not be doing much for you as a witch detective, but maybe I can be a friend."

"*I don't know about this,*" Clara mused softly as Becca drew her a map of the T, jotting her cell number on the bottom.

"Just in case you get lost."

"*Relax.*" Laurel came up beside her. "*She's like a kitten. I can tell.*"

Clara wasn't convinced, and she felt the fur along her back rise as Becca helped Ruby into her coat and hat.

"One thing." Ruby pulled the black cap down to cover the tips of her ears. "Could I leave my violin here again while I go for my bag?"

"Of course," said Becca. "I think my cats are growing fond of it."

Chapter 10

"Becca, have you lost it?" Maddy wasn't so understanding. "You're letting a complete stranger stay with you—a stranger who's been involved in a murder?"

"She wasn't involved." Becca emphasized the last word once her friend had stopped yelling. "Not the way you mean, anyway. If anything, the fact that she was there means she deserves more of our sympathy. Can you imagine opening the door to the apartment where you think you're staying and finding your host…like that?"

"I'm imagining finding you like that!" Maddy had apparently only paused to catch her breath. "I mean, do you know anything about her?"

"She's a student at the conservatory." Becca was speaking with her calming voice, the one she used when Laurel was climbing the drapes or any of them had to go to the vet. "That's how she found me again. And she trusted me, remember? She left her violin with me at the shop."

"That could have been a plant." Maddy couldn't see the confusion on Becca's face, but she must have heard her own words. "I mean a setup, Becca. Something to draw you in. To get you involved."

"I am involved." Becca took the phone over to the table and let the fingers of her free hand run over the violin case. "She came to me even before that—before any of this happened."

"I don't care. I'm coming over. You're not spending the night alone with her."

"But Maddy—"

"No buts. I was thinking I'd come over anyway, and this settles it. I'll sleep on the floor if I have to—that is, if I sleep at all."

True to her word, Becca's friend showed up twenty minutes later, holding a gym bag that was suspiciously lumpy.

"Where is she?" Maddy scanned the room, her usually kind, round face tight with suspicion. For once, she ignored the three cats who had gathered to greet her.

"She's not back yet." Becca reached for the bag, but her large friend held tight. "Okay, what do you have in there?"

"My toothbrush." Her friend continued to eye the room, as if the stranger might be lurking in one of the corners. "And a few odds and ends, just in case."

"You don't have any groceries tucked in there, do you?" Becca laughed. "Look at the way Harriet is sniffing your bag."

"No. Hey, girl." Maddy bent over to give the marmalade a belated greeting, even as Clara rubbed against her leggings in welcome. "I mean, I grabbed some rice cakes and Oreos, but that's all. You want rice cakes? They're cheese flavored." This was to Laurel, who stood on her hind legs to shove her head into Maddy's hand.

"They've already had dinner. But what with one thing and another, I didn't get to shop, and now I don't want to go out in case Ruby comes by."

"Ruby? That's her name?" Maddy paused, looking up at her host. "Ruby what?"

"I'm sure she told me—Grozny, maybe?" Becca's tone was faintly scolding. "There's been so much going on. Hey, why don't we call Zoe's

Chinese. They deliver."

"You're not going to make me feel better about this with some moo shi, you know." Maddy reached down to rub Laurel's ears and then began to unbutton her coat. "But, yeah, I could go for some."

"I'll order extra, for when Ruby gets here. Once you talk with her, you'll see she's just a normal student. A little lost is all."

Before Maddy could respond, Becca handed her the takeout menu. "Here," she said. "Choose a couple of dishes, and I'll make the call."

Once the order had been placed, Maddy got down to business, settling herself onto the sofa. "So, tell me everything you know. " She stroked Harriet absently. "I mean for real, Becca. Not just that you have a feeling about this girl."

"I do, though." Becca paused before continuing. "There's something going on with her, but I don't get any sense of danger from her. More than that, my cats are very calm—they were fine with her and they're fine with the violin."

"Wait, what?" Maddy did a double take, startling the cat by her side. "It's still here?"

"It didn't make sense for her to lug it around." Becca looked like she was going to explain further, but Maddy was already on her feet.

"Where is it? I want to see it."

"It's on the table." Becca led the way, but when her friend reached for the case, she moved to stop her. "I don't know if you should—"

"A stranger left something with you. It could be a bomb. Or drugs. Or…" She'd opened the case by then. "Wow, it's in rough shape, isn't it?"

"She said it was her grandfather's." Becca watched as Maddy picked up the age-darkened instrument and examined it. "It's just a violin, Mads."

"So you say." Her friend pressed her face up to the instrument, squinting into the f-hole.

"Please be careful."

"She wasn't. She left it with a stranger." Despite her words, she replaced the instrument with care back in its worn enclosure, and then proceeded to open each compartment, taking out the sheet music and smelling the block of dark rosin.

"She was jet-lagged, Maddy. She'd been traveling nonstop. She arrived just in time for her audition."

"Great." Maddy tapped a little glass-topped dial that looked like it had been recently set into the stained velvet. "This is probably a drug thing, then."

"It's a hygrometer, to measure the humidity," Becca corrected her gently. "I was reading up on older instruments. They're sensitive."

Her friend snorted, sounding suspiciously like Laurel. "This looks like it's already been through the war."

"It might have been."

Maddy glanced up but didn't respond, and Becca, knowing her friend, let her continue with her examination of the case and its contents, which she only gave up once their food had arrived.

An hour later, the shrimp in the moo shi was gone, to the cats' dismay. But the young violinist still had not appeared.

"You'd think she'd call." Maddy was eying the noodles. As delicately as any move of Laurel's, she reached her chopsticks over to pick out a mushroom. "I assume you've tried to call her?"

"I don't have her number." While her friend was still chewing, she explained. "Everything was so crazy, and I thought she'd be right back. I made a map for her. I hope she didn't get lost."

Maddy coughed, waking Harriet, who had begun snoring beside her. "Maybe," she said in a tone of voice that made Clara turn to examine her broad friendly face as well.

The two friends continued to eat, and if Becca kept sneaking peeks at the door, Maddy pretended not to notice. Still, her friend sighed audibly as Becca laid down her chopsticks.

"I think I'm done." She forced a smile. "You go on. There's no point in saving any of the pancakes," Becca rationalized. "They'll only get stale."

"You might want to put the rest of the tofu in the fridge." Maddy pointed to the half-full container.

"It'll get cold," Becca pointed out.

"I'm not thinking of your houseguests. I'm wondering about your cat." As if on cue, Harriet lurched forward. "I think she might have eaten a hot pepper."

"Harriet?" With one more urp, she sat up straight and licked her chops. "I didn't think cats ate tofu." Becca sounded doubtful, even as she reached for her pet.

"Did you hear that?" Clara felt it only fair to warn her. *"It's not meat!"*

"Stay out of this." Laurel's lip drew back, exposing her fangs. *"I don't have time to explain."*

"She's okay, isn't she?" Maddy asked.

"I think so." Becca stroked the long, silky coat, even as she craned to see into the big cat's eyes.

"This is rather pleasant." Harriet licked her chops.

Of course, Harriet would do anything for attention, especially if that attention resulted in treats. Clara had a sneaking suspicion that more was at work here, but before any of the felines could act, Becca stood, depositing her pet on the rug.

"Maybe I should put this away." She reached for the tofu. "I can always reheat it if Ruby hasn't eaten."

Gathering up their bowls, as well as the leftover rice, Maddy followed Becca into the kitchen. "Becca, I don't think she's going to show."

"Nonsense. You know how long the T takes, and with this cold, with the switches freezing every third day, all bets are off." From her vantage place on the table, Clara could see Becca transferring the fragrant food into plastic containers. "Would you hand me that lid?"

"Becca, look at the time. She's not going to make the T." Clara looked at her person, rather than the clock. Time means little when one can get treats almost on demand. The dismay on Becca's face, however, alarmed the little cat.

"I should never have let her go by herself." She turned to her friend. "Maybe I should call the police."

As if on cue, her phone pinged.

"Is that her? Has she been arrested?" Maddy leaned over.

"It is, but no." Becca looked up from the screen, the relief clear on her face. "She's staying at the conservatory tonight. She'll get the violin from me tomorrow."

"Hallelujah." Maddy threw up her hands in mock celebration. "Or thanks to Bast, or whatever you'd say."

All three cats sat up, eyes wide. Luckily, neither human noticed.

"So, do you still have Netflix?" Maddy sealed the top on the noodles and then licked the spoon, as thoroughly as Harriet would have.

"Don't you have work in the morning?" Becca handed her friend the remote.

"Which is why I brought a bag, silly." Laurel had already investigated the carryon at the foot of the couch. "Besides, I don't trust her not to show up in the middle of the night." Even as she switched on the TV, she fixed her friend with a stare. "If she does, I don't think you should let her in."

"Maddy, you know I couldn't do that."

"Yeah, I do. But please remember, she's a person. Not a lost cat, Becca."

At her feet, Laurel and Harriet exchanged a glance. "*That was too close.*" Clara heard Harriet murmur, and Laurel dipped her head in agreement.

"*And now,*" Harriet's voice sounded softly in Clara's ears, "*where were we?*"

Chapter 11

The heat was intense. The sun, beating down, bleached out all color, so that even the stripes on Clara's forearm appeared pale and gray.

"*Stripes?*" The cat sat bolt upright in surprise and immediately looked down at her snowy white mitts and the sleeves—one orange, one black—on each side. She hadn't been aware of falling asleep, but over here by the radiator, the rug was particularly cozy.

"*Relax, silly.*" Laurel stared down from her perch on the bookshelf. "*It's just a memory.*"

A faint rumble to her right caught her attention. Harriet, eyes closed and with her own white paws tucked under her ample breast, was either purring or snoring. "*A memory?*"

"*Fatso here thought that would be easier, so she put herself into a trance.*" Laurel settled down into her own meatloaf pose. "*Especially since you have the attention span of a gnat.*"

Clara started to protest but caught herself. Harriet had to be really out for Laurel to risk calling her that. Besides, she was curious. Settling down, she closed her eyes and let the dream roll over her once again.

Languid with the heat, the cat strolled slowly over to the high stone wall. Even a desert creature knows to seek shade at high noon, and the tawny blocks cast just enough shadow for one slim feline. From the relative cool, the cat looked out on a woman in a rough linen shift kneeling in front of a reed basket. From where she lay, the cat could see her back, dark with sweat, and how it heaved, her shoulders jerking in a fitful rhythm. Although the cat could hear no sound, it was easy to make out that the woman was crying,

"Poor fool." The cat watched as the woman's sobs subsided and she bent lower, cupping her hands to scoop up what appeared to be small golden kernels from the sandy ground. As she moved to pour the kernels into the basket, the cat got a better sense of what she was doing—as well as the cause of those tears. Some creature had gnawed a hole in the woven reeds, a hole the woman had attempted to patch with rough linen torn from her shift. The patch was barely adequate, however, and the kernels—grain, Clara realized—kept leaking through even as the woman knelt at her task, the linen on her back dark with sweat. *"She should know better than to labor in this weather."*

"She has no choice." The voice, a deep rumbling that seemed to come from the stone itself, startled the cat. *"She must save the grain, or she will be whipped. Your first duty—"*

"Who's there? Who said that?" Despite the heat, the cat jumped up and spun around, seeking the source of that voice.

"Don't you know me?" Deep and low but lightened by—could it be?—humor. *"You should."*

The cat looked up at the stone that sheltered her, the base of a great carving. Bast, the goddess. Could it be? *"Goddess."* She flattened herself before the great statue, chin on the ground in obeisance. *"I know you,"* she said. *"What would you have me do?"*

Perhaps it was the sun. The heat, punishing even for a wild creature. A play of the light, a shadow cast by those giant ears, perhaps, but the stone eyes appeared to flicker. The great muzzle drew back, just for a moment, to reveal a mighty fang…

Chapter 12

A sharp rapping woke Clara. Morning, a watery winter sun was streaming in the window, and the calico looked around for her sisters, eager to share her dream. As the tapping came once more, she found them already waiting by the door.

"*Took you long enough.*" Laurel lashed her tail for emphasis, as her sister joined the line staring up at the locked door.

"*Did you—you must know...*" Clara fumbled for words. "*That was one of us, wasn't it?*"

"*One? You only saw one?*" Laurel turned toward Harriet.

"*I may have rushed that one.*" Harriet was licking her chops. "*There were leftovers.*"

"*You don't like tofu anyway.*" Laurel, Clara noticed, had a touch of black bean sauce on her whisker. At least she did, until a quick swipe of the tongue made it disappear. "*But I was wondering if you were going to sleep through the whole thing.*"

"*What thing?*" Clara scooted out of the way as Becca raced to the door.

"Ruby, I was wondering—" Becca stopped herself. Instead of the pale young musician, she had opened the door to a rotund little man.

Roughly Becca's height, his dark hair, as well as the red wool vest he wore under his brown suit, made him look like a robin. An agitated robin, Clara thought, his beady eyes glaring at Becca out of a face shiny with sweat.

"I'm sorry. Who are you?" Becca pulled her bathrobe collar close. Not, thought her cat, because of the draft.

"You sent us a photo." A breathy voice, rather than a chirp. "I didn't see it until this morning. I came over as quickly as I could."

Becca shook her head, and the man took a deep breath, the red of his vest expanding.

"I'm from the conservatory," he said. He was speaking slowly and clearly now, the breathiness gone. Almost, it occurred to Clara, as if he thought Becca hard of hearing or stupid. "Like I said. I'm here about the violin."

"Oh, you didn't have to bother." Becca eyed him with curiosity. Rather, Clara thought, like Laurel would a bird. "I found its owner."

"The owner?" He tilted his head, those beady eyes shining.

"Ruby. It was her grandfather's, so she knew it right away." Becca stood blocking the door, but she must have heard Maddy come up behind her, her hair still wet from the shower.

"No, that's not possible." The flush spreading to his small, flat ears. "You see, the violin you sent us a photo of is a Guadagnini, and we have reason to believe it's the instrument that was stolen from a collector in New York several months ago."

"Wait." Becca raised her hands to stop the flood of words. "A what?"

"A Guadagnini." The little man leaned in, as if that would make his meaning clear. When it didn't—Becca simply shook her head—he took another deep breath, expanding his belly as if about to break into song.

"Guadagnini was an Italian luthier, an instrument maker, in the eighteenth century," he said, lapsing into a decidedly didactic tone. "Very few of his violins have survived, and the ones that are still

89

around are rather well known. Among afficionados, of course. They are also extremely valuable. This one, as I've said, belongs to a private collector. In monetary terms alone, it's a treasure, worth in excess of half a million dollars. But it's more than that. The collector, the rightful owner, is an extremely discerning man who is understandably upset about the loss of his prized piece."

"That's not possible." Becca's face showed her confusion. "I haven't read anything in the news. Why do you even think the violin I showed you is the missing one? Have you seen this Guad- whatever?"

"Me? No." The man squeaked. "But this is my field of expertise. And this is a very sensitive case. Local law enforcement has not been involved, and even Interpol..." He shook off the idea, frowning. "There's a concern, with a treasure like this, that if the thieves fear being apprehended, they might destroy the piece."

"That sounds horrible, but you really don't have to worry." Becca spoke calmly, but she didn't budge. "Like I said, there's been some mistake. The violin I found is a family heirloom."

"But that photo you sent—" His complexion was verging on purple.

"Maybe it was a bad photo. My phone isn't the newest model." Becca was shaking her head.

Behind her, Maddy shifted her weight from one foot to another. "Becca," she said softly.

Becca ignored her. "The young woman who left it with me just arrived in the States. She's a student."

"She's an accomplice," the round man lisped slightly, his last word coming out like a hiss. "That's what she is. At the very least."

Becca didn't respond, as Clara felt her sister come up beside her. "Uh-oh..." Laurel gave a soft Siamese sigh. Clara flicked her tail once in assent. It didn't take Laurel's skills to pick up the combination of skepticism and doubt playing through her mind.

"But I'll leave that to the authorities, who will be notified in good time. What matters to me is the safety of the instrument. Which I'd like to see now." He paused, as if to master that lisp. "Please."

Still, Becca didn't respond, and Clara looked to her older sister for guidance. But Laurel was staring at the stranger's face, and so the calico looked around for their senior sibling.

"*I don't like him,*" said Laurel.

"*He does smell off,*" agreed Harriet.

Clara felt the prickling as her fur began to rise and hunkered down, ready to pounce on the diminutive intruder. And it hit her: this is what Harriet had warned her about—that their person might get caught up in larger conflict. "*And that,*" Harriet had warned, "*never turns out well.*"

"I don't have it."

Behind her, Maddy gasped. But Becca warmed to her theme as she began to explain. "I sent the university that email last night because I was trying to locate the student who had left the violin with me at the shop where I work. But she came by, you see, and picked it up. That's why I'm convinced that you must be mistaken."

"*She shouldn't be trying so hard to explain.*" Laurel's ears flipped back, never a good sign. Beside her, Harriet coughed.

"There may be a reward." The man didn't seem to believe her, his beady eyes narrowing as he spoke. "Even for information."

"I'm sorry." Becca stood firm. "I can't help you."

For a few moments, the two stood, staring at each other, and Clara could feel the tension between them. She could also, she realized, feel Laurel's concentration, and so she joined in, staring at the little man.

He broke first, licking his lips before lowering his gaze to the floor. "I'm in my office every night till at least eight."

"Thank you for telling me." Becca glanced back at her cats and then pulled herself up to her full height to face the stranger once more. "And now I've got to get ready for work. Why don't you leave your card with me? If I find any other violins, I'll give you a call."

The stranger sputtered as Becca held out her hand, but then he fished in his wallet and came out with a card.

"Norm Brustein, assistant dean," she read. But as he opened his mouth to speak once more, she cut him off. "Thanks so much for coming by, Mr. Brustein. I promise I'll keep my eyes open. Goodbye." And with that, she shut the door.

"What a nasty little man." Becca collapsed against the door as Maddy looked on, aghast. "And he looked rather like a robin too," she added sadly. Her cats, who already had decided opinions about the nature of birds, silently concurred.

Maddy, however, had found her voice. "Becca, what are you doing?"

"I don't really know." She looked up at her friend. "Only, I didn't like the way he was talking to me."

"I don't like this one bit, Becca. You don't know this girl at all. She left her violin with you—it's probably stolen. She's probably not a student at all. She's a criminal, and now she's on the lam. You wanted to call the police last night, right? Well, I think you should. And call that conservatory guy back too. Tell him you were wrong."

"I don't know, Maddy." Becca shook her head. "You didn't hear her talking about her audition. About the conservatory. And the only reason I was tempted to call the police was because I was worried about her."

"She conned you, Becs. You always think the best of people."

"Maybe, Maddy. But it doesn't matter. You heard him: the police don't know anything about this, and I have no idea how to contact Interpol or whatever other agency is involved. Besides, what if I'm right? If she's telling the truth—and I think she is—then I don't want to get Ruby involved in some investigation with the conservatory. She's still waiting to hear if she's been accepted, and I'm not going to be the one to kill her dream."

Maddy sighed. She knew her friend well. "So what are you going to do?"

"The violin is safe here, at least for now. So I'm going to get ready for work." Chin up, Becca walked past her friend into the bedroom to get dressed. "And so, I think, should you."

As the friends dressed, Clara turned toward Laurel.

"Was that your idea?"

Her sister's blue eyes closed in satisfaction. *"You didn't like him either. Admit it."*

Clara bowed her head in assent. There had been something odd about the man. He'd seemed, well, as strained and scared as a bird would in a house full of cats.

"He was a bully, and I don't like bullies." Laurel lashed her tail at the memory. *"Although that does fit with him being scared."*

Clara squirmed. It was always a bit disconcerting when Laurel read her thoughts. Besides, something else was bothering her. *"He did act odd,"* she conceded. *"But Becca lied."* Clara was fundamentally an honest cat, although the feline sense of right and wrong could be a bit subjective.

"Becca stretched the truth." Into Clara's mind came the image of the violin tucked away in the bedroom while Becca had cleaned up after the friends' dinner. Not exactly to hand. *"How do humans put it? Out of sight…out of mind?"*

"I only hope you didn't get her into trouble." Clara sighed as she watched Harriet amble off to the sofa, the history lesson she'd begun to relate vivid in her little sister's mind.

Chapter 13

Maddy took off first, though not before trying one more time to convince her friend.

"All you have to do is call him," she said. "Say you forgot. He won't care."

"Don't you have enough to worry about with Roberts?" Becca hugged her friend, before pushing her out into the hall.

Becca left soon after, and Clara shaded herself to follow. But even as the little cat began to bounce her way down the stairs, she realized Becca wasn't beside her.

Climbing back up, the calico saw her person had frozen in the hall outside the apartment. She was staring at the yellow crime-scene tape that covered the neighbor's door, a haunted look on her face. When she reached into her bag, Clara wondered if she was going to call the robin-like man. Maybe Laurel's influence had worn off. Maybe Maddy's embrace had convinced her. But all she did was pull out a pen and a stickie note.

R – At shop. – B, she wrote. And sticking the note to her door, she turned and descended to the street.

"It's probably nothing." Clara caught up to her in time to hear her talking to her phone. "But maybe I should bring her in? Thanks."

The device buzzed before she could slip it back into her bag.

"Dr. Keller?" she answered without even a glance. "Thanks for getting back to me—"

"So, has she called?" Maddy interrupted, her voice loud enough to carry.

"Oh, Maddy!" Becca glanced down at the phone before scanning the street for the young musician. "We just left. But no."

"Good. Good riddance to bad rubbish!" A pause and the sound of a chime. Maddy, Clara realized, was on a bus. "Anyway, I was thinking. If she doesn't show and you don't want to call the dude from the conservatory, you could just drop the violin off at the police station. I'll go with you."

"I'm sure she'll turn up." Becca ignored her friend's outburst. "I left a note that I'd be at the shop, and I was about to text her back too."

"You—" Maddy's sigh carried over the phone line. "Becca, you can't adopt every stray you meet."

Clara's fur bristled at that. Maddy had always been a good friend to Becca, but that was going too far. Becca seemed bothered as well. "I'm not," she said with a little more force than usual. "But you didn't meet her, Maddy. I did. She's young and she's over her head."

"If you say so." Maddy didn't sound chastened. "I know you have a good heart, Becs. But please think about what I said. You've got to look out for yourself."

Becca was at the shop by then, which gave her an excuse to end the conversation. But even if she led her friend to believe she had to open, she didn't reach for the key ring in her bag. Instead, Clara saw, she knocked on the store's painted glass door, standing on tiptoe to smile in over a yellow and green yin and yang sign.

"Morning!" She waved to Margaret, the store's owner. In response,

Elizabeth's younger, and shorter, sister turned and grimaced, her face pruning up beneath that unnaturally dark hair. Shambling slowly over, she unlocked the door, by which point the grimace had softened a bit to her customary scowl.

"Thanks, Margaret." Becca sounded determined to sweeten the old lady.

"You startled me." The owner waddled away. "I didn't know if you'd be here today." The older woman had walked back into the shop, so she couldn't see Becca's face fall.

"Oh, I'm sorry." Becca quickly shed her coat, tucking her mittens in the pocket. "Didn't Elizabeth tell you?"

"She said you wandered into a crime scene or something. No, don't bother." She waved off Becca's explanation as she bustled past. "I gather this came from your running off after some girl like she was your long-lost sister." The answer came from the shop's back room.

"Kind of." Becca struggled to explain as she followed her. Hanging her coat, she began again. "We had a customer and she left something in the store. That's why I took off, but then, well, something happened with my neighbor—well, the man I thought was my neighbor, and I had to talk to the police—"

"Forget I asked." Margaret waved away Becca's explanation like a pesky fly. "This girl, she didn't buy anything, right? So she wasn't a customer, was she? You certainly have a knack for finding trouble, young lady."

Becca opened her mouth to respond before deciding better of it. "She's only venting," Clara heard her say to herself, even as the little cat braced for what was coming next.

"Coming!" Becca called out as the bells in the front room jingled, rushing back to the front room as Elizabeth strode in. "Oh, hi!"

"Good morning." The taller sister smiled with real affection. "Did my sister interrogate you yet?"

"No." Becca managed a smile, even as her eyes darted to the back room. "She didn't want to hear any of it. I gather she didn't believe what you told her?"

"Oh, I didn't give her the details." Elizabeth breezed by. "She wouldn't have cared. Family, you know? It's never perfect."

"Is that Bitsy?" Margaret came out of the back. "Finally! Some obnoxious man was here, asking questions."

"I hope you didn't tell him when Becca was coming in."

"What? No." Margaret thumped past her sister. "I don't know when she'll be here half the time."

"Margaret, I'm sorry." Becca was doing her best to keep her tone pleasant, her smile fixed. "Elizabeth and I both thought I should go after her—the customer, that is."

"Huh." Margaret snorted, pursing her lips. "Well, maybe if you can catch one, it will be worth it."

"This was important, Margie." Clara could have sworn Elizabeth's smile was as forced as Becca's. It softened when she turned toward the shop girl. "I'm going to help her with the inventory, Becca," she said. "I'll make sure she understands. Give a yell if you need me."

"Thanks. Do you want me to wait on the window display?" Becca called as she disappeared into the back.

"Of course," Elizabeth called over her shoulder.

"Anything in particular you want?" Becca sounded a little shakier than usual.

"Trust your instincts, Becca." The older woman's voice carried from the back room. "I do."

Elizabeth must have managed to make her sister understand about the murder—and Becca's role in discovering it—because the owner didn't bother her employee again that morning. Two hours later, when the sisters were leaving for lunch, Margaret even went so far as to approach Becca, patting her arm as if she were a cat. It hadn't been that long ago, after all, that Becca had helped her deal with a series of crises that had resulted in the death of her husband.

"Thanks." Becca acknowledged the awkward kindness.

"We're going to lunch," her boss replied, the moment over.

Once the two were gone, Becca took advantage of the quiet to focus on the display. She was in the back, choosing between two statues of Ganesh, when the bells announced a visitor.

"Coming," she called, grabbing the more colorful of the two elephant-headed gods and proceeding to the front of the store, only to find Marcia and Ande had entered, propelled by a gust of wintry air.

"Hey, Becca." Ande was hugging herself as she looked around. "Seems we brought the cold with us."

"Honestly? A draft is kind of welcome. That window concentrates the sun. Even with the paint, its usually broiling in here."

Marcia, meanwhile, was staring, transfixed. "That is so cool." She reached for the statue.

"I'm going to use it in the window display," Becca explained, handing it over. "What brings you out in this weather?"

"We were talking." Ande returned her friend's smile. "And it came up that you could use some help."

"How did you—?"

"We hate the idea of you losing your place," Marcia broke in. "Hey, it's selfish. We both love having the coven there."

"I know you said you can't afford to buy your place. But I've been looking at some options." Becca began to protest again, but Ande cut her off. "Please, Becca, this is what I do. I've run the numbers."

"And I just tagged along to lend some moral support." Marcia set the Ganesh down beside the register and leaned over the tray of gemstones, running her finger through the offerings, so that the colorful stones made a pleasant rattle. "And maybe look for a ruby."

Becca did a double take. "Do you know her?"

"What? No. Wait, do you have any info?"

Ande looked at her two friends. "What are you two talking about?"

"This girl who came in—"

"Oh, no, I meant that big jewel heist."

"Wait, what?" Becca stopped first. "Marcia, what are you talking about?"

"Didn't you hear?" Marcia selected a red stone and held it up to the light. Polished as smooth as beach glass, it glowed like fire. "The crown jewel of Monrovia or something was stolen from a museum exhibit. It's all over the news. Hey, if it ended up here, it would certainly cover your down payment." She winked. "I mean, the reward money, of course."

Becca managed a smile, but Ande was studying her face. "What is it, Becca?"

"It's complicated." Becca hesitated on that last word. "Something happened last night."

Two sets of eyes waited, but Becca looked down at the tray.

"I sort of can't talk about it anymore. Not if I'm going to make it through the workday." Summoning a smile, she touched one finger to the stone in Marcia's hand, as if taking strength from its smooth and glowing surface. "And that's a garnet. Sorry."

Ande and Marcia exchanged a glance that both Becca and her cat could read too well.

"But tell me more about this robbery." Becca summoned an enthusiasm that had been missing earlier. "I could use a good heist story."

"Well," Marcia leaned in, clearly willing to humor her friend, "the news reports were talking about how the jewel might have been smuggled out of the country. Sounds like they could use a witch detective, Becca."

"I think they have Interpol for that." Her friends' concern, as much as the distraction, had brought some color back to Becca's face. "Besides, wouldn't it have been cut into pieces by now and sold?"

"Actually, probably not," Ande responded. "More and more, when something famous is stolen—and the Vér ruby is a big deal—it just kind of disappears."

The tall, dark-skinned woman took in her friend's surprise. "Someone from Interpol was interviewed in a forensic accounting journal," she explained.

"Is that something you're thinking of going into?" Becca regarded her friend anew.

"She's got a crush on the lead detective." Marcia grinned. "Some French dude named Salieri or something."

"Sanglier. And I do not." Ande ducked her head but not fast enough to hide the flush that swept up her neck. "I just admire his methods. He's a proponent of the theory that they're going into private collections, or maybe used as markers in underworld deals. Almost like currency, since everyone has a pretty good idea of what its value is."

"There you go, Becca." Marcia warmed to the topic. "If you did find it, then you could use it to get a mortgage."

"Only from a drug lord." Becca managed a laugh, which Ande took as her cue.

"Seriously, Becca, there are a couple of different paths you can take here." She must have seen something on Becca's face, because she then pulled two pamphlets out of her bag and pushed them across the counter. "Would you take a look?"

"Sure." Becca's smile wobbled as she pulled the papers toward.

"And if you want to talk." Ande's dark eyes were kind.

"Thanks." Becca nodded as they headed toward the door. "And thanks to both of you for coming by. I promise, Marcia, if I find any rubies, you'll be the first to know."

"I'd say you've found something priceless already."

Becca whipped around, startled. She'd been focused on her friends as they headed out to the street, and Elizabeth's approach had been masked by the bells.

"My friends, you mean?" Becca smiled up at her manager. "Yeah, they're pretty great."

"Yes, they are." Elizabeth returned her grin. "But I was thinking of other treasures as well."

With that, the older woman pulled a cardboard box from a lower shelf and disappeared back into the storeroom, leaving Becca alone in the shop. The visit from Ande and Marcia had lifted her mood. Even though she hadn't told them of the horror of the night before, their mere presence—and, yes, Ande's generous offer—had done their work. Even the tray of gemstones looked duller now that Marcia wasn't flipping them over or holding them to the light. Although she picked out a particularly pretty one, another garnet with an interior flaw that made it flash like fire, Becca's shoulders sagged.

The accompanying sigh might not have been audible to anyone whose hearing was less acute than Clara's, but to the little calico, the exhalation, and its meaning, was loud and clear. Becca was distressed, and her pet felt powerless to help her. Invisibility could be so frustrating. If they were at home, Clara could simply jump for that red gem and bat at it. While Harriet might covet something so sparkly, Clara would be doing it to distract her person. Her sisters' teasing nickname, Clown, wasn't always a negative.

But shaded as she was, Clara could do little but watch, dispirited as Becca leafed through Ande's pamphlets without really seeing them. What Becca's boss had said had touched her, her cat realized, and for the first time Clara wondered if Laurel had a point. Maybe Becca did need more human companionship. She certainly deserved to be treasured.

Could that have been what Elizabeth meant? There was something uncanny about the older woman, a tendency to say things that sent a prickling along Clara's spine and made her fur rise just thinking about it. Elizabeth might be friendlier than her sister. She was certainly more interested in Becca, as well as the shop. But that interest could be unnerving. The calico had not forgotten how the older woman had appeared able to see her, for instance, even when she was sure she was shaded to be invisible to humans.

That couldn't be the problem for Becca though, the little cat thought as she stared up at her person's face. Elizabeth interacted with her like most humans did. Or, no, the tingling in Clara's fur alerted her, almost like all humans. While most of the bipeds were fairly predictable, at least to a cat, this one was different. How, she couldn't exactly say, and watching the play of emotions across her person's face, Clara once again wished that she'd heard more of Harriet's story. Her history had hinted that there were humans who were different. Special somehow. Clara had automatically assumed that Harriet was referring to the ones like their Becca. Even if their person hadn't the magic of a day-old kitten, surely she was special in other ways. But maybe she meant humans like this Elizabeth, with those dark, hooded eyes that seemed to perceive so much.

How could they see her? Clara hunkered down to work this through, her black-tipped tail wrapping around her white front paws. As she pondered, Becca went through her usual morning routine in the shop: checking the cash register and watering the two plants that sat in the window. She had had problems with plants here before, but these were harmless—an aloe, which probably would have benefited from less water, and a geranium, which Clara would have liked to nibble on if she weren't pretty sure it would upset her tum.

By the time Becca had finished with the plants and summoned some gentle music out of a machine in the back, Clara was giving this problem her undivided concentration. And if she was not asleep on the pile of soft fleece sweatshirts with the image of Bast on them as she mulled, then she was most assuredly in that deep meditative state that cats can assume when they're thinking. Almost like a trance, as if Laurel and Harriet were still with her, lulling her to sleep…

"Your first duty…" The words, like an echo, stayed in her ears, even as the cat sensed that years had passed. The woman had not become a queen. It was not to be. But since that day she had power of a sort. She was certainly no longer to be whipped.

The cat had made quick work of the mice in the granary, as the pointy-eared goddess had decreed. But there was more as well. Whereas the others of her kind had only thought of themselves, feasting at will on the wheat-fattened prey and moving on to other amusement once their hunger was sated, this cat had stayed true, standing sentinel on the woman's baskets, even while she slept.

One evening, early in her vigil, two of her kind joined her.

"You need your rest." The more slender of the two addressed her first, a spark in her sky-blue eyes. *"We will watch the woman and her wares."*

"But why?" The cat looked from the speaker to her companion, a large animal with unusually thick fur. She was tired by then, but wary. *"Was your kill not sufficient?"*

"Have you no memory, Foolish One? We come from the same mother." The second cat spoke in a low rumble, her reprimand like a growl. *"A daughter of Bast who brought us here to serve."*

"To serve?"

The two newcomers looked at each other as the smaller cat waited.

"Did you not sense it?" the slender one responded at last. *"Did you not see the great fang?"*

"We are to be guardians," her companion—her sister—explained,

103

her voice weighted with import. *"Of the grain, but so much more."*

And thus it began. The three cats made themselves known to the woman. Through thought and touch, they revealed mysteries. How the yeast, summoned from the air, could make beer as well as bread. How some plants could ease cramps and others rashes on the skin. Soon, she and her two sisters became known as the woman's companions, a point of honor. Beloved of Bast, the woman was called. Beloved of the small cat, in particular, who sought her out at night to sleep curled by her side...

Only when the bells jangled once more did Clara wake. The young violinist, her heart-shaped face pale and drawn, had entered the shop and was looking around. She was searching for Becca, Clara realized, her human senses unable to hear the soft humming that Becca kept up as she sketched, a set of markers resting on the top of the ladder where she stood.

Becca had been waiting to speak to this woman, Clara knew, and so she mulled over how to alert her—her shaded ears twisting this way and that—until a soft cough caught her attention. Relaxing back onto the cushion, Clara watched as Becca turned and descended the ladder to greet the newcomer.

"Ruby! I'm so glad to see you." Becca sounded breathless. "Please wait there. Don't move."

Even before Ruby could respond, Becca folded the ladder, carrying it to the back room. When she returned, she smelled strongly of the marker that had colored her outstretched hand blue.

"I'm sorry." She withdrew the offending hand and wiped it on her jeans. "We're—I'm redoing the window. But please, Ruby, what happened last night? I confess, I was worried."

"I am the one who should apologize." The dark-haired woman looked down at the floor. "And I do. By the time I got to the conservatory,

I realized I should simply stay there. Your subway system—I read that it closes. Besides, I have already involved you too much."

"You haven't done anything." Becca examined the other woman's face. "But you do look exhausted. I think some tea is called for."

With a glance at the front door, Becca led the other woman into the back room and put the kettle on. Ruby immediately slumped down onto the worn-out sofa, and Becca regarded her silently for a few moments.

"Okay, Ruby," she said. "What really happened?"

"I spent the night in my practice room. I did," Ruby began, rousing enough to protest. "But first, I walked for a while. There is a café by the train station, but until I know what I will be doing…"

"You didn't want to spend any money. I get it." Becca spoke softly. She pulled up the room's other chair, waiting for the water to boil—and for some answers. "After we have some tea, I'll get us both something to eat. But first, you've got to tell me what's going on."

The other woman slouched further, as if the old sofa would swallow her up. Just then, the kettle began to whistle, and Becca set about making two mugs of tea. By the time she handed one to Ruby, either the fragrant steam or the friendly fussing must have done their job. Ruby took a deep breath and began to talk.

"My family… we don't have much." Ruby must have sensed that Becca was about to say something, because she held up a hand and kept talking. "I am not asking for sympathy. We are happy. My mother works, and her sister, my aunt, she lives with us, too. But we do not have a lot of money. It was not always so. Before the war, we had standing. My grandmother was a professor. My grandfather played violin in the symphony. Then…" She waved her hand, showing how quickly that could all go away.

"We lost everything. Almost everything, but somehow, my mother kept my grandfather's violin. And when I was very little—I do not

105

remember, but I am told I was four—I found it and started to play. Not well, of course." A quick, shy smile. "But well enough. And some of the old friendships remained. My mother found one of her mother's former students. We had no money to pay him, but we would feed him. He became like a member of the family. He was the one who told us about the conservatory. He wrote to a musician he knew, someone who came here after the war, and he told me I could audition. That if I was accepted, I would be given a scholarship. I would be given work. I could study and I could play.

"Of course, even to come here…" She broke off, looking around. But Becca remained silent.

"My grandfather's violin was the only thing of value we had. But to sell—well, that is like that famous story, yes? But it must be done. We spoke to a dealer, thinking to trade it for a lesser instrument. Something that I could play, but then…" The other woman took a deep breath and let it out with an audible sigh, staring at the floor. If Clara didn't know better, she might have thought the other woman could see her, the way she was concentrating. But a certain wide glassiness to her eyes let her know that the young woman was really looking over events in her own mind. Her options, Clara thought, though a glance up at Becca reassured her that her person was aware that the newcomer might be making up a story.

When Ruby began again, she spoke so softly that Becca had to lean forward to hear her. Even Clara turned her ears.

"The dealer did not want it. He said he could not help us. Mementos of the time before the war are everywhere, and they are not valued maybe as they should be. We were ready to give up, but then he sent a message. He told us he had spoken to a wealthy man. Someone I had only heard of—no, you would not know his name, but in my city, he is known.

"He asked us to his house, my mother and me. He asked me to play

106

for him." She broke off, lost in her reverie. "It was like an audition, only for one man. After, he had us stay. He fed us and put us up, the two of us, in a beautiful room."

She sighed at the memory. "He thanked me afterward. And he said he thought it was important that I attend the conservatory. He would buy my grandfather's violin for enough for me to travel. He told me I could keep the case, for sentimental purposes. In the morning, I found he had fixed it up, fitting it with a travel sleeve and the hygrometer that modern cases have. And when I opened it, there was a new instrument inside. Student quality, such as many of my colleagues at the conservatory will probably be playing, but very nice."

She managed a smile that was wobbly at best. "It was a kind gesture, more than I expected. I did not see him again. But he made it all possible."

Becca was about to follow up—Clara could see she had more questions—when the familiar sound of the store's bells summoned her instead.

"Welcome to Charm and Cherish." Clara heard her person's familiar greeting and, after taking a last look at Ruby, the cat followed Becca into the front of the shop to find her addressing an older man in a zip-up leather jacket. "May I help you?"

"Oh." He squinted, heavy brows pushing down over deep-set eyes, as if he didn't quite see Becca. "You work here?"

"Yes, I do." Becca stepped behind the counter, as if to assert her proper place. The move also put a barrier between her and the man, Clara was relieved to note. As he frowned and looked around, she became increasingly certain he was not here for a candle or even a book. "Are you looking for anything in particular?"

Becca appeared to be on the alert as well.

"I was hoping to find the other girl. You know." One paw-like hand gestured to where his heavily pomaded hair curled around his ear.

"The one with the dark hair?"

"If you mean Gaia, she doesn't work here anymore." Becca's predecessor at the store had left town after a tumultuous series of events.

"I don't know what name she's using." The man stared at Becca, as if waiting for more.

"Well, I'm here now." Becca was straining to sound reasonable. Clara could hear the tightness in her voice.

"Alone?" He looked toward the open door that led to the back room.

"My manager and the store's owner live right upstairs." Becca reached behind her for the landline mounted on the wall. "Would you like to speak to either of them?"

"No." He frowned. "I'll come back." And with that, he turned and left.

"Whoa." Becca slumped onto the counter.

"Who was that man?" Ruby came out of the back room. "What did he want? You seem…upset."

"Yeah, I didn't get a good feeling from him." Becca turned to the girl, a quizzical look on her face. "You didn't recognize him, did you?"

"I didn't see him." Ruby shook her head.

"There's more to your story, isn't there?"

Ruby nodded slowly, her eyes on the floor, and followed Becca back to their tea.

"After that, everything happened very quickly. Everything took more money, more time, than I thought. I went to the conservatory first, of course. I needed to confirm my audition and that man—the one I thought was the landlord—he had left the room key there. He was gone when I finally found the apartment. It was after midnight, but what with the flights and all…"

She waved her hands.

108

"Besides, I wanted to do well, and so I practiced. Softly, of course, with a mute on my bridge. I did not bother you, did I?"

"I didn't hear you at all," Becca reassured her.

"I am glad." A ghost of a smile lit up Ruby's face. "I did sleep, finally. And, well, when I woke, it was later than I thought. I grabbed my violin and ran. I made it to the audition. Only, when I opened the case…"

She stopped, biting her lip.

"It was my grandfather's violin. Not the new one I'd been given. That is why I came into your shop. Why I wanted to talk to you. I do not know how my grandfather's violin made it back to me, but I do know it must have been magic."

"Are you sure?" Becca didn't mean to sound harsh. Clara could feel the effort she was putting into keeping her voice gentle. Still, she was glad her person was skeptical. Clara didn't have Laurel's gift for reading people, but even she could tell that something didn't add up. "I mean, you haven't slept much. You're in a strange place. Jet-lagged."

Ruby was shaking her head. "My new violin is factory-made. Czech. The kind schools rent for children. As soon as I opened the case, I saw, but I doubted too. Then I picked it up. The sound! The violin I brought with me can be played. My grandfather's violin almost makes its own music. It almost…yes, it seemed like a miracle, and after I started to talk with you, I thought, why not? Perhaps I should not question it. Only then I returned to the apartment and saw—I found—"

"My neighbor," Becca filled in the blanks.

Ruby nodded, her eyes filling with tears. "Then I knew. What I thought was a blessing was the opposite. My grandfather's violin makes beautiful music, but it has become part of something evil."

Chapter 14

At moments like this, Clara sorely missed her sisters. They might tease her, but the calico knew they shared her allegiance to Becca. Even if they didn't love her like Clara did, they would want what was best for her. And in this case, what was best was beyond her powers. While Laurel might be able to implant the idea of escape into Becca's mind, and Harriet could possibly change this Ruby into something unthreatening—another pillow, perhaps—all Clara could do was stare up at her person with growing alarm. True evil existed, Clara knew. More to the point, she was learning from her sisters' stories, it often came through the actions of human beings. Whether or not this Ruby was herself bad or simply a conduit through which trouble could be channeled, Clara did not care. She wanted Becca safely away, and for this dark-haired young woman to disappear.

Becca, however, was not cooperating. "That's nonsense," she scoffed. "I don't believe a musical instrument could be evil. There's obviously been some kind of mistake." Her words trailed off into a thoughtful silence. "Though…no, that doesn't make sense."

"Please," the young musician leaned in, her face drawn with fatigue, "tell me."

Becca hesitated. "I had a visitor this morning," she said at last. "A dean from the conservatory. He said that your violin belonged to a collector, and that it had been stolen."

"A collector? Did he say who?" That wasn't the question Clara had expected. Becca, either, from the sudden rise of her brows.

"I'm not sure," she admitted. "Someone in New York. The dean gave me his card. I could ask, I guess…"

But Ruby was shaking her head. "No, that is not possible."

"What's not?"

"The man who bought my grandfather's violin. He is a collector. He has many fine things, but he is not in New York, and he only bought my violin a few weeks ago. So even if he sold it…" She turned a puzzled frown to Becca. "You said this happened this morning?"

Becca nodded.

"Did you give him the violin?" Ruby spoke haltingly, as if each word hurt.

"No. I didn't even show it to him."

"I do not understand."

"He…I guess I just didn't like him. And I thought, well, it's your violin. I said I would hold it for you."

If Becca expected this to cheer her visitor up, she was disappointed.

"I think I do need your services now," she said, her voice low.

"You can't really think a musical instrument can be evil, do you?"

The other woman simply shook her head. "I do not know what is going on. But this violin—it keeps coming back. Already one man has died. And that man who was just here…"

"I thought you didn't see him." Becca's face grew grave.

"I heard him." Ruby looked up at her. "He was asking about a girl. He did not sound like a friend."

"He was creepy." Becca gave her that. "But this is Cambridge. It's a big city. There are creeps everywhere." She sounded like she was trying to convince herself. Then, taking a deep breath, she reached a decision. "Look, Ruby, you must be exhausted, and I've got to work. Why don't you lie down and see if you can get some sleep? We'll go back to my place when I take my break. Your grandfather's violin is safe in my bedroom. Maybe you can take a look at it and figure something out." She paused, considering. "Then again, maybe you'll open the case and find that it's not there at all."

Ruby started to argue, but Becca was having none of it. "You're dead on your feet," she said. "If my boss comes by, I'll explain. She's not bad—well, her sister isn't anyway."

Leaving her new guest to nap, Becca returned to her post, and Clara with her. If she could have communicated with Laurel and Harriet, she would have. Her sisters had skills enough between them to figure out what was going on with this strange young woman. Whether they'd be willing to part with the violin was another story.

Becca's generosity did her credit, Clara thought. And even without knowing that her feline minders had her best interests at heart, she seemed confident in her decision. But after the most cursory dusting of the candles—the expensive ones had sat on the shelves for months— she suddenly stopped, stepping into the corner before she pulled out her phone.

"Maddy." Becca was almost whispering, one eye on the door to the back room. "She showed up just like I said."

Her friend's voice was so loud that Becca muted it with her hand.

"It's complicated, Maddy. She—well, she's not some kind of international thief. She's a broke student, and she's sleeping in the back room. She needs my help, Maddy. I think she may need some witch detecting after all."

112

Chapter 15

Clara listened to Maddy sputter, feeling as frustrated as a kitten who can't reach the ball under the bookshelf. She felt for Becca's friend, but although she and her sisters would do anything to protect their person, the cats' powers were limited. And, as Clara was learning, there had been times in their history when both felines and humans had come to harm despite the cats' best intentions.

Maddy's worries proved groundless, as an hour later, Ruby emerged, hair tousled. "Thank you," she said, smoothing her dark locks back with one hand. "I feel much better."

"I'm glad." Becca appraised her guest. "Are you hungry? I've got another hour or so before I can head out, but if you want, I could loan you a few—"

"No, no, please." The musician was adamant. "You have already done so much. I will wait and go with you and get my violin. Then I will be out of your hair."

"But…" Becca bit her lower lip, a sure sign, Clara knew, that she was holding something back. "Okay, we'll talk about it once I finish up here."

With that, she went back to the window, pulling the ladder up to the right. But whether because the morning had been an odd and broken one or because the musician was wandering around, a quiet but obvious presence, Becca didn't seem able to regain her former groove. Time and again, she started to paint, only to stop, muttering that some element was wrong. The design unbalanced or the color off.

"Maybe the top banner was beginner's luck." She sounded almost embarrassed as she wiped off the wet paint, wetting a large sponge from a bucket by her feet.

"What is it supposed to be?" Ruby emerged once more from the back room and looked up at the smear of blue.

"Fish—for Pisces, you know?" Becca pointed, jostling the sponge, which sent a spill of blue-tinted water down the window. "Bother." She hopped off the ladder and began grabbing magazines off the window shelf. As she reached for the sponge, Ruby bent to lift the Ganesh out of harm's way, and the two bumped heads.

"I've got it," Becca snapped, grabbing the figurine.

Ruby stepped back, her hand on her forehead. "I am sorry," she said as she backed away. "I am in the way. I should leave."

"No, please." Becca replaced the statue a safe distance from the spill. "I'm the one—are you okay?"

"Yes, yes." Ruby nodded, fingertips gingerly touching her forehead. "I think I will go lie down again."

"That's a good idea." Relief flooded Becca's voice. "I'll wake you when I can leave. I'm almost done here anyway."

The rest of the morning was quiet, with only two customers coming in—one asking about candles and the other simply to browse. Becca turned the accident to her advantage, finishing the blue zodiac sign without any further delay and cleaning the rest of the window to let in the winter sun, now diluted by clouds. The work was good, bolder and more detailed than the previous painting, but Becca's cat could tell she wasn't happy. The set of her mouth and the line between her eyes dismayed the calico, who tagged along as Becca stepped out into the cold to check her work.

"Maybe it's the weather." Becca spoke softly to herself as she glanced up at the milky sky, unaware that her pet was listening. Digging her hands into her pockets, she glanced at the window, stepping back to the curb to take it in.

Cambridge, even in winter, was alive. Behind Becca, a bike messenger, earbuds in, pumped furiously against the rising wind. Two older women in designer couture stopped in front of her, blocking her view. But if she hoped they would proceed into the shop, she was disappointed.

"It's all in the point of view," said one, turning to face her companion. "Completely unbelievable."

"I thought it worked," her companion argued, waving her hands and almost taking out an oblivious jogger as he passed. A onetime rocker, looking both too old and too cold in his black leather jacket, ducked around them, as he chatted with a tweedy academic whose sensible wool hat was pulled low.

No, Becca wasn't leaving Cambridge, her city. If Clara couldn't hear her person's thoughts, she could see her determination as she turned, chin up, back into the shop. With a few quick dabs, she outlined an optimistic-looking sun and then, checking the clock, brought the rest of her supplies into the back.

"Ready to head out?"

"Yes, and thank you again." Ruby looked up from her phone. "I was hoping to hear about the scholarship," she explained as she tucked the device into her purse.

"These things take time," Becca improvised as she washed her hands. "And there's a storm watch too. We're expecting a nor'easter, so maybe they've closed early."

Ruby responded with a tight-lipped smile, and Becca let the subject drop as the two donned their layers. Putting up her break sign—*Back in an hour!*—Becca led the way, locking the door behind them.

"Your mother must be very proud of you." The two had stopped at a light.

"She made all this possible," Ruby responded, looking around at the busy street in awe. "Are you close to your parents?"

Becca chuckled. "I guess so. My mom wants me to return home. I grew up in the Midwest—in the middle of the country—and she keeps pushing me to look for a job back there," she explained. "My mother isn't a big fan of cities."

Ruby nodded, her face grave under that black tam. "My mother worries as well," she said, her head still swiveling this way and that as the light changed.

Lost in their thoughts, and propelled by a gusty wind, the two hurried on, and Clara, shaded to avoid detection, broke into a lope.

So intent was Clara on keeping up that when Becca came to an abrupt stop about a half a block from her building, her pet had to scramble to keep from running into her. Hard on her person's heels, the cat heard her sudden intake of breath with barely a second to spare. She soon saw what had provoked it. The nasty neighbor was standing in front of the building, speaking to a tall man wearing a tweed jacket. That jacket gave him a professorial look—common enough in what was essentially still a college town—but it wasn't up to the weather. Although a natty scarf was knotted around his throat, his ears, peeking out from behind slightly too long sideburns, had turned bright red. The brunette before him, kitted out in what appeared to be ski wear, began playing with the ends of her glossy curls, either not noticing or not caring that that man she was addressing was freezing.

Clara looked on, trying to understand such puzzling behavior, when Becca pulled Ruby aside.

"Change of plans," she said, speaking quickly. "That's one of my new neighbors, and we've been quarreling."

Ruby nodded. "They do not want to see me. Not after…"

"Probably," Becca admitted. "But it isn't you. It's her. Let's give it a minute."

Backing behind a hedge at the corner of the brick building, the two waited, watching as the conversation on the stoop continued. Soon both were shivering, and when Becca sneezed, Ruby backed away.

"I should go. It is too cold," she said, her own lips rimmed with blue.

"No, really, Ruby." Becca reached to stop her. Too late, the man in tweed had looked up. Forcing a smile, Becca waved, then dug into her bag. "There's a backdoor," she spoke quickly as she fished out a keychain. "Just go around the block. You'll see the alley between the two triple deckers over on Ellery. You can go through there and let yourself in."

Ruby started to protest, when Becca detached one key and pressed it into the other woman's hand. "I'm going to go talk to them. I'll try to distract them, and you can go up the alley. You can't miss it: number six. I'll be up in a minute."

Her shivering companion didn't need any more urging, and after a brief pause, Becca continued walking in a slightly more deliberative manner toward the front door of the building she called home.

"Good afternoon." Becca waved as she walked up, her voice even. "Ready for the storm?"

"Hope so." The man gave her a quick glance, his blue eyes beseeching. His lips, Clara noted, were turning blue.

The neighbor looked at Becca too, her pretty face turning sour in a flash. That passed quickly, though, as she realized the man was once again focusing on her, and she smiled, tossing her hair as if to shed the fit of pique she had just displayed.

117

"You were saying?" She reached out so that her gloved fingertips just touched the man's sleeve. But although Clara was curious about what exactly was going on, Becca had mounted the steps to their building and so the cat turned to follow.

"Excuse me." Hand on the door, Becca paused, and then turned to acknowledge the summons from the man, who was striding quickly toward her. "Do you live in this building?"

"Yes." Becca was trying to sound forceful, but Clara could hear a quaver in her voice that didn't come from the cold.

"I thought I'd seen you here. Do you mind if I ask you a few questions?" The man in tweed pulled the door open, and the two stepped into the shelter of the building foyer. Out on the sidewalk, Becca's neighbor scowled. "I'm Matthew Wargill. I represent the new management association."

"The management association?" Becca's face clouded with confusion.

"For the condo association." He pulled a card case from his pocket, extracting one with clumsy fingers. "I didn't expect to get into a conversation outside," he explained with a sheepish grin that lit up his angular face.

Becca examined the card before responding. "I'm sorry," she said. "I don't understand why you're here."

He nodded. "You're one of the renters, aren't you?"

"She is." The nasty brunette came in with another gust of cold. "She lives in number six, right above me. Which means I can hear everything. And next to... you know."

"Excuse me." Becca rarely got angry. When she did, however, she pulled herself up to her full height, throwing her head back in the human equivalent of spiking her fur and arching her back. If she had a tail, Clara thought, it would be fluffed out like a bottle brush. "I don't see how my living situation is any business of yours—either of you."

The brunette gave the management representative a look, brows raised as if to say, "I told you so."

"I'm sorry." The representative ignored her, his face softening. "I didn't mean… It's just that I've met most of the new owners already. You must know Deborah, Deborah Miles." The brunette pursed her lips, but he kept talking. "Please, call me Matt."

"Becca Colwin." She shook his hand, and Clara edged closer to sniff the cuff of his pants. "What is this about again?"

"May we talk somewhere private?" He smiled. "Perhaps upstairs, in your unit?"

His voice was gentle, but Becca's eyes narrowed, much like Laurel's did before she struck. Clara felt a surge of pride. No smooth-talking man would get the better of their person.

"I'm fine speaking here." As if to accentuate her point, Becca crossed her arms, leaning back on the closed door.

"Her place is a wreck." The brunette—Deborah—didn't even try to disguise her malice. "It's filled with animals. Unclean."

Becca took a deep breath. To Clara's surprise, the man did too, before turning to the spiteful brunette. "Thanks so much for speaking with me, Ms. Miles. I've really enjoyed meeting you."

It was a clear dismissal, but the brunette still lingered a moment, as if searching for just the right scorching comeback. When none presented itself, she sniffed audibly and pushed past Becca, tossing her hair once more for good measure.

"I'm sorry." He dipped his head, revealing a bald spot. In a cat, that would have been a submissive gesture, but Clara wasn't convinced. Neither, she was gratified to see, was Becca. "I understand that sometimes, when someone moves from the suburbs back into the city, there can be tensions."

"That's one word for it." Becca laughed softly and shook her head. "I'm sorry. I recently took a new position, and, well, it is possible that my cats have been making more noise than previously."

"Your cats?" He pulled a handkerchief from his pocket and dabbed at his nose.

"They're allowed according to my lease," Becca asserted, unnerved, Clara could tell, by the question.

"No, I'm sorry." Now it was Matt's turn to chuckle. "It's just, I've fielded complaints about many things. Dogs, exercise machinery, but cats?"

"They can be very energetic." Becca relaxed. "I adopted three littermates—sisters. But they're all clean and up to date on their shots and everything." Maybe she wasn't completely relaxed, Clara thought. What was it Harriet had started to tell her about their history? Something about women who lived with cats, she recalled. Something bad.

"I'm sure." His sharp features once again pulled into high relief by his wide grin. "I mean, I'm a dog man, myself. But if I don't get home at just the right time to walk Tiger, he can tear up the place. Luckily, my roommate always gets in before I do. Do you have a roommate, Becca?"

"Me? No." Becca squeaked, ever so slightly, and she stiffened, as if willing herself to stay focused on the man in front of her. She was thinking of Ruby, her cat realized, although why the young woman's presence should be of interest to this stranger was not something she understood. In the pause that followed, Clara peered up at him. He didn't know her person, and his ears were certainly not as sensitive as a cat's. Still, he screwed his eyes up ever so slightly, and Clara could almost hear his pulse start to race.

"Occasionally, I have a friend stay over." Becca must have sensed this too. Clara could hear the effort she was exerting to keep her voice level. "But I value my privacy."

A pause, slightly too long to be natural. "I'm with you there," he

120

said with another, softer laugh. "Well, I've taken enough of your time, Ms. Colwin. I hope to be seeing you at a condo association meeting soon."

Becca watched him as he walked off. "Values his privacy," she repeated softly as she climbed the stairs.

Her relief proved to be short-lived. The third-floor hall was deserted, so she leaned into her apartment door. "Ruby?" she called, keeping her voice low. "Can you hear me?"

Nothing.

"Ruby?" Becca knocked, but the only answer was Laurel's distinctive yowl.

"*There's no one here.*" Clara's ears perked up at that, and she looked up at her person. Surely, this hadn't been expected.

"*That other girl, the one with the violin, was supposed to come here.*"

"*Well, she didn't.*" Laurel's matter-of-fact statement came out more like a howl. "*Come see for yourself if you don't believe me.*"

"*No, I do...*" Clara paused, looking up at her person, dismayed to see the worry creasing her brow as she called again for Ruby and rattled the knob. "*Maybe we should stop talking. Becca thinks something is wrong.*"

"*Something is wrong.*" Laurel didn't bother to mute her distinctive Siamese meow. "*Becca can't get in to feed us.*"

"*But...*" Clara broke off. It was no use pointing out to her sister that, in fact, they had been fed only a few hours before. If Clara knew anything, it was that Harriet would have already scarfed down the crunchies that were supposed to hold them until their regular dinner time, hours from now.

Besides, Becca had turned away from the door and was busy with her phone.

"Ruby? Where are you? I'm at my apartment—and you have my keys."

121

A moment later, she tried again.

"Maddy? No, I know you're at work. Do you still have my extra key?"

Fifteen minutes later, Maddy was calling up the stairs.

"I grabbed a Lyft." Even though she had just emerged from a car, Becca's friend sounded breathless. "I didn't want to risk you being alone with her."

"That's just it," Becca said with a shrug. "She's not here."

Maddy only shook her head, her round face serious as Becca explained. "I cannot believe you gave her your key," she said once Becca had finished. "After last night, too."

"She texted me last night, Maddy, and we've talked since. You haven't met her. If anything, I'm worried about what might have happened to her. Maybe she fell or—"

"Maybe she grabbed your laptop and ran."

"*No!*" Laurel's yelp carried through the door as Maddy fiddled with the lock. "*Nobody here!*"

"Well, at least your cats are okay." Maddy glanced at her friend. "The Siamese-looking one always sounds like that, right?"

"Yes, she does." Becca took the key from her friend and opened the door. "Ruby? Are you here?" Ignoring Maddy's outstretched arm, she walked right in, only to stumble over Harriet.

"Becca, are you okay?" Maddy reached for her, eyes wide.

"Yeah." Becca scooped up the marmalade cat. "But I nearly tripped over Harriet. Are you okay, girl?"

Harriet closed her eyes, basking in the attention. "*I am a queen,*" she purred. "*Fetch me lunch.*"

Whether Harriet shared Laurel's powers of suggestion or the sisters simply had Becca well trained, she started toward the kitchen. Only Maddy's hand on her arm stopped her.

"You can't just go in there."

122

"It's my apartment."

"That you gave a stranger the key to." Maddy glowered. "Wait here," she said as she pulled her own keys from her bag. Grasping them in her clenched fist so that one stood out between each knuckle, she made her way toward Becca's bedroom.

"Does she think she's being quiet?" Laurel sauntered into the foyer. *"What does she think she's going to catch?"*

"She thinks there might be a person hiding in there," Clara explained.

"Nonsense!" Harriet struggled to be let down. *"If someone were here, we'd have been fed already."*

Clara held back from pointing out the obvious—that Harriet was perfectly capable of consuming multiple back-to-back meals—as Becca gave her own explanation.

"Maddy, relax." She followed her friend into the bedroom. "If there was a stranger in the house, I'd know it. The cats would let me know."

Maddy's muffled response came from her closet. "They're not guard cats, Becca."

"No, but I know their behavior. They'd be acting differently if someone was in here." Becca knelt. "Nothing under the bed either. I don't know what happened to her." Pulling herself up, she headed toward the kitchen.

"Finally." Harriet trotted off, tail high. Laurel started to follow, albeit at a more dignified pace, when she stopped and turned toward her younger sibling.

"Good work bringing her home safe, Clown," she said, her blue eyes closing slowly in an approving blink. *"Now if you could just get her to bring one of those interesting men with her..."*

"Which men?" Clara asked. *"And what was I keeping her safe from?"*

But Laurel had already moved on, eager as Harriet to queue up for the unexpected bounty.

"First things first, you need to get your locks changed." Since Maddy had already left work early, claiming an emergency, she accepted Becca's invitation to lunch.

"I need to not jump the gun." Becca stood at the counter spreading mayo on the bread she had just toasted as the cats circled. They had already had a can each, but Maddy wasn't the only one who loved how she made turkey sandwiches. "We don't know what happened. I was talking quickly, and my directions might not have been clear. Maybe she got lost. It's not like she knows the city yet."

Becca followed the mayo with a swipe of mustard, causing Laurel to rear back in disgust. Harriet, undeterred, pushed her aside. Neither noticed how Maddy had frozen, a quizzical expression on her face.

"If she was heading off on her own, why did you have to come home in the middle of the day at all? I thought the point was that you were finally going to get her out of your hair."

Becca explained as she layered the sliced turkey. "It's not that simple, Maddy. I'm worried about her. She just seems so lost."

Maddy rolled her eyes. "She seems very good at getting people to look after her."

Becca laid a finishing touch—a pickle slice—on each sandwich before slicing them neatly on the diagonal, focusing on arranging the halves just so instead of responding. Maddy took the point, even as she followed her to the table.

"So, are you going to hang out here all day, waiting for her?" she tried again.

"No, I'm worried about Charm and Cherish too." Becca took a big bite, chewing thoughtfully. "We made one sale all morning—a candle," she said at last. "I don't know how it's going to survive."

Maddy gulped down hers. "You know you can always—"

"Sorry I even mentioned it," Becca broke in, rising from the table. "I wonder if I have any chips."

"Did you ever find out why she wanted to hire you?" Maddy had waited until her friend shook the chips onto a plate, but clearly she wasn't going to let the matter drop.

"You mean as a witch detective? She thinks her violin is haunted or something. I doubt it." Becca ate a chip and licked her fingers. Almost, thought Clara, like a cat. "But it did occur to me that perhaps Ruby was the intended victim of the killer next door."

Chapter 16

Maddy had a lot to say to that. If she were a cat, Clara knew, her back would be arched and she would be spitting, she was so upset. Only, before she could marshal a response, Clara and her sisters went on the alert. Someone—or something—was approaching.

"What's with your cats?" That wasn't what Maddy had intended to say. Clara would have bet on that, had felines been the kind of animals that gambled. Still, she cocked an ear toward the round brunette, even as she loped after Laurel toward the door. Even Harriet came forward, parading at a stately pace that befitted her dignity.

"*About time.*" Harriet took a seat by the door and began arranging her fur. "*Now perhaps this silliness will cease.*"

"*Doubt it.*" Laurel looked back over her shoulder at the two humans. "*Sometimes I despair of our Becca.*"

"*She's doing the best she can.*" Even at the risk of angering her siblings, Clara felt the need to stand up for their person. The fact that she had her own doubts did nibble away at her confidence.

"*See?*" Laurel's blue eyes were on her now, and her sister was concentrating so hard she had gone cross-eyed. "*You're wondering too.*"

"Do you think it's mice?" Maddy's question interrupted Clara's

126

attempt at a response. From the quaver in her voice, it almost sounded as if Becca's friend was more afraid of vermin than of a killer in the building. "I mean, your cats are acting super weird."

Before Becca could answer, the sound of footsteps—audible even to human ears—and then of a key in the lock had them both stepping back.

"Oh!" Ruby opened the door to find the two humans and three cats staring at her. "I'm sorry. I would have knocked, only I thought—"

"That you'd have the place to yourself?" Maddy no longer sounded afraid.

"What happened, Ruby?" Becca took her visitor's arm and led her back into the living room. "Did you get lost? Didn't you get my message?"

"No, I am sorry." She shook her head. "I was walking around the block, like you told me, and I thought I saw someone. I'm sorry."

"It doesn't matter, but you gave me—us—a scare." She shot a look at her friend.

"Because of my violin?" She followed Becca's gaze. "You told her?"

"Some of it. Maddy, Ruby. Ruby, this is Maddy. But no, Ruby. Not because of the violin. Because of what happened next door."

"You cannot think…" Ruby suddenly swayed, and Becca found herself supporting her.

"Maddy, help me." Together they walked the young woman over to the sofa. "Here, lie down."

"I am sorry." Ruby allowed herself to be led over to the couch, even letting Becca slip off her shoes as she lay back on the pillows. "I am just…tired."

"You must be exhausted." Becca pulled the old afghan off the sofa's back and laid it over the prone girl. "Why don't you try to get some sleep. I've got to go back to work."

Maddy gave Becca a pointed look, but her friend shook her head and retreated to the kitchen, Maddy close behind.

"Convenient, don't you think?" Maddy's whisper was more of a hiss.

"She's exhausted. Jet lag, not sleeping last night, and shock as well." Becca's voice was soft, but Clara could hear the pain in it. "Have some sympathy."

"Have some sense," her friend countered. If Maddy had a tail, it would be lashing.

"Look, I don't know anything about her." Becca glanced back into the living room, where Laurel perched on the sofa's back, surveying the girl who lay motionless below her. "But I'm not entirely defenseless. You might think it's crazy, but I trust my cats. They'd let me know if anything was wrong. They're good judges of character."

"Your cats?" Maddy burst out.

Becca shushed her, her eyes growing wide. Clara's sensitive ears could hear that Ruby's soft snore hadn't broken its gentle rhythm, but she had no way to reassure her person.

"You don't know, but I do." Becca spoke softly, but with urgency. "Please, Maddy, you've got to trust me on this."

Maddy only shook her head. "I can't stay, Becca. But I don't like this. I don't like any of this. Look, if you're really going to leave her here, at least take your laptop and any jewelry you've got. Okay?"

"The most valuable thing in this apartment is the violin." Becca smiled. "And that belongs to Ruby."

Bowing to her friend's request, Becca packed her laptop as well as her small jewelry box in her bag as she readied to leave. She also wrote a note, which, thanks to Maddy's comments, Clara learned was about the oven and the shower, which could be tricky.

"Do not tell her when you're going to be home." Maddy insisted. "You might as well give her a deadline for clearing you out."

Becca only sighed at that, but Clara figured she must have given in from her friend's satisfied snort. Only then did she leave the apartment, watching as her friend locked the door behind her.

"Talk about barn door and all that. I don't know why you're bothering."

"She asked me for my help, Maddy." Becca was losing her patience. "She's alone in a strange city, and she happens to be asleep on my sofa. I'm not going to leave her in an unlocked apartment. Especially not when a man was killed next door."

Maddy was muttering something as the two descended the stairs. But although Clara's inclination was to follow her person, she wanted to check in with Laurel first.

"What did you get?" Clara might not have had quite Laurel's grace. Laurel was, after all, a slightly longer and leaner feline, but the calico did make it up to the sofa back in one leap. *"Can you read her thoughts?"*

"Of course I can." Laurel sat back and folded her tail neatly around her brown toes, and Clara's heart sank. When her sister assumed that rather superior look, she had learned, it was a sure bet she had failed at whatever mental feat she had attempted. *"Do you think you could have done better?"* Laurel whined. If nothing else, she clearly picked up on Clara's doubts.

"I'm sorry." Clara ducked her head submissively. *"Only, so much is riding on what we can find out about this girl."*

"I know." Laurel turned to look at the sleeping Ruby, attitude temporarily at bay. *"All I'm getting are images of that stupid instrument."*

Clara waited as patiently as she could. Finally, she broke. *"Does she know anything about how it showed up here?"*

"No." Laurel's tail lashed. Frustration, her sister realized. Not temper. *"She's dreaming about playing it. Only, there's something wrong."*

Clara cocked her head at an inquisitive angle. Laurel always did like to amp up the drama. This time, though, her baby sister really thought her part-Siamese sibling was trying to puzzle something out.

"She's playing it, and then she's putting it in its case. She's sad. I can feel that."

"Because she's putting it away?"

Laurel's tail flicked in annoyance. The sealpoint hated to be interrupted. "No, silly, it's memory. The violin makes her sad, but it also scares her."

Clara waited, her own tail twitching with the strain of keeping silent. "She did tell Becca she thinks it may be haunted."

"Bast, you're annoying." Laurel was a master of side eye. "You should know by now that humans don't have any sense of what may be haunted or not. For all I know, it's Harriet's pillow that's giving her these dreams. Our big sister sheds like nobody's business."

With that she turned and jumped to the floor, sauntering off to the bedroom with her chocolate-tipped tail held high and leaving Clara to observe the young woman sleeping on the sofa.

"If only I could eavesdrop on her dreams." Clara stared down at the pale face and concentrated. All she managed to do, however, was make one dark-lashed lid twitch a bit. For all Clara knew, Harriet's dander might have been responsible. There was an awful lot of it.

"I beg your pardon." The calico looked over to see Harriet staring at her icily from the ottoman. "I happen to have a most luxuriant coat."

"And beautiful fur it is, too." Clara leaped over the sleeping girl to land on the rug below Harriet. There was no use in antagonizing her fluffy sister further. To make matters worse, the sleeping girl's head was resting on the marmalade longhair's special pillow. With a slight grunt, the big cat turned to glare at Ruby, concentrating so hard that Clara thought she could feel it. All she succeeded in doing, though, was to make the sleeping girl shift and turn on her side.

Harriet's ears flicked back.

"Would you tell me more?" Clara wasn't sure why she wanted to protect Ruby. The girl was an interloper, and she appeared to have brought trouble into their quiet world. Maybe it was that Becca had spoken up for her. Maybe it was some feeling of kinship with a smaller creature, alone in the world. *"About our family history?"*

Harriet shot her a glance, her yellow eyes hooded with suspicion. *"You're trying to distract me."*

Clara couldn't directly disagree. Not when it seemed like her sister would know. Instead, she offered an alternative explanation. *"I'm worried about Becca. About who she chooses to trust. And I had a dream..."*

Harriet closed her eyes, settling down on the ottoman. For a moment, Clara thought she had fallen asleep, and although she had, in fact, asked her sister about their shared history primarily as a diversion, she found she was disappointed by her sister's silence. Not only was Clara concerned about Becca, the little calico really did want to know more.

"Always so impatient." A rumble from the white and orange cat, more growl than purr. *"Yes, there have been lapses. Times when we failed in our duty, at times with tragic consequences."*

Clara could feel the fur rise along her back in horror, but she kept silent.

"Often, as in great-great-granddam's time, it would begin when someone would seek our aid. Strangers, coming to our people, asking them to intercede, with our aid, of course. Now, in the old days, these requests were made in the proper fashion."

A scent like pine resin flooded Clara's mind. Smoky, only infinitely more pleasing than the incense Becca's coven sometimes burned. At the same time, tastes—meat, milk, and...was that honey?—had her licking her chops. She felt once more the desert sun. Only that heat was muted now, held back by the thickness of stone walls around her. As her eyes adjusted to the darkness, the only illumination coming from the small glowing braziers, she could make out pictures on the painted stone. Images of—yes—her sisters, their eyes painted large and bright in vibrant blues and greens, the enamel reflecting back the firelight, sparkling amid the shadows.

"We were respected. Even feared." Harriet's voice took on a rumbling resonance, filling Clara's head. *"Only after we followed our people north and west, traveling over the oceans, did the troubles begin."*

Clara felt the rug pitch beneath her, as if she were being tossed on a stormy sea. So her family had traveled from another land. Rather like Ruby, who now lay on her side, her breath gentle and even.

"Not like this stranger!" Harriet's anger cut in. *"We did not bring danger with us. We journeyed out of loyalty and a sense of exploration. We were bidden to protect."*

Clara ducked her head, acknowledging her sister's rebuke, and as she did, she felt the cool wind off the water. The warmth of a more moderate sun. A new home, more green than gold. A place of safety and community. Her person respected for her learning. Her understanding of the plants that grew there. The rhythms of nature. Until…

"The first strangers respected this. They respected us. Only, they grew jealous. Suspicious of our powers, which they wrongfully attributed to our people—our great-great-granddam's person, in particular."

The marmalade fell silent once more. And as her breathing became as even as the girl's, her stub nose emitted a gentle snort that let Clara know Harriet had, in fact, fallen asleep. Already, the calico was picking up dream images—that green shore—which receded as her ear twitched. *"Danger?"*

Too late, she felt her own head begin to nod.

Chapter 17

She was walking alongside a woman. The woman's scent was familiar. Her warmth welcome, but when Clara looked up, she saw a different person than she expected. This woman was lighter skinned than the one she recalled, her hair a rich russet, like the leaves she held out in her open palm, offering them to another person. A woman that even in this dream state Clara did not know.

"Here," she was saying as she displayed the leaves, before folding them into a cloth. "This will help your cramp, and then, next time…"

Her words fell off into silence, swallowed up in a palpable sadness. A fog, almost, enveloping the two. The second person, a younger woman, still weak as if from the loss of blood, accepted the bundle, her eyes searching the older woman's face. She wanted more, the cat could clearly see. That need was so sharp it frightened the small cat, but she made herself sit still. Willed her tail to wrap around her white front paws. A useful mouser, nothing more.

"Can you promise me a next time?" Her eyes were wide and pleading as she broke the silence.

"I cannot promise more than my aid." A smile softened the words, but the younger woman didn't appear to see it. She was staring down at the ground, her forehead furrowing with growing anger.

"I thought you had power." She spoke softly, but her words were audible to the cat. Her bitterness as well. "If you chose..."

The cat moved closer to her person. Leaned her soft fur side into her shin, as if she could turn her aside. The younger woman may be weak, but there was a note in her voice that alarmed the cat. She looked up to see the young woman staring. Her eyes smoldering with... frustration? Anger? Whatever, it was veiled, as if by smoke.

She looked around for her sisters. Surely, they would be here. They would aid her. For now, however, she was alone.

She bowed her head, letting the wave wash over her. Could it be... guilt?

Clara woke with a start and bristled, shaking off the dream—the vision—as if it were a pesky bug. Was this a memory? A warning? Harriet had said something about danger, even as she was fading out. Perhaps this was what she had been referring to. Clara had always been told to shade her magic. To keep her person from seeing what she could do. Could it be that others saw and felt...what? Jealous? Afraid?

She needed to know more.

A snort drew her attention to the big cat by her side, still sleeping. Still dreaming, possibly, of the distant past. Harriet could explain, Clara knew, but she also knew how irritable her sister could be when she was woken. Besides, her biggest sister would deny napping, even in the service of sharing memories, and her embarrassment would make her grumpier still. For the space of a minute, Clara considered her options, but none of them involved jollying either of her sisters into helping her out. And so with a last look at the sleeping Ruby, Clara hunkered down, wiggled her hindquarters in preparation for a leap, and launched herself through the apartment's locked front door in pursuit of Becca.

She was halfway down the apartment stairs when a muffled shriek made her jump. Turning, she realized she was passing the landing by Deborah Miles' apartment. Her timing couldn't have been worse, as the nosy neighbor had apparently just left her apartment. Keys in hand, she stared, frozen, the pink blush on her cheeks standing out on unnaturally white cheeks and her false lashes frozen open in shock. A flash of fear. The dream, the memory. Cursing herself silently for her carelessness, Clara quickly shaded, only to see those oversized lashes blink like frightened birds.

"What?" One syllable squeaked out as her manicured nails clenched around her keys. But Clara knew there was no way to explain. Vowing to be more attentive—in all ways—she went on her way.

Becca hadn't gotten far. In fact, Clara's person was walking so slowly by the time she caught up with her that the calico looked up, worried. Was something really wrong in this, their waking life?

No, she realized. Becca simply wanted to make a phone call. But after fishing her device out of her bag and staring at it, she stowed it once again. Shaking her head, she kept walking, picking up her pace as she turned onto Mass Ave. Middle of the day, on a weekday, the street was always busy, but Clara heard her person gasp as they neared the little storefront.

A small crowd had gathered out front, and at first Clara knew that Becca would blame herself if the shop lost sales. Certainly, she shouldn't have closed the shop at midday. But she had left a sign saying that she'd be back, and, besides, hours often went by without anyone coming in at all. Although Clara had grown accustomed to the incense and herbs Charm and Cherish sold, she'd come to realize that it was the dust, especially on the bookshelves, that tickled her whiskers the worst. Charm and Cherish was far from bustling, even in better weather. Whatever that buzzing crowd might be on about, Clara told herself as she trotted to keep up, it was unlikely to be Becca's fault.

"There you are!" a familiar caw broke through, and Clara looked up to see Margaret emerge from the pack. Despite her short stature, the store's owner parted the crowd like curtains, her fierce gaze and lipsticked glower causing bystanders to draw back even before her arms reached up to push them aside. "Elizabeth said you'd be back any minute, but the police wouldn't wait."

"The police?" Becca stopped so quickly, Clara had to scramble not to run into her.

"Didn't you get my message?" The painted-on brow sank into an angry V.

"I'm sorry." Becca reached for her phone. "I was trying to reach a friend, and—"

"Never mind." Margaret waved her off. "Maybe it's just as well you weren't here. You could've gotten hurt. Come on, then."

Without any further explanation, she turned, and, after a moment's pause, Becca followed. Shoving her phone back in her bag, she pulled out the keys. Not that she would need them. As the crowd once more parted for the diminutive owner, Clara could see that the door of the little store was propped open. A tech wearing gloves was busy examining the frame, as well as the broken glass within. Becca's sign— *Back in an hour!*—still clung to a jagged fragment and swiveled back and forth in the breeze.

"One moment, please." The tech held up his left hand, palm out, to stop them, even as he continued to brush the door's metal frame with his right.

"What happened?" Becca's head swiveled as well, from the broken glass to her boss. A uniformed officer had appeared and was moving the crowd, which continued to creep forward, back almost to the curb. Becca looked like she was ready to follow them, but Margaret had rooted herself to the spot. "I don't understand."

"They broke the glass." Her boss shrugged, as if the answer were obvious.

"I see," Becca pressed on. "But why? Was it an accident?"

Margaret made a sound like a passing bus, blowing the air out from between those carmine lips. "Accident? No way. Maybe they thought we actually had some money in the register. Or, I don't know, that some of those crystals were worth something. Like we had emeralds in there."

She shook her head, though whether in disbelief or to dismiss such a foolish idea, Clara couldn't tell. The idea of anyone breaking the law over a rock of any kind, even a very pretty one, seemed foolish to the cat. It wasn't like you could eat a rock, and most of them weren't even much fun to play with. But as she watched Becca and her boss, another idea began to take shape in her mind.

The painting Becca had been working on—the fish and the sun. They were all symbols, pictures that Clara knew were supposed to summon power for the people inside. What if those pictures, newly bright and visible, had prompted this violence? Even now, Clara could see the green and gold letters that remained above the broken glass. "Magic," she had heard Becca say, as if those lines and shapes could conjure.

Clara's dream had not explained everything, and she had left before Harriet or Laurel could have filled in the blanks. But Clara knew the truth of what she had seen—the rage in that other woman's eyes. Humans wanted power, wanted the gifts that their cats could bestow. The other side of that wanting, though, that was dangerous. Clara could still smell the smoke.

Harriet hadn't finished with her story of their family, and of the people they had long befriended. But Clara had heard enough to understand that some people reacted badly to others, especially to special people like her Becca.

Becca often talked about how open and friendly this city was. After all, she had noted, Cambridge was the kind of place where a coven of would-be witches advertised for new members in a laundromat. But what if she were wrong? What if—Clara shivered—the burning times had come back again?

Chapter 18

The police had their own theories. Once the tech waved Becca and Margaret into the store, urging them to step carefully, Clara leaped to follow, easily clearing the shards.

"You're the owner?" A woman in a dark blue suit emerged from the back room. With her black hair pulled back into a slick bun and a pale, stern face, she looked like another tech. Like the tech, she was wearing gloves, with which she waved the two back from the window. Her voice, however, suggested authority. "Leave that, please. We haven't finished," she said. "And you must be the salesclerk?" She turned her deep-set hawk-like eyes on Becca.

"Yes." Becca nodded. "Becca Colwin. And this is Margaret Cross." She motioned toward her boss, who had waddled over to stare at the open register.

"I'm sorry." She addressed the owner but didn't stop her as she pulled the drawer out further. "That was the first thing we looked at. You've been cleaned out. Do you have any idea how much was in there?" Dark eyes met Becca's. "Either of you?"

Becca inhaled. "I only made one sale today. A candle, and she used her card. So, maybe twenty dollars in small bills?"

139

The cop raised one brow.

"We try to keep change," Becca explained. "A lot of our customers come in for a charm or a bundle of herbs, and we're pretty much a cash business."

Without comment, the cop turned back to Margaret.

"It would've been twenty-eight dollars. A ten, two fives, and eight ones." The owner rattled off the numbers with a frown. "Even with insurance, fixing that door is going to cost me."

"And valuables?" She turned her head, taking in the packed shelves and the dish by the register. "I see what look like gemstones. And you mentioned herbs?"

"They're crystals. Quartz and semi-precious stones," Becca explained as Margaret made her way over to check the back shelf. "And the herbs are pretty basic."

"Nothing medicinal?" A slight pause made her meaning clear.

"No, not really." Clara saw a small, sad smile play at the corner of her mouth. "I mean, sage is good for lifting depression, but not in the way that you mean."

"It's still here." Margaret spoke from the corner.

"What?" The detective walked over to join her.

"My gong. It's an antique. Cost me, too."

The detective's lips tightened, but she only nodded before turning back to Becca.

"You had locked the store up and left for lunch. How long were you out?"

Becca checked the clock. "No more than an hour ago. I'm pretty sure."

"And only one customer had come into the store all morning?"

"I didn't say that." Becca's voice rose as she corrected the woman. "And, I'm sorry, who are you again?"

"I'm Detective Branch. "

140

"I know a Detective Abrams." Becca paused until the silence grew awkward. "There was something that happened…a while ago." She let her explanation peter out.

"So, this morning?"

"We only had that one sale, but we do get folks browsing." Was Becca going to mention Ruby? Clara stared at her person, wishing once again that she had Laurel's powers.

"Anyone stand out?" Those dark eyes narrowed slightly, as if she could see what Clara couldn't.

"There was one man who seemed, well, a little creepy." The detective feigned surprise. "This is Central Square," Becca explained. "We get some odd people. It's a city. At the time I didn't think anything of it. But now…"

"What was creepy about him?" She pulled a pad from her pocket and waited, pen poised.

"I'm not entirely sure. He was asking about someone who used to work here, Gaia Lindstrom."

"That girl…" Margaret butted in, scowling. "She was trouble. But she's been gone a while now. Left town, and good riddance."

The detective nodded but she didn't put the pad away. "Was that it?"

"No." Becca frowned in concentration. "He said something about me working alone. That's what freaked me out. So I mentioned that the owners lived upstairs, and he left."

"Do you think I'm in danger?" Margaret piped up, her voice tightening with fear.

"This is probably just a smash and grab," the detective reassured her. "Although it's possible that this man you spoke to was casing the store, and you let him know that nobody else was working today."

"So it's your fault." Margaret turned on Becca once the detective had taken their contact information and left. "And then you took off.

You practically told that man that the store would be unguarded."

"I locked the store," Becca protested. "We're right on Mass Ave, and it's always busy."

"Becca did nothing wrong." Elizabeth stepped in from the back room. "She has a right to take a lunch break. Besides, he didn't take anything."

"How can you be sure?" Margaret wheeled on her sister. "He emptied the register."

"That was for show." Elizabeth shook her head. "And I know because I've just been looking through the storeroom."

Becca opened her mouth to protest and then caught herself. Only after Margaret herself rattled off into the back did she approach the taller sister. "How can you say that?" She kept her voice low. "It's such a mess back there."

Elizabeth smiled. "There's nothing here a man like that would want. Personally, I'm glad you weren't here when he came back."

"Wait, so you think…" Before Becca could finish, Margaret was standing in the doorway.

"Someone was back there." Clara couldn't decide if the short woman was angry or scared. "The place is a mess."

"But nothing's been taken." Elizabeth went to her, placing her hand on her short sister's back. "I promise. So why don't we go back upstairs and have a cup of tea? I've already called our insurance agent, and they're sending over someone to board up the door."

Margaret sputtered but let herself be propelled toward the door. Elizabeth looked back over her head toward Becca. "The glass will be replaced tomorrow. If you'd let them in, Becca? And start thinking about what you want to paint on the new door."

Once they were gone, Becca got to work, sweeping up the glass fragments from the shattered door. With the uniformed officer outside, she was left in peace, the curious crowd kept at bay as she moved from the broom to the vacuum. Only Clara's deep love for her person kept her around once that came out, and only because she found a safe, deep shelf to shelter in. When the horrendous roar finally stopped, the little calico was shocked to realize that she'd missed another set of vibrations—a bearded man in a blue jumpsuit was standing at the door, a sheet of plywood leaning against his leg.

"Didn't mean to startle you." He was speaking to Becca, who was staring open-mouthed, but Clara came gingerly forward. "Hatch Insurance sent me to board up a window?"

"Sorry, yes. I was—I should have been—expecting you." She nodded to the door. While Clara sniffed his work boots and the green metal toolbox he'd placed on the ground. "You're standing by it. I guess we should be grateful they didn't break the big window."

"Different M.O." He stepped inside and sized up the damage, pulling a tape measure from his box to take the height and width of the shattered pane. "This was someone who wanted to get in quickly."

"It happened right in the middle of the day."

He shrugged. "Maybe it was vandalism, then. But by the look of your rug, I'd say they came in and did a pretty thorough search."

"A search?" Becca turned to look.

"Look." He pointed with one gloved hand. Sure enough, a tell-tale sparkle caught the afternoon light. "There's glass fragments going down each aisle."

Twenty minutes later, he was done, but Becca was vacuuming for the second time, running the horrid machine back and forth between Charm and Cherish's packed shelves, her brows knit. Concerned, Clara had forced herself to watch from a safe perch on the counter. Becca seemed to be taking this quite personally, but this time, almost all the glass had been sucked up, her pet would have told her if she could. And the few splinters that remained were hidden well enough to not threaten any wayward human. No, something else was bothering Becca.

Knowing how her human worked, Clara wasn't overly surprised when she took out her phone. To humans, the little cat realized, speaking to the device served much the same function as grooming. What did surprise her was who she called

"Elizabeth? It's Becca." When Becca bit her lip like that, lifting one foot behind the other leg, she felt uncertain about something. "I had an idea I wanted to talk over with you. Would you call me back?"

Throughout the rest of the afternoon, Becca kept checking the device. From her frown, Clara could tell it was not providing the satisfaction she sought. But at least Becca had put the vacuum cleaner away, shutting it in a closet and safely closing the door—and freeing Clara to explore. She needed none of her power when her superior senses would do, and she leapt from her safe haven to take in the odd assortment of scents that had taken over the little shop.

The most obvious, to the sensitive feline, were the traces of various people. The man with the boards, for sure, with his interesting boots and the pine-y smell of the wood he'd nailed in place. He had dogs, she could tell, but she assumed he couldn't help it.

She had a harder time getting a read on that detective. She was polished and professional, but Clara sensed little of depth about her. It didn't matter. What she was seeking was more elusive. Doing her best to discount the smell of deodorant and shoe polish of that detective, as well as the doggy smells of the repair man, Clara got to work. Closing her eyes and opening her mouth, she breathed in deeply. There—a wisp of a scent. Scents, really. The first was familiar, an itchy, ashy smell. A smoker, she thought. Or someone who had been near fire. Faint hints of leather and motor oil. Along with that, a deeper, stronger scent. Sweat, she thought, only a particular kind—bitter with fear, she suspected. Whether these traces came from the same man or from

144

more than one was hard to tell. Human men, she had learned, were an odd bunch, and unlike Laurel she was just as happy to have Becca steer clear of them.

At that, the memory of the earlier visitor came up. A man, older, wearing a leather jacket from another era, was not the usual client of a store like Charm and Cherish. And although Becca, and Clara as well, had been relieved when he had left, the calico had to wonder. Could that be whose scent she now traced?

Becca had mentioned the man to that detective, only she had seemed to downplay her gut impression. That, Clara knew, was something a cat would never do. In fact, she made a mental note to talk to Laurel about it. If her sister could convince their person to pay more attention to her instinctive reactions than to her reason—to be more like a cat, that is—then Clara would rest easier. It would also, she mused, make her person a better detective, even if nothing could actually make a human, no matter how well intentioned, into a witch.

If only Becca would trust her cats. Between the three of them, Clara knew, they could be quite good at detecting. Laurel with her powers to suggest and read the thoughts of various humans. Clara with her ability to go out into the world. And Harriet, well, Clara wasn't sure exactly how her big sister's facility with pulling objects out of the ether could actually improve an investigation, but she was sure it would. Family, she was learning, worked together. In fact, she could imagine Laurel quizzing her now, asking her every little thing about the man who had been here.

And—it hit her like a sharp clap—who had then left. That man, the one who had unnerved Becca so, hadn't come far into the store. Clara remembered Becca tensing as he approached her station. She'd sensed a threat, the calico was quite certain. She had also felt protective of the girl Ruby, who was sheltering in the back room. But the man had stopped when Becca spoke to him, and retreated, departing the store and leaving Becca and her cat relieved.

Had he returned once Becca had left? Nose to the linoleum, Clara searched for further traces. Too much had happened, though. Too many people had come and gone, all with their particular aromas. As she concentrated on identifying the various scents, Becca had come out from behind the counter and was pacing. Only a quick move by Clara kept her from getting stepped on, her person was moving in such an agitated manner. But that movement had stirred the air, and much as she was loath to admit, Clara caught another whiff. Sweat, that bitter scent, once more. The man had trespassed further in the store than she had known. Yes, following her nose made it clear—he had been down these aisles, each one of them. Though there was another scent. Another human had been here first, and whatever either had been seeking was as much of a mystery as before.

It wasn't a puzzle she had time to work out. Becca had ducked into the backroom and emerged with her coat and hat. Keys in hand, she pulled tentatively on the board that now filled the top of the door, and, finding it nailed tight, she locked the door behind her, unaware of the cat who leaped through that plywood barrier to jog along at her side.

Chapter 19

Ruby was still asleep when Becca got home, but neither of Becca's two remaining cats had slept a wink.

At least, that was the implication as they caught their youngest sister up.

"She's been like this all day," Laurel told Clara. The two cats were perched on the back of the sofa, looking down at the girl who lay, mouth slightly open, below them. *"I haven't left her side."*

Harriet, who had lumbered up to join her sisters, snorted. *"One of us kept watch, at any rate."* While Laurel peered down at the slumbering girl, dangling a paw close to her open mouth, Harriet arranged herself into a more sphynx-like pose, pulling her head back into her ruff, a sure sign that she felt proud of herself. *"I never closed my eyes."*

Clara wisely declined to comment, and instead jumped lightly down as Becca tiptoed past the couch where her houseguest sighed and turned in her sleep. Once her sisters realized that Becca was heading toward the kitchen, they quickly followed suit.

"What happened?" Laurel mewed, even as she twisted around Becca's ankles. *"I can tell you're upset, you know."*

"She can smell strangers on you." Harriet pushed in between them. *"Also, you've got dust in your fur."*

Clara didn't want to spoil their meal telling them about the vacuum cleaner. But she quickly caught them up on the break-in and the all-too-cursory investigation that followed. *"Whoever broke the door walked all over,"* she said. *"The humans in charge didn't seem to realize that."*

"I don't see what the big deal about that is." Laurel had an affinity for walking the perimeter of any room she entered. Usually via the highest shelf she could reach.

"I don't know why they bothered breaking in at all." Harriet, on the other hand, moved as little as possible.

"I don't either, exactly." Clara couldn't explain why this oversight troubled her, but by then Becca was laying down their food dishes—Harriet's first, of course—and the time for conversation was over.

"You're up." Clara glanced up to see the dark-haired girl enter the kitchen, stifling a yawn. "I hope I didn't wake you," Becca said.

"No, I sleep very well." Ruby rubbed her eyes and smiled, suddenly looking younger. "Though your cats…"

"I know." Becca winced. "They can make an awful ruckus. The woman downstairs has already complained."

"No." Ruby shook her head. "They were quiet. Only, every now and then I would wake up and they were staring at me."

"Told you." Laurel smirked.

"I didn't say…" Clara caught herself. She had suspected her sister of stretching the truth. And anyway, Becca was still talking.

"If you don't mind," she was saying. The other girl's smile had faded, and now she simply looked lost.

"No, that is fair." She glanced around, and when Becca motioned to the living room, led the way. Although she'd folded the blanket and sheets, stacking them on the sofa's arm, she squeezed herself in at the end, as if afraid of taking up too much space.

"I guess I still have some questions." Becca spoke gently, but the

148

other girl hung her head. "Would you tell me again about the violin?"

"It is my grandfather's," Ruby responded forcefully. "And we had to sell it. That is the truth. I did not think…" She broke off, and a crease appeared on her brow.

"There's something you're not telling me."

"I could have told her that." Laurel jumped up on the sofa back and began to wash, and Clara had to resist the urge to shush her. Too late, the sealpoint looked up from her neat front paw and snarled ever so slightly, revealing one ivory fang.

"Ruby?" Becca prompted, unaware of the feline drama taking place behind her.

"Please." Clara ducked her head in apology. *"I want to hear this."*

"If you'd just listen to their thoughts…" Laurel began, breaking off as Ruby sniffed loudly.

Blinking back tears, she nodded. "I did find the violin, but it was not in my case." Even Laurel looked up at that, although Clara was careful to not even think of commenting.

"I had exchanged text messages with my landlord, your neighbor. He wanted to know if I was in the apartment, and I said I was going out. I had my audition. I wanted to talk to him about staying, and he said we could talk in the evening."

She rubbed the back of her hand against her eyes. "I was getting ready when I saw the case—the other case. I did not realize he was a violinist too." Another sniff. "I could not resist. I opened the case, and then I saw it. My grandfather's violin."

"You recognized it?"

She gave an emphatic nod. "I would know it anywhere. The carving of the scroll, the color of the varnish, so deep and rich. Only, well, someone had been rough with it. There were scratches, and the bridge was ever so slightly out of line." She looked up at Becca, eyes wide. "Something like that throws the alignment off entirely. So, I picked it up—the bridge was only slightly off true, and I knew I could slide it back if I was very careful. Only, once I had it in my hands…"

Her wide, wet eyes said it all.

"You took it." Becca filled in the blanks, her voice oddly flat.

"Just to borrow. Just for the audition." Ruby was insistent. "I told myself that it was fate that it had showed up just then, and that my landlord did not care for it. Not properly. The new case was all very nice. But my grandfather's violin fit so naturally in the old one, even with all the patches…

"From what he had said, I thought he wouldn't be back until the evening, and I was only going to be out for a few hours with it."

"Only you didn't bring it back. You left it with me, at the store."

Ruby hung her head, her dark hair hiding her face.

"Did you text him? Leave a note?"

"I thought he might say no." Her voice was so soft even Clara had to strain to hear it. "I left my new violin, just in case. I thought, maybe, he is a student too. Maybe he also had an audition."

She choked on a sob, but although Clara waited expectantly, her person offered no words of comfort. "Justin Neil didn't even mention that his employee was a musician," she said instead, her face unreadable. "He didn't know anything about him."

The two sat in silence for a minute, until Ruby pulled a handkerchief out of her pocket and blew her nose. Looking up at Becca, she seemed to have gathered strength from her confession. "I have been thinking, maybe he received my violin as a gift," she said. "Maybe he too came from my town."

She colored and looked aside.

"What?" Becca pressed. "There's something else, Ruby. Tell me."

"That is how I found the room."

"Your benefactor set you up with the rental?"

A quick shrug. "He knew people. I thought it was fate."

150

"Like 'finding' your violin again?"

She hung her head.

"Have you tried to contact your benefactor? At the very least, it sounds like he probably knew this Larry, whatever their relationship."

"I have to." Her voice was mouse soft. "I will. I know what I did was wrong. But I never meant—" She broke off, biting her lip.

"So you're thinking the same thing I am," Becca said thoughtfully. "Whoever killed Larry Rakov was after the violin."

Chapter 20

"That makes no sense." Ruby looked more confused than before. "I am sorry, Becca. I know I did wrong. I should not have taken the violin, and I feel awful because now I cannot return it. I will never be able to explain. But even here, in Boston…"

"People will do crazy things for money."

Ruby kept shaking her head. "I love this violin. I love how it sounds—how it sounded before. And it reminds me of my grandfather, of course. But it is not worth a life."

"Well, no, of course not."

Ruby cut her off. "Would someone really kill a person for five hundred euros? I understand there is street crime, but in the apartment there was a television and a computer that were surely worth more than—"

"Wait, what?" Becca was a little slow to jump in, perhaps because it was her turn to be confused. "Five hundred euros?"

Ruby nodded. "And we considered ourselves lucky to get that."

"Your mother sold your violin for less than seven hundred dollars?" Becca was turning into a parrot.

Ruby nodded. "We were so happy. That was enough for my airfare

152

and for the room."

"So there's no chance that your grandfather's violin was that collector's piece?"

"No." Ruby was firm. "The luthier in my city would have known. Besides, that violin was stolen when? Several months ago? We did not even know I would be invited for an audition until the first of the year."

"I thought maybe..." Several responses appeared to be going through Becca's mind, none of which she got a chance to voice before a sharp rap on the door made her turn. It also caught Clara, who had been monitoring the conversation, by surprise.

"*Who is it?*" The calico raced over to the door, where Laurel waited. "*What do they want?*"

"*What do any of them want?*" Laurel stalked off, leaving Clara to stand guard alone. Another series of knocks, and she turned toward her person, but Becca was busy shooing Ruby into her bedroom.

"Coming!" she yelled toward the door, even as she ran back to the table, grabbed the violin, and shoved it into Ruby's arms. As Clara watched, she stood for a moment at the door and took a deep breath, almost, her cat thought, as if she were readying herself to jump. Then she opened the door.

"Oh!" She sounded, Clara thought, like someone had stepped on her tail. But as the little cat twined around her ankles to get a better look, she found no cause for alarm. Confusion, yes. The man in tweed was standing there, although his friendly face was now drawn down into a frown. And right behind him stood Deborah Miles, arms crossed, with a look on her face very like Laurel's the time she'd swallowed a dust ball thinking it was a moth.

"Ms. Colwin," the real estate manager said with a nod. It wasn't much of a greeting. It was certainly a departure from his friendly chatter by the door earlier.

"Mr. Wargill." Becca didn't invite either of the visitors in, Clara

153

noticed. Harriet, meanwhile, had lumbered up beside her. "May I help you?"

"*I thought you dispatched these two,*" Harriet grumbled at her baby sister, even as she sat heavily on her tail.

"*Dispatched?*" Clara turned, confused, even as she tried to slide her tail from under Harriet's bulk. "*Why? And what was I supposed to do?*"

Harriet sniffed. "*If you can't suggest that they leave our person alone and you can't summon up a decapitated mouse, then I guess you have to find your own methods. But really, Clown, there must have been something you could do.*"

Clara started to respond but then decided against it, the memory of that last vision, of the feeling of responsibility it had left her with. *Was there something she could have done?*

She looked for Harriet, but her sister had stalked off, pleased to have had the last word. Besides, the calico wanted to hear what her human was saying.

"You think I'm running a hotel?" Clara looked up at her, but Becca seemed as confused as her cat. "In a one-bedroom apartment?"

The real estate manager and the neighbor exchanged a weighted glance. "Ms. Miles asked me to speak with you again. She is understandably concerned about noise."

"That's just my cats." Becca shook her head, searching the manager's angular face. "I told you—I told you both, I've started a new job, and they're not used to my new hours."

"She's probably the reason why her neighbor was killed," the glossy brunette interrupted before he could respond. "Letting strangers in here at all hours."

"Wait," Becca broke in. "I thought you wanted me out because of my cats. Now you're saying it's not my cats?"

"I'm afraid we are going to have to revisit the policy on pets at our next condo meeting." The real estate manager sounded wooden.

Almost, Clara thought, as if he were reciting a speech. Becca did not seem to be fazed.

"You can decide what you want," she said, standing a little straighter. "It won't affect me. I've got a lease that permits cats, and legally that takes precedence over any decision by any new owner."

Deborah Miles' generous mouth drew up into a pout, screwing up her eyes as if she was about to leap. Clara readied herself, prepared to counterattack, but it was the realtor who responded.

"That's true, of course. But you're a tenant at will, I believe." As he spoke, he cast a sidelong look at the glossy brunette, and she bared her teeth in what was probably intended as a smile. "That means that your lease can be cancelled by either party with sixty days' notice. And if you've been running an illegal short-term rental or subletting without express permission, you're already in blatant violation."

"But I'm not," Becca protested. "You're thinking of…" Her answer trailed off.

"Of course!" Clara lashed her tail. *"She's thinking of Ruby."* The cat might not be sure of the dark-haired girl, but she had to admire her person for her care and concern.

"Speaking of…" A familiar yowl behind her caused the calico to whirl around. *"That girl is acting strange."*

For a moment, Clara hesitated. Becca was talking, trying to suggest that it was her neighbor's late employee who had been involved in illegally renting out his space without mentioning how she might know such a thing, or even how the trans-Atlantic referral had come to be. But Laurel's comment was just too tempting. Her sealpoint sister wasn't the kind to ask for help, but that observation sounded awfully like a request. Besides, Becca was likely to be busy with these unwanted visitors for a while, which left her cats to supervise the stranger.

"What's she doing?" Clara touched her nose to Laurel's and then followed her sister back to the bedroom to find Harriet curled up on

the bed.

"There you are." The marmalade yawned, drawing out the words into a high-pitched squeak. *"Watching this one is exhausting."*

As her big sister stretched, arching her back like a Halloween cat, Clara followed her gaze. On the other side of the bed, she could see the curve of Ruby's back. The girl was bent over something on the floor.

One of the advantages of being a cat, Clara had learned, was that humans tend to discount their curiosity. They might have odd sayings about it, but did they ever pause to consider that perhaps their felines were inquisitive for a reason? They did not, Clara knew, and so acting as casually as a cat can, she sauntered around the side of the bed, ears up and tail perky, almost as if she found a stranger kneeling by her person's bed every day.

"What is this girl up to now?" Laurel asked as she sidled up to Clara, and together they watched the young woman bent over the open violin case. *"She was only looking at it before."*

"I'm not sure," admitted Clara. *"Do you think she'd going to play?"*

Laurel shivered, her sleek café au lait fur shimmering. *"I hope not."* Cats have very sensitive ears.

"I hope not, too." Clara didn't relish the idea of a high-pitched instrument either. More to the point, she had seen Becca shoo her guest into this room. Any sound she made would give her presence away. As it was, Clara mewed as softly as she could, not that Laurel's distinctive Siamese vocalizations could be mistaken as coming from anything but a cat.

As if she could understand what the two felines were saying, Ruby turned and smiled, lifting the instrument from its velvet bed. "Hey, pretty girls," she said. Such an address made Clara sit up straight in shock. Laurel, however, blinked slowly, accepting such praise as her due. "Are you watching me?" She fished a square of paper out of one of the case's pockets and held them out for the cats to sniff. "Not to worry,

156

kitties. These are steel-wound strings."

"*I think she's gutting it.*" Harriet, leaning over the edge of the bed, looked ready to pounce.

Clara suspected something else was going on but watched as the young musician shoved the case under the bed and sat cross-legged, violin in her lap. With a look of intense concentration, she pushed back the dark hair falling over her face, tucking it behind her ears as she began turning the instrument's black wooden pegs. Harriet was right, the cat thought, as Ruby started pulling the violin's strings from their housing. Only then, to the cat's confusion, the young musician extracted new ones from the package, wound into a tight circle, and began to feed them into the instrument. The work appeared to take all her concentration, and the cats stayed clear of her swinging foot, even as it pushed the opened case further beneath Becca's bed. Quickly, however, the new strings fell into place, and the young musician was tightening the pegs as Becca entered the bedroom, almost as quietly as the cats.

"They're gone," she said, sitting on the bed beside Ruby to watch her work. "My downstairs neighbor was complaining, and the manager seems to think I was running an Airbnb. I tried to steer them toward my neighbor, but I didn't want to bring you into it."

"Thank you." Ruby plucked softly at a string before turning the peg. "I am sorry I lied to you."

"I understand you were drawn to your grandfather's violin." Becca spoke slowly. "But, Ruby, I need you to be honest. Are there other things you're not telling me?"

The violinist hung her head. "You mean, about renting the room?"

"I was wondering."

"I did not know there would be a problem," she said as she reached under the bed for the case. Still shaking her head, she lay the instrument in its well-worn place. "I was told it had been arranged, that I should

157

come here. That's the truth."

"Do you think the owner—the real owner—knew his manager was renting it out illegally?"

Ruby frowned. "I do not know. I only met that poor man when I got here." Latching the case, she looked up, eyes wide. "I never meant any of this to happen, Becca. And I would have returned the violin to him, I swear."

Chapter 21

"*Blasphemy!*" *the voices shouted, but the cat heard another cry, fainter than the rest. Her person calling out...for her? For her friend? That young woman, bitter and broken, had already turned away, her scowling face obscured by the rising smoke. Her person called out once more as the flames rose around her. Separating them. Frantic, the cat circled, dodging the rough hands that had grabbed them both, though they'd loosed her in the scuffle, eager to secure the woman. Desperately, she searched for a solution, a path to her person, aware all the while of four eyes—two blue, two yellow—watching from the rafters, bitter with rebuke.*

"*We told you. Warned you, again and again—*"

"*Blasphemy! Blasphemer!*" *In the voices, the cat heard the truth.*

"*Daughter of Bast, indeed,*" *her sisters scoffed.* "*Your pride, your carelessness...*"

The voices faded, and in her deep sorrow, she saw the basalt eyes glistening.

The younger woman had pleaded, desperate for a remedy, and so she had revealed herself. Shared the power.

As now she shared the pain.

Clara slept fitfully that night, her dreams a series of broken images, but she really couldn't blame Becca. Her person had insisted that Ruby stay over, even as she promised to help her look for a more permanent arrangement the next day. It was Clara's sisters who kept the calico awake. Laurel, specifically. The slender Siamese spent much of the night on alert, leaping down from the bed to spy on Ruby and then leaping back to report.

"*I don't like this.*" Even if her nimble landing hadn't woken Clara, her lashing tail would have. "*There's something off about that girl. She's not telling Becca everything.*"

"*I agree.*" Clara hesitated, unsure how to explain. Their person had taken her laptop into her bed, displacing the calico. Becca did that sometimes, and her cat had learned to accept it. This time, however, her person wasn't peacefully reading. Instead, she kept tapping away, at times with increasing fervor. From the muttered exclamations, Clara could tell that whatever she was seeking in the flat device was proving elusive. "*Becca knows something is off.*"

"*Sounds like you're finally learning about trust.*" Harriet broke off into a yawn. Their oldest sister had been dreaming too, Clara noted, her big hind paws kicking out as if she were leaping, or in a fight. "*Not that either of them is going to do anything while they're asleep, not with you patrolling like a dog.*"

"*If you'd stayed awake during your turn to watch, you'd sense that something is off,*" Laurel sniped.

"*You're about to be off.*" Harriet lumbered to her feet, growling.

"*Please! Sisters!*" Clara nuzzled up between them. "*Becca needs her rest. I'll take the next shift.*"

That offer calmed things down, Harriet's complaints fading into snores as her yellow eyes slowly closed. Laurel, for her part, settled on the bed by Becca's feet. That was Clara's usual place, but she ceded it with a dip of her head, seeing an opportunity to question her sister.

"What did she mean by trust?" The memory of smoke came back to her and the image of a woman who turned away. *"Who can we trust? How do we know?"*

Clara tilted her ears forward in vain.

"Huh." The sealpoint pulled a tuft of fur from her tongue. *"Haven't you figured out anything, Clown?"*

The calico looked around. With Harriet and Becca asleep, everything seemed peaceful, and yet… She dipped her head. *"Please."*

"This is why we hide our powers, runt." Her toilette completed, Laurel arranged herself into a disc. *"Why you shade yourself. The dangers…"* Her voice began to fade. *"Can't see everything…"*

For a count of breaths, Clara waited, hoping her sister would explain. But the slender sealpoint was fast asleep, her own high-pitched snuffle playing counterpoint to Harriet's deeper snorts. The calico longed to join them. The knocking of the radiator served to remind her of her promise to keep watch, however, and she found herself recalling a winter long ago. Kittens, then, they had huddled together under their mother's watchful gaze. Waiting, she now realized, to be sent off. For their human to appear…

"Your first duty…" The phrase echoed as she woke. Shaking off her own sleepiness, the little cat jumped to the floor, determined to stay alert, the rules echoing in her mind. *"Protect your person. Learn. Observe, while being unobserved."*

Clara made her way into the living room. Eschewing the armchair, she leapt instead to the table, where the violin case lay. From here she could see the top of Ruby's head, just over the edge of the sofa. Any outsider in the house made the confirmed housecat uneasy, and this one had already proved she could not be trusted. Although Becca seemed to care for this one, her cat would rest easier once this Ruby had moved on.

"Protect your person."

Retreating to the bedroom, Clara jumped up onto the nightstand, the better to keep an eye on Becca. The little table was crowded with books, none of which were particularly soft. She wasn't dozing at all, therefore, when a slight movement by her feet alerted her. Becca's phone had whirred ever so slightly, and unable to resist, Clara had pawed at it, causing the little beast to awake.

"What's that?" Becca propped herself up and yawned. "What are you doing up there, Clara? No, that's not a toy."

The tiny beast had buzzed again, jittering across the tabletop. Clara was only right to try to trap it.

"I thought I turned notifications off." Becca reached for her phone, fumbling in the half light. "Is Ruby Grozny at this address?" She squinted at the device. "Must be the dean. I guess they need to send her registration materials."

She tapped a few buttons and replaced the phone, sliding back under the covers.

"Thanks, Clara." She reached to fondle the base of her cat's ears. "Maybe we'll have a nice surprise for Ruby in the morning."

The banging, an hour later, woke them all. Clara, aware that she was supposed to be on duty, sprang up first. Back arching, she positioned herself at the foot of the bed, where she could defend her person.

"Hang on." Becca slipped around her and reached for her robe. And although Clara did her best to stop her, twining around her ankles as she left the room, her person made her way to the front of the apartment. "Who is it?"

Ruby was sitting up on the sofa, eyes wide as she grasped the blanket to her.

"Cambridge police," a brusque voice called out. "Open up."

"What?" Becca's foot caught Clara in the belly as she reached for

162

the door. Before the calico could plan a next move, her person had opened it. "What's happened?"

The tall detective from the shop stood there, a portly uniform behind her, matching her glower for glower. "Becca Colwin?"

"Yes, we met at Charm and Cherish."

But the detective wasn't done. "I believe I warned you about withholding information. That includes knowledge of any person of interest who may be wanted for questioning."

"Person of interest?" But her confusion cleared as the detective pushed past her. "Wait, you can't come in here."

The detective didn't spare her a glance. "Ruby Grozny, I'd like you to come with me."

The wide-eyed girl looked from the detective to Becca and back.

"You can get dressed first." The detective turned to her portly colleague. "Turndale, can you give us some privacy?"

The detective pulled the door closed, and Clara was on her, sniffing at her thick-soled shoes and trying to get a take on the intruder. Pavement, an office, the scent of other humans, sad and sweaty both, and she looked up at Becca in concern. Her person was no longer standing behind her, however. She had gone over to Ruby, and although she was speaking softly, Clara's sharp ears could hear her talking softly to the girl. She was telling her not to worry, although both their faces were drawn in panic. She also sounded like she was promising something, but her words about "spring" and "a solution" didn't make much sense to the disconcerted cat. Determined to uncover anything that would help, she turned back to the detective's black shoes, aware all the while that the woman was ignoring her because she was so focused on Becca and Ruby.

"*You're not going to get anything.*" Laurel stood in the bedroom doorway. "*She may look stern, but that's just how she is. Kind of like that bulldog down the block.*"

"But can't you make her go? Suggest that she leave?" Clara looked up anxiously. Becca was wrapping a sweater around Ruby that Clara was sure was one of her own favorites. *"Becca doesn't want her here."*

"She doesn't?" Laurel stretched, showing her front claws. *"Are you sure? Because this person seems to believe that Becca invited her in."*

"She did not!" Clara hissed. She didn't mean to, but Laurel's comment had unnerved her. In response, the detective looked down.

"Ms. Colwin? Would you remove your animal?" She did not, Clara noted, move away.

"Now you've got her." Laurel sauntered over. *"She's afraid you're going to attack."*

Becca must have been as well. She raced over and grabbed Clara, hoisting her by her middle. "She's not used to strangers," Becca apologized, holding her a little too tightly.

"Really?" Skepticism dripped from the detective's one-word reply, and Clara strained to face her. Something was going on, and she didn't want Becca to have to face it alone.

"You must have startled her." Clara gave up trying to maneuver. Every move she made only prompted Becca to squeeze her closer. "She's a very sweet cat."

The detective didn't bother to respond. "Ms. Grozny? Shall we?"

"Where are you taking her?" Becca's heart was beating so loudly Clara had to flick her ears to hear the response.

"We'd like to ask her a few more questions." It was a non-answer. Clara could only hope that Laurel was getting more. "As you may have guessed."

"Becca?" Ruby's voice, closer now. The girl must have finished dressing, Clara realized, and was standing by the door.

"It was your host who informed us of your whereabouts." The slight squeak of the door and a waft of air as the detective ushered the scared girl out into the hall. "You didn't know? She reached out to us by

164

text this morning, even if she's doing a good job of hiding it."

Clara didn't have to imagine the shocked look on Ruby's face. She could feel Becca recoil as if she'd been struck and, as the door closed, heard the intake of breath that was more of a sob.

Chapter 22

"Not only did you disabuse my trust, you acted unethically toward a student—a potential student!" Becca was pacing as she yelled into the phone. "And you said the police weren't involved!"

Clara didn't know who her person had called, but whoever was on the line was getting a tongue lashing. "What do you mean? Who else could it have been?"

Although Clara couldn't make out the response, the tone sounded even and calm.

"I'm sorry. No, of course." Becca sounded appalled. "I thought— Please, Dean Brustein, don't hold this against Ruby."

She hadn't calmed down much by her next call.

"But, Maddy, I didn't mean to tell the police anything. I didn't recognize the number and I was half asleep. I assumed it was the dean, reaching out about her application. It looked like a conservatory number. I should've asked…" All three cats were watching as Becca paced. She was supposedly dressing—Clara got that from the clothes she kept pulling from the closet and throwing on the bed—but clearly her attention was not on getting ready for work.

"He's still convinced that Ruby is involved with that violin heist."

From the sounds on the line, it was clear Becca's friend had strong feelings about this. "But that's just it, Maddy. I haven't been able to find out anything about the missing violin, so how can I argue? So, I was wondering—you have a lot more access than I do, these days. Do you think you could poke around some of the legal databases and see if you can find anything?"

Clara could hear the squeak of Maddy's response but she didn't bother to decipher it. Becca's friend was loyal, even when she disagreed.

"Thanks, Maddy. Honest, I'm just curious. I won't do anything." Becca had managed to get her jeans on. The socks were proving a challenge. "At this point, I feel like I'm involved, even if I didn't mean to be."

Even through the phone, Maddy's irritation was clear.

"My key? I don't know, Maddy. They hustled her out of here so quickly. It's probably in her bag. At any rate, she's with the police. Surely, you can't think that she's any threat to me now."

The call ended without a resolution, leaving Becca in a foul mood. "Was one of you sleeping on my sweater again?" With rougher strokes than she would ever use on any of the cats, Becca brushed several strands of white fur from her black mohair sweater. "Clara, bad girl!"

Clara sat there, wide-eyed, but silent. Her person needed to vent. Otherwise, she'd surely have noticed that the errant hairs were longer than her own.

"*If she doesn't want us to sleep on her clothes, she shouldn't leave the drawers open,*" Harriet purred, unfazed, as she kneaded the comforter on Becca's bed.

"*But she didn't. That was in the box under the bed.*" Fundamentally lazy, Harriet could be quite deft with those mitten-like paws. "*And now she's blaming me.*"

"*Whatever, it was warm.*"

Curling into a neat circle, Harriet was soon dozing once again, her big head bobbing with each breath. Becca paused to watch her, one hand reaching out as if to stroke the wide white head. When she held back, Clara studied her face. As the big marmalade's baby sister, Clara would rarely choose to wake Harriet, knowing full well how much her oldest sibling valued her rest. Becca, however, had never scrupled to pet her cats, almost as if she understood at some level how they vied for her attention, and to the calico her reticence seemed to stem from a private concern. As Clara watched, Becca's lips tightened, a worry line appearing between her brows that seemed at odds with Harriet's peaceful snore. But Clara had no time to consider the cause for such distress. Becca was heading out the door.

"See you later, kitties," she called, unaware that Clara was readying to join her. "Try not to destroy the apartment. Okay?"

With that, she grabbed her hat and slipped out the door, locking it behind her as Clara, with a shimmy and a leap, slipped out beside her, shading herself from sight. While she couldn't clear her name in the case of the mohair sweater, she could at least accompany her person and make sure she stayed out of trouble.

What a relief, then, that Becca headed straight to work, and that the little shop appeared to be in no more disarray than the day before. Although the door's window was still boarded up, its lock was intact, and when Becca opened it, the pleasantly toasty interior gave up the slightly spicy, musty scent of the candles and herbs within. Nobody had been here, Clara noted with a sigh. Becca seemed to sense this too, though she locked the door behind her and checked the back room and bath before once more flipping the lock, as well as the sign that announced Charm and Cherish was open for business.

"Good morning." The jingle of bells announced Elizabeth, who entered swathed in a colorful patchwork cloak and holding two steaming mugs of peppermint tea. "I thought you might want something soothing to start the day, so I brought these down. My special blend."

"Thank you." Becca accepted the mug, wrapping her hands around its warmth, but kept her gaze on the older woman. "But how did you know?"

Elizabeth smiled and raised one untamed brow, but before she could answer, Becca chuckled. "Of course. The police must have called you as well. Did they come by here?"

"They had no reason to."

"Of course not." Becca shook her head. "I can't believe I led them to her."

"Are you sure you did? She's old enough to be responsible for her actions."

"You mean, borrowing the violin? Did I tell you about that?" Becca smiled ruefully. "She's paying an awfully big price for a small act."

"Small things matter." Elizabeth looked down. She might have been thinking, but Clara couldn't help but feel that the woman was staring directly at her.

Becca, preoccupied, barely seemed to notice.

"I'm going to make some queries," she said. "She's doesn't have anyone else here to help her out."

"Help who out?" The jangle sounded more dissonant as Elizabeth's sister Margaret pushed her way in, dressed in a camel wool coat and matching hat that must have been the height of fashion four decades earlier. The shop might be hers, but she looked out of place among the mystical and religious ephemera, and as she removed the hat, perching it atop a black basalt cat statuette, Clara bristled as if an intruder had invaded the space. "We're not running a charity here."

"No, of course not." Becca stood up straight, tucking the mug out of sight. "I was just talking."

"Humph." The shorter woman looked down her long nose. "Well, I don't have time for chitchat. The glazier will be here within the hour.

169

Keep an eye on him, won't you? I gave him the exact dimensions and specified safety glass. If he tries to install anything else, or wants to sell you anything, call me right away. Elizabeth?"

Giving Becca a look that Clara couldn't quite interpret, the older sister brought her empty mug into the back and then followed her kid sister out of the store.

"I guess it's good that we're getting the door fixed." Becca might have been talking to herself as she carried the empty into the back, but Clara liked to think her person could sense her presence. "Though, I wonder if I have time..."

A moment of staring into space must have supplied the answer. Or maybe it was the tea, because, as Becca drained her own mug, she fished out her phone and punched in a number that she seemed to know well. "Hi, Becca Colwin, calling for Detective Abrams. Yes, I'll wait."

As she stood there, the bells rang again, and a big man in a work jacket and worn jeans stepped in with a gust of frosty air. Although a turned-up collar hid most of his face, his black knit cap, pulled low, couldn't quite hide the scar that split one eyebrow, dragging the corner of one eye down.

"Hello." Becca pointed to her phone. "I'll be with you in a minute. If you want to get your tools and get started, that will be fine."

Just then, a tinny squawk announced someone had picked up her call, and she turned away to give herself some privacy. The man, meanwhile, seemed in no hurry to get started. Instead, he was taking in the store, peering up at the tops of the shelves and back at the intact front window with a frown on his piggish face.

"Just the door," Becca called over her shoulder. "Mrs. Cross was very clear."

She turned back. "No, I can't really. It's personal and it's kind of complicated."

Becca was talking softly, and the store was quiet. But Clara noticed that the man was quiet too. With only the slightest squeak of his boots, he took a step toward Becca, paused, and then took another. For reasons she couldn't quite explain, Clara felt the fur rise along her spine. If he could have seen her, he might have backed off. Instead, he crept forward with the slow, deliberate tread of a hunter.

"Detective Abrams? I've been trying to reach you."

The man froze, and just as silently, although a sight more quickly, he stepped backward. Taking care not to jostle the bells, he opened the door, slipped out to the street, and disappeared.

Chapter 23

"So, in brief, if I can offer any kind of testimonial or, I don't know, character witness…" Five minutes later, Becca was running out of steam. "Anyway, I wanted to reach out. I feel responsible, you know?"

Clara couldn't quite make out the rumbling voice on the other end of the line. Feline ears are more attuned to the higher pitches of birds and rodents, or female humans. She did get a sense of the rumpled, burly man whom Becca had encountered before. And while it may have been a memory, the calico got a strong sense of barely concealed impatience.

"No, I didn't mean—" Becca was trying to cut in. "No, I—I understand. That's funny."

The change in her tone must have elicited a question from the other end. "No, I'm sorry. I'm at work and there was a technician here and now he's—never mind. No, I don't have to go. Really. Oh, well, thank you. And please remember—"

With a deep sigh, Becca put down her phone. Just then, a gentle rap sounded on the door frame, and a head poked in. Salt-and-pepper hair, with a moustache to match, set off round wire-frame glasses.

"Hello! I'm here."

"So you are." Becca couldn't help but smile. "Please, come in. We're open."

The man unzipped a parka, revealing a denim coverall so spattered with paint it matched his hair. Rather, thought Clara, as if he were a calico too.

"I'm here about the window." He turned back to take in the board. "Is this the entire job?"

"That's it. Your colleague must have stepped out to get his tools."

"Colleague?" He turned to take her in, the glasses making his eyes owlishly large. "For a job like this? I'll have this fixed up within the hour."

With that, he stepped out, leaving Becca, her mouth gaping like a goldfish. She rallied before he could return, however, and raced back out to the sidewalk.

"I'm right here, miss." The bespectacled tech was pulling a tool kit from a truck clearly labeled Saldana Glass. "I'll be right back."

"No, I…" Her head swiveled. "I was looking for the other man. A big guy with an eye…" With one finger, she drew down the corner of her eye.

"Are you sure he was a glazier?" His bushy brows hunched together. "Did you call another company?"

"No, I didn't, and I don't think my boss would have either." Becca peered up the sidewalk and then turned to look the other way, shaking her head. "I don't think he was here about the door at all."

With that, she turned and walked back into the shop, ignoring the puzzled look of the glazier.

"Detective Abrams, please." Tense fingers beat a tattoo on the countertop, rattling the dish of colored stones. "Yes, this is Becca Colwin again, but I have something new to report."

The rat-a-tat-tat of the nails was almost too percussive for Clara's ears. But the set of her person's jaw kept the little calico alert and by her side.

"He's not? Did you tell him there was something new?" Becca stared down at the counter, but Clara had the distinct impression that she wasn't seeing the collection of colored charms in the bowl before her. "Well, then, yes. Yes, please. At his earliest opportunity," she said forcefully. "I need him to know that I'm not crying wolf."

As soon as she put the phone down, it buzzed once more.

"Thank you for—oh." She stood up, turning to check out the clock. "Yes, that should work. All three? I'll be there. Thanks so much."

Clara braced herself to run. Becca had a wild look in her eyes as she grabbed her coat. Only just then, the glazier came back in with a pane of glass and the intoxicating aroma of glue.

"I'll have this up in a jiff." A smile appeared under the moustache, and then he turned to his work. Becca, still by the counter, barely registered the technician and stared instead at something even Clara couldn't see.

"I can't tell you how much I appreciate this, Maddy. It's Guadagnini." Becca shrugged into her coat as she spelled out the name. "Maybe the dean was wrong?"

"Brustein," she said after a pause. "Norm Brustein. Sure, add his name. It can't hurt. Speaking of, I owe him an apology. His manner was kind of off-putting, but who knows? But if you can find out anything. Maybe Ruby didn't understand…"

Becca broke off, interrupted by her friend. As Maddy spoke, she glanced toward the front of the store, where the glazier was finishing up. With her eyes on the mustachioed man, her voice dropped to a breathy murmur.

"No, I'm not trying to get her out any longer. In fact, I hope they don't release her any time soon."

From the squawk on the line, Clara could tell that Maddy agreed with this last statement.

"No, it's not what you think, Maddy." Becca's eyes darted to the front of the shop, where the technician was gathering up his tools. Standing, he pulled on that parka and a pair of gloves.

"Miss?"

Maddy was still talking, but Becca nodded.

"Hang on a minute, Mads. I've got someone here. Yes?"

"I'm done, but this should really be let to set for at least an hour." He eyed the door. "Is there another entrance you can use?"

"There is!" Becca's enthusiasm clearly startled him. "In fact, I'll put a sign on the door. Thanks so much."

Shaking his head, he let himself out, bracing the door behind him. Becca smiled through the new glass as she clicked the lock back in place and turned the sign to *Closed*.

"I've got to run." Back on the phone, Becca was already heading toward the back room. "No, I'm not going to bail Ruby out. It's Harriet. She's developed this odd occasional cough. It's probably nothing, but the vet had a cancellation and can fit us in. If I hurry, I can make it."

Clara's ears went up at that. The vet? Her sisters would weigh in on that, but Laurel, in particular, would be intrigued. Her immediate concern, however, was the key that had just turned in the locked front door.

"She's innocent—well, she's innocent of murder, at any rate." Becca, pulling on her coat, was oblivious to the door opening behind her. "But all things considered, I think this may be a good thing. I think she may be safer in custody."

Chapter 24

"You're simply leaving? In the middle of the day?" Margaret frowned as she looked around. "This is getting to be a habit. A bad one."

"I'm sorry, but this is an emergency. A pet emergency." Becca was trying to be reasonable, but Clara could hear the strain in her voice. "One of my cats has been having some health issues, and my vet had a cancellation. Besides, the glazier said we shouldn't use the front door."

"I used it," her boss protested, as if that made it all right. She waved a gloved hand toward the entrance as she waddled down the first of the little shop's aisles. "We could leave it propped open."

"In this weather?" Becca softened the question with a smile. "You know, they're predicting snow."

The logic was inescapable. That didn't mean her boss liked it, her displeasure clear as she scanned the room. Her scowl relaxed briefly as she located her hat. But then, grabbing it off the statuette where she had left it as roughly as if the stone cat were somehow to blame, the angry little woman retreated back to the counter, eying her employee with what was probably supposed to be an intimidating stare. To Clara, she looked like an angry sparrow.

But Becca was no worm. "I promise I'll come right back, as soon as I drop my cats off."

"And in the meantime, what do you expect me to do?" Margaret flapped dismissively, as if the turmoil of the last few days could be so easily brushed away. "Run the shop myself?"

"Of course not." The deeper voice of Margaret's older sister made them both turn. Elizabeth had come in through the back and was already tying back her wild gray hair. "I'll do it. I'll post a sign explaining about the door. I've been meaning to finish the inventory, and it will be easy enough for me to hear if anyone knocks."

"Why are you covering for her?" Margaret's tone grew waspish, even as she arranged the brimmed topper. "It's not like she has a family emergency."

"Not an emergency, but family." Elizabeth, already a good head taller than her sister, pulled herself up to her full height as she spoke. Particularly, Clara thought, so she could look down her nose at her sister. It was a move Harriet often used, though Elizabeth's Roman nose was much more intimidating than Harriet's Persian pug. "And family," she reminded her baby sister, "looks out for each other."

Margaret had no response to that, none she would vent in front of Becca, anyway. And so with a bit more grumbling and another dismissive wave, she walked out to the street, closing the door behind her with exaggerated care. Becca, however, remained rooted in place. Unsure, her cat thought, whether she had been given permission or possibly if she would have a position to come back to.

"Go on." Elizabeth nodded toward the door. "I really do have inventory to look into, and you don't want to be late."

"No, I don't." Becca broke into a grin, which Elizabeth returned, as Clara looked on in wonder. "Thanks, Elizabeth. You don't know how much—"

"I have an idea." The older woman headed back into the storeroom.

"And if you want to take the rest of the day, that's fine. I suspect your cats are in tip-top shape, but I meant what I said about family. And they'd do the same for you."

So set on gathering up her pets and making the appointment, Becca didn't even look back as she called out her thanks once more and made her own way out via the back. And so she didn't see Elizabeth look up as she left. She certainly didn't see the smile on the older woman's face—or the quick wink she gave to Clara.

That threw the calico, and she had to hurry to catch up to Becca, who had rounded the corner and was race-walking down the street. Her person was spurred by the cold, Clara knew. But she was also anxious, and as her pet trotted unseen by her feet, she thought of all she wished she could share. For starters, that the three sisters didn't usually mind going to the vet, weighing the attention—and the inevitable follow-up treats—as adequate recompense for the discomfort of the carrier and the unfortunate recurrence of shots.

More important, Clara wished she could ease her person's worries. The three litter mates, she knew, were young and generally healthy, and Clara had reason to believe that her oldest sister's powers helped protect them from various threats and illnesses. That was why she hadn't worried much when she had heard Harriet coughing, a short, bark-like sound more fitting to a canine than a majestic cat like her sister.

Actually, Clara thought, Harriet's grandeur might be what concerned their person. While neither of her sisters would ever dare mention it, Harriet was on the heavy side, and with her tendency to overindulge, she would occasionally barf up some of the many treats she had heedlessly scarfed down. And while Laurel considered the well-placed furball a respectable form of expression, Harriet's cough *had* become more frequent. Add in that the older cat's flattened Persian features made her more susceptible to respiratory issues, and Clara understood her person's concern.

More to the point, as Becca hurried through the city crowds, Clara found herself wondering if another factor was at work. Clara had seen the way Laurel and Harriet had looked at each other when Marcia had mentioned the cute vet. Plus, she suspected, at times her sisters played at being normal cats in part to keep their person occupied. She herself tried never to worry Becca, though she had caused her distress on occasion just through the normal chain of events.

Still, the three knew what was expected of them. And so, once Becca brought out the big carrier, they led Becca on a merry chase for several minutes.

"Oh, please." Becca reached to pull Laurel from the upper bookshelf, just as Harriet managed to unlock the carrier's catch to free herself. "Not you too."

"*Laurel*," Clara called out as she squeezed herself into one corner of the big plastic box, to leave more room for her sisters. "*She's getting upset.*"

"*You've let her get soft,*" her sister complained, even as she let Becca lift her into the box. "*Besides, this vet isn't that cute.*"

Clara didn't respond. Better to let Laurel win this round, even if she disagreed. Dr. Keller might not be as dashing as the sealpoint would have preferred. Although tall, the vet was lanky, rather than muscular, with a long, weathered face dominated by large, sad brown eyes that, along with his slightly shaggy hair, reminded her of the elderly retriever who used to live next door, a good dog if such a thing were possible. Even if there weren't—and Clara knew Laurel would surely have argued that case given the chance—there was a gentleness to the veterinarian that made the calico trust him.

"*Gentle, huh!*" Harriet grunted as Becca lifted her back into the carrier, an exhalation that turned into a cough. "*Injecting us without*

179

our explicit permission. As if we would allow ourselves to get rabies. I may bite him if I get the chance."

Again, Clara held her tongue, trusting that, in Harriet's case, at least, some combination of dignity and lethargy would prevail and that her cough, as worrisome as it sounded, would prove to be nothing at all.

Chapter 25

Forty-five minutes later, Clara stepped cautiously out of the carrier. Unused to being carried, she felt a little wobbly from the back and forth and was still waiting for the cool, sterile room to settle down.

"Car sick?" Laurel had by then perched herself on the edge of the metal examination table, from which she could view the room. *"What a pity. This place is fascinating."*

"I consider it an affront." Harriet, of course, refused to leave her case, though whether that was in protest of simple inertia was hard to tell. As the vet lifted her onto the table, she went limp, letting her hindlegs hanging down like fluffy white bloomers.

"She's a big girl." The vet placed her carefully beside Clara.

"I try to watch what they eat." Becca sounded apologetic. Harriet, on the other hand, preened at what she considered a compliment. "It's been challenging. Harriet does tend to hog the food."

"And these two let her?"

Laurel stretched, flexing her claws in silent rebuke to his assumption. Not that the humans noticed.

"Clara, the calico, does. I try to keep an eye on them, but there's been a lot going on. I've got a new job so I'm away from home for so much of the day, and I may have to find a new place to live."

He turned to her with a questioning gaze, even as he reached to pull Clara closer to her siblings. His hands, Clara was relieved to note, were warm.

"My building's going condo, and I'm a renter, so…" Becca shrugged and turned away, blinking back the tears that had sprung to her eyes.

The vet's voice grew soft. "I'm sorry. I do see how that might be difficult, especially with three cats."

Becca managed a weak smile. "Thanks. That's one of the reasons I'm worried. Maybe I missed something…" She broke off.

"I understand." The room grew silent as he lifted Harriet, peering into her eyes and then into each fluffy ear. "Better to be careful, especially in winter, with the heat on. Cats are prone to respiratory viruses much like we are," he said as he thumbed her mouth open, taking in her glistening fangs.

"Very good, my girl."

Harriet smiled, her eyes closing as she prepared to shuffle off. She was stopped by a large hand on her back as, with the other, the vet lifted the diaphragm of his stethoscope, breathing on it to take off any chill. Holding the marmalade under her front legs, he raised her, almost to a sitting position, while with his other hand he moved the stethoscope around.

"She's not coughing now." While Harriet's eyes grew wide, he shifted again, pressing the disc against the softness of her belly.

"Cough? I'm so going to bite him." Her annoyed mew alarmed Clara, who silently begged her sister to behave. *"Or maybe just barf."*

"Everything sounds okay. I'll do some tests, to be sure."

Placing the big marmalade back on the table, he reached for Laurel. "Let's see what we've got here." He palpated her velvety midriff, and her eyes crossed. "This pretty lady seems to be in good shape."

"*I am,*" Laurel purred, her eyes closing with pleasure at the compliment. In contrast to Harriet, the sealpoint accepted the vet's ministrations gracefully, even quieting her purr briefly as he listened to her heart and lungs.

"And how's this little one?"

"I've been a little worried about Clara, to be honest," said Becca.

The calico stiffened at the sound of her name, but the vet's only response was to grow more solicitous, one warm finger moving to stroke the smooth fur beneath her chin, as his otoscope parted the long hair in her ear.

"She's been, well, jumpy lately. Nervous."

"Is she off her food?" He frowned as he stared into one green eye.

"No." Becca frowned. "At least, I don't think so. It's hard to tell with the three of them. But she seems to be underfoot more recently."

"Is it that she wants more attention?" That finger now circled the base of Clara's ear, and she began to purr. "If your new job is taking you out of the house more, she may be suffering from separation anxiety."

Through her purr, Clara could hear Laurel's scoffing cough. Both the vet and Becca looked over, and the Siamese licked her chops, blue eyes wide and innocent. Clara could sense the vet's interest diverting and was anticipating a lecture about furballs, when she saw Laurel's eyes crossing.

"*You heard nothing.*" The suggestion was so strong, even Clara began to believe it. "*Go back to rubbing the clown's ear.*"

Turning obediently back toward Becca, he did just that, to Clara's relief. It wasn't simply his careful touch—the light massage rubbing just the right spot—it was also that she wanted to hear more of their conversation. Something was bothering Becca, that much was clear. If Clara was acting in a way that disturbed her person, she needed to stop it.

"It's not that she's seeking attention, exactly." Becca stared at a spot on the wall over the vet's shoulder, as if she could read something there, her gaze so intent that Clara turned to look as well. "In fact, half the time I don't know where she is. But then suddenly she'll appear underfoot. And, well, it's almost like I feel her with me all the time, even when I can't see her. Like I'm about to trip over her, but she's not there. I don't know if I'm making any sense."

Clara froze, the fur along her spine bristling with horror. Becca couldn't know. Could she? The petite calico had always believed that Becca was special, a particularly sensitive human and almost cat-like at times. But this? It had been ingrained in Clara from earliest kittenhood that cats had to hide their magic from their people. She had always accepted this dictate, even before she understood why. Now that Harriet had begun to share their history, and that of their often ill-fated humans, Clara understood just how dangerous it could be for humans to concern themselves with the affairs of their feline companions. Bad enough that Becca kept involving herself in perilous situations with questionable characters, like that girl Ruby. Worse still that she assumed she had powers. If she actually found out…

Clara was brought to her senses by the vet's hand. It had stopped moving, she realized belatedly, holding the tender velvet of her ear between his index finger and his thumb. Unlike Laurel, Clara didn't think this man was dense. If he had noticed how she froze at Becca's words, the result could be just as bad.

She looked up at his kind brown eyes, pleading silently for him not to comment. For him to move on as if nothing had happened. Surely, as a veterinarian, he was accustomed to cats displaying what he would call extraordinary empathy. Wasn't he?

"Sorry, kitty." His voice was soft and seemed to be talking directly to her, and her heart sank. But then he began that lovely circular motion again and it hit her: the kind man thought he had caused her reaction. Maybe even that he had pinched her tender ear. She leaned into his hand and ramped up her purr. Whatever Laurel thought about Dr. Keller, he cared.

And he wasn't quite as smart as she had feared. In fact, once she butted her head against his hand a second time, he chuckled, redoubling his efforts until her ear grew a bit irritated. No matter, she shuffled slightly to remove herself from his attentions. Better he think she was an oversensitive house pet, reacting simply to his ministrations. But while he kept talking down to Clara, as if she were the focus of his thoughts, it was soon apparent that his words were directed to Becca.

"That does sound disturbing," he said. He was speaking slowly and softly, more as if he were calming a spooked pet than a woman as accomplished as Becca. "But I wonder. Sometimes, you see, we use our pets as a substitute for ourselves, and it does sound like you've had a good deal of upheaval in your life."

Becca made a noise like she was about to cough. Clara didn't think she was prone to furballs, but for a moment she wondered. He might have heard her slight gasp, Clara couldn't tell, but he refrained from commenting. He glanced up and quickly looked down again. As he continued to speak, he examined the tray of utensils on the table beside the cats' carrier, selecting a syringe. That was just as well, Clara thought, bracing herself for the needle. The vet had a sure hand, she told herself. He also had a very feline sense of privacy.

"Well, my first impression is that everyone is healthy." He broke the silence a few minutes later, speaking even as he inserted the needle into Clara's forearm. "Though I'll give them each a complete blood workup to be sure."

The two other blood samples weren't taken entirely without incident. Laurel felt it a matter of honor to howl as if violated, and Harriet, not to be outdone, drew her head back in the most ferocious snarl. That didn't stop her from accepting treats from the vet once the vials had been labelled and set aside. Treats that she shared with her sisters only grudgingly.

"*You're only here because of me, you know.*" Having snarfed up three in rapid succession, she eyed the one Clara was still licking.

"*It was my idea,*" Laurel growled, prompting Clara to look up.

"Now, now." As Harriet had swooped in, two large hands grabbed her around the middle, pulling her back. Those same hands then scooped up Clara's treats, holding them up to her face.

"*He smells nice.*" Aware of the honor, she gobbled them down.

Harriet wrinkled up her nose. "*If you like disinfectant.*"

Clara knew better than to respond, but as she washed, she eyed Laurel, her question at the forefront of her mind. Her sister only yawned and licked her chops, however, her big ears flicking back and forth as the two humans spoke softly above them both.

"In the meantime, if I can do anything, Ms. Colwin," she heard the vet say. "Anything else, that is, please do let me know."

Chapter 26

The visit didn't entirely ease Becca's mind, Clara could tell. Once they were home, Becca doled out treats even before taking off her coat. "He did say that Harriet's cough was probably nothing, and that you all appeared healthy." She spoke more to herself than the cats, not knowing they understood every word.

"*Better eat up,*" Harriet urged. "*We don't want her to worry.*"

"*You can have mine.*" Clara was still a bit nauseous from the carrier. Besides, Becca was already pulling her hat low over her ears. While her person was obviously anxious—to her cats, at any rate—she also was clearly readying to head back out

"I won't be too late, kitties," she called. "I'll come straight back after closing."

"*If you really cared, you wouldn't be going out at all,*" Laurel, mouth full, mumbled.

"*Please, she's having a hard time.*" Clara pleaded with her sisters, but she couldn't linger. Becca was already out the door.

Despite Clara's lingering concerns, tagging along beside Becca offered a welcome change to being cooped up. Although the shaded cat had to watch out for pedestrians as her person strode purposefully into the heart of Cambridge, the brisk air was bracing, especially after the almost overwhelming blend of smells inside the animal hospital. The temperature seemed to have risen a bit, as well, losing the harsh dryness that had made her nose sting.

The newly moisture-laden air held scents better as well, and Clara closed her eyes, the better to take in its hints of the river and the ocean beyond. So intoxicating was the mix that the little calico forgot her concerns for a moment, feeling briefly the call of the wild.

Until, with a shock like a splash of cold water, she realized where Becca was heading. Clara froze in horror, staring up at the large grey building before her. Looming over the sidewalk like a stone owl, it appeared to stare back, watching the creatures scurrying back and forth before it. If Clara could have stopped Becca, even at the expense of her whiskers, she would have. As it was, all she could do was shiver in fear as she watched Becca pause—"Elizabeth did say I could take as much time as I needed"—and then mount the steps to enter the building itself.

Fighting her own urge to flee, Clara dashed up the stairs after her, shimmying through the glass doors to find herself in a cavernous waiting room.

"Detective Abrams, please." Becca was standing by a wooden counter, speaking to a stout woman with a moustache.

"Do you have an appointment?" The woman stared past Becca. Not at Clara, the little cat decided, but at some middle point in space. Nearsighted, she decided. Unless she could spy something beyond even the feline's acute perception.

"No, but we've spoken." Becca leaned forward, as if to give her words more weight. Her person didn't like to lie, Clara knew, but she would stretch the point when it seemed important. "I'm following up on an earlier discussion."

The woman nodded in a way that didn't inspire confidence. "Wait here."

Becca visibly relaxed as the woman waddled off. Leaning back on the counter, she took in the waiting area, and it occurred to Clara that her person felt safe in this large cage-like building—a worrisome thought. There were too many strange odors circulating here, many carrying the stink of fear or of pain. And as much as Becca appeared to trust the rumpled detective, the calico could not help but remember all the discord that had followed in the wake of the large man.

While Becca waited, Clara did what surveillance she could. Leaping soundlessly to the counter, she peered out over the crowded reception area, searching for the large man or any other familiar face among the shifting crowd.

Her instincts had been right. Over by the door, a short man. Collar up, he must have just come in from the cold, and his head swiveled back and forth, deep-set eyes taking in the waiting area. In a moment, he would see Becca. Clara surveyed the room, seeking an exit or a place to hide.

Too late. A sudden stillness alerted the cat that her person had seen and recognized the man. Worse, Clara saw in a flash of horror, Becca was going to approach him. As her person stepped forward, the cat considered her options. She could jump down and trip her. Scratch a stranger—someone who might scream. Anything to keep Becca from confronting the stranger. Only, before she could act, she found her own fur starting up in surprise.

Becca wasn't heading toward the small dark man who had been prowling through Charm and Cherish, inquiring about her predecessor in a most unsettling way. No, her person was in pursuit of a tall, lean figure whose slick hair reflected blue in the light. With a shock that shook her nose to tail, Clara realized who he was, and why Becca was pursuing him. It was the man the police had questioned after they had found the body of Larry Rakov. Her absent neighbor, Justin Neil.

"Excuse me!" As Clara watched, the dark-haired figure walked swiftly through the crowd. He must have come from the side of the waiting area, where a door opened onto private offices. Now he was heading to the street, either not hearing or not acknowledging Becca's calls.

"Hello? Excuse me." The man was taller than Becca by far and managed to weave through the crowd while Becca found herself blocked first by a woman with a crying child in tow and then by two teens, seized by the sudden urge to kiss. "Coming through!"

Head down, Becca pushed by, but by then the man she knew as her neighbor had made it outside, as quickly as if he had been able to pass through the dirty glass of the door. Unwilling to leave her person, Clara, meanwhile, had hung back, waiting for Becca.

"Wait," Becca called once she emerged from the crowded building. "Justin? Justin Neil?"

The name did it. Halfway down the steps he paused, turning, his eyes growing wide as he spied Becca tripping down the steps toward him.

"You!" He drew back. "Haven't you caused enough trouble?"

"Excuse me?" Becca stopped short, her customary smile evaporating. "What are you talking about?"

His mouth puckered like he'd bitten into something sour. "Harboring a fugitive, I believe they call it."

"Ruby? She's an innocent bystander." Clara heard the slight stumble as her person pronounced "innocent." She couldn't tell if the man facing her did. He stared down his nose at her. "She didn't do anything. We found that poor man together."

"That poor man…"

It must have been his tone that made Becca snap. "That man, Larry Rakov, worked for you. He was a musician. He had a life."

"I know that." Neil reared back, affronted. "I also know he was a

190

fraud and a fake. He was taking advantage of me. Illegally renting out my apartment."

"I'm sure he had his reasons." Becca grew thoughtful. "Have you spoken to his family?"

"I do not maintain that kind of relationship with my employees." He frowned.

"Well, he must have given you someone as an emergency contact." She paused, undoubtedly feeling the heat of his glare. "You see, I met the man, and—and I borrowed something from him."

"What?" A bark of command, rather than a question.

Chin up, Becca held firm. "I'd rather talk to his family. Do you have his contact information? Do you know where he was from?"

"I don't have to answer any of your questions." He turned, giving the building behind him the same disdainful stare. "I've already wasted too much time on this project."

"This project? The apartment, it's another investment for you." Realization dawned on Becca, and her eyes grew wide. "You're not even curious about why that poor man was killed."

His eyes narrowed further, meeting Becca's with an intensity the cat by her side could almost feel. She stared back, unblinking, and with a dismissive grunt, he turned aside, continuing down the stairs.

"Wait," she called once more, nearly tripping in her haste to catch up with him. "You can't just walk away from this. You own the unit that was illegally rented out, and now a man is dead."

"So says an angry renter," he snapped back, his voice sinking to an angry growl. "A woman with an ax to grind who is already involved with the primary suspect."

Becca retreated into the cage-like building after that. But after another futile attempt to reach Detective Abrams, she satisfied herself with leaving a note before trudging back to Charm and Cherish.

191

Letting herself in, she yelled a greeting back to Elizabeth, and set to work on decorating the new glass. But even though she did her best—stenciling a new mandala on the door and rearranging a set of crystals to catch the thin winter light—Clara could tell her heart wasn't in it. Elizabeth seemed to sense this also. Although she had called back her own greeting from the back room, she left Becca to deal with the three customers who came in.

"So you're open!" The first visitor, bundled into a full-length purple plush coat, barely navigated the first aisle without knocking over a candle or a statuette. Still, she managed to squeeze down all three, her eyes on the ceiling rather than the shelves the flanked her. "Are you new here?"

"Me or the shop?" Becca managed a perky smile. Despite the playful style of that big coat and its matching boots, as fluffy as puppies, the woman inside looked deadly serious, and closer to fifty than fifteen. "Charm and Cherish has been around for a little over a year. I've only worked here a few months."

The woman nodded, even as she scanned the counter, apparently intrigued by the clock and the wall-mounted land line beneath. "It's a good space. Thanks."

"*She wants the shop.*" The thought came to Clara as clearly as if she had Laurel's powers. More likely, she told herself, she was simply getting better at reading people.

"Gracie, come here." Clara figured the two schoolgirls who came in next as browsers rather than buyers. But Becca kept her eye on them as they made their way around, picking up every candle and figurine.

"These are pretty." The shorter of the two, her pigtails matching the figure on her anime backpack, ran a black-lacquered nail through the gemstone tray. "What do they do?"

"Well, tradition has it that different stones have different properties. But it depends what you want to believe." She concluded the abbreviated pitch with her best professional smile, and a glance toward the back room. Elizabeth had emerged and was standing in the doorway.

"Take a look at the rose quartz," the older woman said. "The pink one."

"This one?" The girl held up the translucent stone. "Gracie, check it out."

"And for you, the jadeite." Elizabeth came over and pointed to a dark green disk.

"I like it." The taller girl cupped the stone in her palm. "It makes me feel, I don't know, calm."

"Jadeite is centering." Elizabeth glanced over at Becca before retreating, leaving her to complete the sales—her first of the day.

"Thanks for that." When the pair had taken off, giggling, Becca found her colleague bent over a carton the back room. "I'm never sure how far to push the powers."

"You don't believe?" Elizabeth's brows rose, though whether in skepticism or surprise, Becca couldn't tell.

"I don't know anymore." She sounded so forlorn her cat stared up at her with concern. "I used to think I could help people. Or at least read them."

When the other woman didn't respond, Clara turned to her. Elizabeth was staring at Becca and nodding slowly.

"I get it," she said, her voice soft. "There's so much we all still have to learn."

"Isn't that the truth." Despite Becca's quick response, Clara had the distinct impression that the older woman's comment had been meant for her own multicolored ears. Elizabeth was an uncanny woman. Unnerving at best, and Clara could not forget that large, dark volume that Elizabeth had been on the verge of lending Becca only two days before.

As a cat, Clara understood that magic wasn't something that could be taught, even with an old book. She also sensed how badly Becca wanted magic in her life. But her pet could not feel entirely comfortable with this new relationship. Becca was a mere human, and power was a dangerous thing. What Elizabeth offered might be more than guidance, and the little cat knew her first responsibility was to keep her person safe.

Chapter 27

Becca's shift ended soon after, and she headed out, walking quickly through the early winter dusk. The temperature had fallen once more, although the air still held a damp heaviness that had the other rush hour pedestrians scanning the skies. It wasn't simply the cold—or the thickening cloud cover that reflected the gray light—propelling Becca along, her cat suspected, especially as her pace picked up as she neared their building. And while Clara wanted to think it was anticipation of seeing her littermates, piqued by concern for Harriet, a prickling feeling along her spine alerted her to other forces at work.

Indeed, although Becca was appropriately enthusiastic in her greeting of Harriet and Laurel once she got in, she was clearly preoccupied. She'd barely noticed that Clara had appeared later than her sisters, hung up as she was in sniffing the stairs as Becca bounded up. And although she had fed her pets before doing anything else, as was only proper, she didn't follow up with a snack for herself or even a cup of tea. Instead, she headed toward Ruby's bag, which had gotten tucked under the coffee table in all the fuss when the police had arrived.

"Please be here." Becca rummaged through the bag, like Laurel looking for a bug. Moments later, she squeaked as if she had found one, as she pulled out a metal ring with a paper label attached, and—yes—a key.

"Number five! Thanks to the Goddess," she said, holding the label up to the light. When she headed back to the front door without donning coat or hat, Clara's heart sank. She had figured out what Becca was about to do, and she knew there were dangers her person could not comprehend. With no way to warn her, the little calico had no choice but to follow along

"*Where's she going?*" Harriet, who had already finished her food, stuck her head out of the kitchen. "*She hasn't eaten.*"

"*She's going next door.*" Clara, her tail twitching nervously, explained. "*I'll report back.*"

"*Good. You do that.*" Harriet licked her chops. "*And since she'll probably feed us again when she comes back...*"

"*Enjoy,*" Clara called, knowing her sister would likely clean her dish, whether she gave her blessing or not. And with that, she was off.

The yellow crime scene tape should have given Becca pause, even if the paper seal that covered the door jamb had already been cut. Clara had learned enough about humans to know that. But once she had unlocked the door, Becca ducked under the tape as easily as any cat. That's where she froze, with a gasp that caused her cat to look up in alarm.

There was no danger. Nothing confronting her person that the shaded cat could sense, and nothing stirred beyond a few beetles deep in the door's wooden frame. Becca had gone white, however, her breath quick and shallow. Following her gaze, Clara realized what had startled her so—a dark patch, its uneven edges smeared to faint streaks on the pale wood of the foyer.

Blood. Clara could have prepared Becca if she'd had Laurel's powers. Its sharp iron tang was obvious to the felines next door. Of course, it hadn't occurred to the cat that her person would be so taken aback by the crusty brown spot, which had already begun to stain the wood beneath. The man it had come from was dead, and whoever had killed him was gone. There was no threat left in this room.

Unless… Clara's whiskers twitched. As the currents stirred up by the opening of the door disturbed the stale air, a faint scent had reached her. A hint that she could only hope would evade her human.

If only Becca would back out of the apartment. Follow her instincts and retreat from this place of death. But the young woman whom Clara loved was nothing if not determined, and so, after a few deep breaths that returned the color to her cheeks, Becca walked into the apartment proper, skirting the dark spot to enter the living area itself.

Her growing sense of dread making her tail droop behind her, Clara followed. It wasn't only that horrible stain that set the neighboring unit apart. Even without that reminder, the apartment was as different from Becca's as could be. Bare brick walls made the main room appear larger than Becca's, an impression aided by the extra windows made possible by the unit's placement in the corner of the building. That sense of space was furthered by the spare, clean furniture—two sleek chairs set before a glass table, and that new leather sofa the cats had seen coming up the stairs not that long ago. The kind of style Clara could only think of as "shiny."

Sniffing at the leather, Clara could barely pick up any trace of the animal that it had once belonged to, while the glass table looked to be good for neither sitting or scratching. In fact, the only positive about the cold modern décor was that it appeared to have distracted Becca from the mess in the entry.

"Wow." Becca walked slowly through the long living room, running a finger along a bookshelf bare of books. "Is that…?" She picked up

197

an oddly shaped vase and looked at its underside before replacing it on the shelf with exaggerated care. Laurel, Clara knew, would have a heyday with that. She could visualize her sister strutting down the shelf and how, with one well-aimed paw, the delicate porcelain would go crashing to the floor.

To her, it all looked uncomfortable. People weren't cats, she well knew. But lacking their own cushioning fur, wouldn't they want something soft? Some pillows for that sofa, like Becca had? She watched her person as she made the rounds, seemingly admiring the slick surfaces. Some things about humans she would never understand.

"Maddy would love this place." Becca was talking to herself to keep her nerve up, Clara suspected. Despite having a key, her human was here without permission, and she was essentially a law-abiding creature. As a cat, Clara obeyed a very different set of rules, but she was anxious too. In part, she was picking up on Becca's emotions. Cats, after all, are naturally empathic. In part, Clara had realized something that Becca had apparently forgotten. She had given shelter to the woman who, if not a suspect, had been staying here. If anyone reported an intruder, Becca would be the first person they would look at.

Maybe Clara had some of Laurel's powers of suggestion, or perhaps these thoughts had occurred to Becca too. Having made a complete tour of the place, she stopped, seemingly reconsidering whatever mission she had in mind.

"Poor Ruby." She looked around. "She's probably told them about the violin…"

She paused at that and then began to search in earnest. First casually and then with increasing fervor, Becca checked the closet and under the bed.

"Maybe they took it. Maybe it was evidence, or a motive for Ruby. But wouldn't he have had music? Or even a music stand?"

She was standing by this point, staring into a second closet that,

198

like the first, was empty of everything but a few wire hangers. "How odd."

As Clara watched, Becca renewed her search. More methodical this time, Becca went room by room, opening drawers and looking under every piece of furniture. The kitchen, she found, was well stocked with matching dishes and glassware. But the cabinet, like that closet, was empty. A small chest in the living room held a few mothballs that stank in a way that set Clara's ears back. She was grateful when Becca closed that and crouched to peek under the sofa. Grateful, as well, that the faint trace she had picked up on first entering had grown dilute. So weak, in fact, that she had trouble placing it, only recalling a sense of danger and the unknown. Closing her eyes, the calico concentrated, trying to remember. No, it was no use. When she looked around again, she had a moment of panic.

Becca was gone.

A heartbeat of fear, and then she relaxed. A familiar smell and a low hum drew her back to the bedroom, where Becca was pulling open the drawers of a bureau, each sticking with misuse.

"Maybe the police took his things and sent them to his family?" She stared at the bureau as if it had the answers. "Or maybe Larry Rakov wasn't living here either."

Chapter 28

When the phone rang the next morning, Becca jumped for it, abandoning an active search through her sock drawer that had piqued intense interest from Laurel. She'd slept poorly the night before, tossing and turning, to the distress of her cats, and now, they'd discerned, she was running late.

"Ruby, are you okay?" She set the phone to speaker, one wool stocking in hand, as she continued to dress. "I didn't recognize the number. Where are you? What's happening?"

The laughter that emanated from the device seemed to confuse Becca, and Clara jumped onto the dresser beside her sister to observe.

"Yes, yes—to everything. I am fine. I am calling from the station." Ruby, her oddly stilted phrasing sounding surprisingly joyful. "The police had more questions, but what could I tell them?" She punctuated her question with a nervous laugh, and her voice dropped to a near whisper. "Oh, but, Becca, I do not want to have to deal with your police again. They kept me for so long."

"They can't do that. That's wrong," Becca fumed. "I've got to get you a lawyer. Where are they holding you? Have they said anything about charges? An arraignment? Bail?"

"No, please. All is well. I am leaving here now, and I have the best news."

Becca paused to listen.

"The conservatory! I am admitted. I used the phone here to check in and was told that being a student, I have a place to live."

"That's wonderful." Clara could hear the relief in her person's voice. "I didn't know the conservatory had student housing."

"They do not, exactly, but there is housing for students." Ruby paused. "When I called, I was put through to an official, and that is what he told me. I may not be saying that right."

"No, I understand." Becca went back to rummaging through the drawer, ignoring the sealpoint who hovered. "I'm so happy for you. Where is it, and when can you move in?"

"What is it?" Clara couldn't resist. *"Moths?"*

"You wish." Laurel lashed her tail. *"No, something was dropped here."*

Clara peered into the open drawer. *"Catnip mouse?"*

"Focus, Clown." Laurel's blue eyes went steely. *"Have you forgotten how to be a cat? If we only relied on what we could see, we'd be as helpless as they are."*

Clara sniffed the air, but all she got was the wool from those socks and the beguiling pine scent of a balsam sachet. She did feel a certain warmth, but that was to be expected, from those socks. Distracted, she focused instead on the continuing conversation between the humans.

"Maybe your grandfather's violin brought you luck."

In the pause that followed, Becca dug out the other sock. Perhaps it was suggestion—Laurel wasn't above playing tricks on her sister—but Clara thought she caught the echo of a slight thud, as if something hard had slipped between the bundled stockings as the drawer closed.

"Maybe."

Ruby's subdued response seemed to spark something in Becca. "Hey, can we meet later?" She hopped over to the bed, her second sock

201

half on, and sat. "I have an idea I'd like to talk over with you. I could bring your stuff over. See the new place?"

"That would be wonderful."

"Great." Becca paused to jot down an address. "I'm working until four today, but I'll come by after."

Chapter 29

Her ancestors may have been denizens of the desert, but Clara was grateful for her fur as she watched Becca bundle up. In addition to those wool stockings, she added a thick mohair sweater, and when she pulled a pair of big red mittens from the closet, her cat began to worry about her leaving the apartment at all.

Her concern—and the fact that the mittens resembled plush toys— led Clara to bat them from the bench where Becca sat to pull on her boots, a bout of cat-like play that earned a scornful stare from Harriet and a scolding from Laurel.

"Must you be such a clown?"

"I thought that was part of my job." Clara, who'd been up on her haunches, settled down and turned toward her sister. *"Besides, don't you want her here at home for as long as possible?"*

"Clueless," the Siamese muttered as she walked away.

Confused, Clara would have pursued her sister, only with a final flourish—a scarf that matched those mittens—Becca was already shouldering her bag, and Ruby's as well.

"Bye, kitties." She reached for the violin. "Please try not to destroy everything. Okay?"

Once outside, Clara was grateful for Becca's care. In fact, she would have wished her own lush fur on her person. Although the wind of the day before had calmed, it had left in its wake a brooding cold, almost as if the sky were waiting for some climactic event. The pedestrians on the street appeared to share this feeling. So many were racing along with their eyes on the clouds that Clara wondered if her shading made any difference at all. But if the lessons from her sisters had imparted anything, it was that she could endanger Becca by breaking the rules. Better to stay unseen, she told herself as she dodged a heavy-soled boot, than to risk bringing trouble to the human she loved.

By midday, the cat was wondering why her person had ventured out at all. When Becca had opened the shop, there had been a brief flurry of activity. Two women had come in asking about candles, both wrapped in matching shearling coats that gave off an exciting wild aroma and set the calico's whiskers tingling.

"In case we lose power," the taller of the pair had explained, picking several of the biggest beeswax pillars off the shelf. These were, Clara knew from previous customers, among the priciest candles in the shop. She would miss their sweet scent, reminiscent of a particular vine that often trailed out of Becca's window box. But seeing the mix of pleasure and relief on Becca's face as she rang up the purchases more than compensated.

Her person was wrapping the heavy candles in tissue paper when the shorter of the two customers noticed the plate of gemstones by the counter.

"Oh, is this a ruby?" Pulling off a woolly shearling mitten, she picked up a dull red stone that came to life as it caught the light. To Clara, it appeared to glow faintly, emitting a faint glow that drew the sensitive feline.

"A garnet, I think." Becca offered a gentle correction, as Clara crept closer. "It's supposed to help circulation."

"That's funny." The woman held the stone in her palm, smoothing it with an outstretched finger, before extending her hand to her friend. "It feels warm to me. Does it to you, Linda?"

"If it warms your heart, dearest, I'm happy to get it for you. How much?" That latter was to Becca, who smiled as she rang up the total.

"Would you like me to wrap that?"

"No, thanks." Linda slipped her mitten back on over the stone. "This weather, I can use it like a little heat pack."

Soon after, an older man stepped in, setting the bells jingling. Frowning, he looked around, checking out every aisle with a concentration that drew his heavy brows together and made his large nose appear even more hawk like beneath his thick knit cap.

"May I help you?" Becca called as he strode down another aisle. "If you're looking for candles, they're right up front."

"Yes, yes. Thank you," he said, with a trace of an accent, and returned to the counter with a five-dollar pack of votives.

"Have we met?"

"No, no." That accent growing heavier as he pulled his cap low, throwing down a bill before rushing back out.

Becca stood watching, a thoughtful look on her face. "Life in the city," she said softly after a minute or two had passed. Since then, nobody had even ventured into the shop, and while Becca had taken out her stencils, adding detail to the smiling sun in the center of the door's new window, she had spent more time looking up at the sky than filling in the drawing.

That sky must have wanted the day to pass quickly, growing darker even as Becca finished her lunch. By the time she had cleaned the front window, the usual bright colors had grown dim. Becca switched on the overheads, but as she watched them flicker and buzz, Clara could sense her growing discontent. Most days, Becca would have lost herself in one of the thick books that lined the back shelves, and Clara thought again about the volume Elizabeth had briefly brought downstairs. Today, her person seemed more interested in the street outside than any history or compendium of spells. Frustrated by her inability to do anything but watch, Clara curled up on one of the larger tomes, a reference work that lay on its side, and let her mind wander. Not into sleep exactly, but something close.

The light, she thought as she began once more to dream. *Like today, it was gray. The clouds dark and closing in.*

Clouds? Her nose twitched, and her waking mind recalled those candles. Not the sweet honey-scented ones, but others. *Not clouds*, she realized. *Smoke, and through it all, voices.*

"She helped me."

"No, please. She saved my child."

"She's innocent."

Innocent? Clara's ears pricked up. *What was this talk of innocence in a haze of smoke and noise? Who were these voices, and who were they pleading with?*

Why was the smoke so thick?

"It's as dark as night out there."

Becca's voice woke her, and she sniffed the air. Although the shop was toasty—a welcome byproduct of the lack of customers—her sensitive nose picked up the slight draft that still had managed to leak beneath the closed door. Clouds, she thought as she took in the moisture and some ineffable heaviness in the atmosphere. That moisture she had sensed earlier. Snow, she realized. Not smoke.

"The French Toast Alert must be off the charts. Early on, we had some customers looking for candles. But nobody's come by in the last hour." She was speaking on the phone, the store as still as it had been all afternoon. "I was wondering what you'd think about me closing early."

A pause. "You are? Thanks, Elizabeth. I'll lock up so you don't have to rush. And if you want to wait, I'll help with the inventory tomorrow. Do you want me to bring some candles up to you two in the meantime? Okay, then. Stay safe."

As soon as she hung up, Becca locked the front door and headed into the back room, where she'd stashed her coat along with Ruby's violin and bag. She had already drawn those tempting mittens from her pocket and was in the process of winding the red scarf around her neck when she paused, staring at the violin case on the floor beside the coat rack.

Good, her cat thought. *She's being careful.*

She didn't think that Becca could have heard her. No matter what her sisters said, Clara knew she lacked that power. Still, her person appeared to hesitate, looking down at the instrument as if considering its fate.

Clara didn't know why she felt a wave of relief when Becca hung the bag back on the rack and tucked the instrument on a shelf, pushing it deep behind a box of gemstones. All she knew was that while her person might not have any magical powers, she was acting with care. For that, the little cat was grateful. And so with a level of restraint that she hoped her foremothers would be proud of, she resisted the urge to jump up as Becca pulled those big plush mittens from her pocket and, donning them, pulled the back door shut behind her, listening for it to lock before she headed out into the darkening day.

Chapter 30

Striding briskly through the frigid afternoon, Becca set off down Massachusetts Avenue. Not, Clara realized with drooping whiskers, to their home, where her sisters waited. But also not across the river toward the conservatory. Instead, she was heading into Harvard Square, the chic student-filled center of the city.

Clara had always liked the square. Not only was its preponderance of red brick warm, but its age meant every corner had nooks and crannies likely to hold mice or, at the very least, some interesting scents. This trip felt different, however. As the sky continued to glower and darken, the streets were unusually empty, the few other pedestrians hurrying by with an urgency that reminded Clara of her dream. Becca's quick steps echoed that anxiety, her pulse racing loud enough for her cat to hear, even beneath all her layers of clothing. The oncoming snow had the city spooked, Clara suspected. There was more going on, however.

When Becca's phone buzzed and she jumped, her cat knew she'd been right. Becca was not herself. She was—the little cat felt her own heart sinking with the realization—anxious.

"Maddy? I can't talk right now." Becca spoke with hushed urgency as her eyes swept the street. Already, security gates were coming down and curtains being drawn. "I'm heading into the Square. I figure everything's closing early because of the nor'easter. Call you back?"

Her friend's response, tinny and faint over the phone, sounded just as stressed, the volume rising as she spoke. Clara strained to hear more, but the wind had begun to pick up, tossing paper and dust as it whistled between the big brick buildings.

"I'm sorry, Mads. I can't really hear you." From the way she spoke, Becca was interrupting her friend. "Later?" She tucked the phone back into her pocket.

The building, right in Harvard Square, might have been anywhere in the city. In contrast to its red-brick neighbors, the slick tower, all steel and smoked glass, looked cold. *Like a trap,* Clara thought. And yet when Becca pulled open the glass front door, her pet followed. *If Becca needs help getting out of this, I may as well be with her.*

After checking in with the bored security guard, Becca headed to the elevator. Such things made Clara anxious. Cats may like boxes, but the subtle vibration as the lift ascended reminded her too much of the trap that took her and her siblings away from their mother early on, before she had any awareness of her powers. Entering that metal box with its springing door had been her mother's intent. *"You have a destiny and a duty,"* she had told her three kittens. That hadn't made the parting any easier.

Memories, and her own lingering questions about her history, distracted Clara to the point where she almost didn't notice when the elevator stopped.

Luckily, the steel doors posed no problem to the talented calico. And so when the machinery started up again with a shudder, Clara gathered herself up, hindquarters twitching, and leaped, landing on her feet in the sixth-floor hallway, just in time to see Becca disappear into an office at the far end.

Racing to catch up with her, her claws scrabbling on the slick tile floor, Clara missed Becca's first words. Her person must have had an exchange with the receptionist, however. She was shaking her head, and the petite woman behind the desk—her hair as sleek as Laurel's—was speaking in the exaggerated tones humans used when they had to repeat themselves more than once.

The receptionist pulled back, and Clara braced herself, unsure whether the sleek woman was retreating into her shell or preparing to strike.

"Is there a problem here?" A familiar voice broke her concentration as a man in a tweed suit emerged from a hidden door. "Ms. Colwin, isn't it?"

"Yes." Becca studied the angled face of the man who had just appeared. "Mr. Wargill?"

"Please, call me Matt." He strode forward, hand outstretched, and Becca quickly tucked the card back into her pocket before she accepted his hearty shake. "Thanks, Francine. I'll take over from here."

With a smile as bright as the reflection off Francine's desk, he gestured toward the now open door. "It's so great to see you again, Ms. Colwin. I'm so glad you came in."

"I'm a little confused." Becca followed him into a long room dominated by an oval table that ran nearly its full length. While prints on three walls showed scullers on the river, the windows that made up the fourth wall opened on the real thing, a few blocks away. Over the black roofs of the neighboring buildings, and an oversized HVAC unit that almost ruined the view, the river reflected back the marbled gray of the sky. "The sign says Student Stay. I thought your firm was Red Brick Realty."

"We share a conference space." Still smiling, he took a seat at the head of the table, motioning for Becca to sit facing the windows. "I'm so glad you came in. Does this mean you're ready to take that next step?"

"Excuse me?" She'd been staring at those clouds.

"Aren't you here to discuss purchasing your unit?" His voice grew serious. "You must know that the resident discount is considerable—and time limited."

"I do. But—"

"You should know, we have some very creative options." He leaned over his desk, blue eyes intent. "Very creative."

"No. Thank you, though." Becca drew back slightly. "I'm looking to contact my neighbor, Justin Neil."

Wargill's face went blank.

"Do you have a number for him?"

The realtor tilted his head, scratching at one sideburn. "Why do you need to speak to Mr. Neil?"

"Well, really, I'm trying to reach the family of that poor man who worked for him, Larry Rakov," Becca explained. "Mr. Neil hasn't moved in yet, and I would imagine that after what had happened, it might be a while."

"Oh, yes. Of course." The smile was back, this time in apology. "I'm afraid I can't simply share his information, as I'm sure you'll understand."

"I know he and I got off on the wrong foot," Becca offered. "But we are going to be neighbors."

"And when you are, you'll be able to cultivate your own relationship with him, I have no doubt." Wargill nodded, as if this settled everything, and started to rise. When he saw that Becca remained seated, he paused, looking down at her. "I have my own relationship with Mr. Neil," he added.

"Of course." Becca nodded as the tall man sat back down. "He's in venture capital. Is he considering buying other units?"

Wargill paused, and so Becca kept on speaking. "Because if that's his plan, and he's looking for another unit in our building, one that has a tenant in place…" She waited, but Wargill's face was once again unreadable. "I've been a good tenant," she added. "I'm never late with the rent, and I don't cause any trouble."

"I'm sure you're lovely, Ms. Colwin." He pulled a phone from his pocket, missing the flash of consternation as Becca heard—and reconsidered—her own final claim. "I do have your contact info, and I'll be sure to let Mr. Neil know of your interest."

"And that I'm trying to reach the family of Larry—" Despite rallying quickly, she didn't get to finish. The realtor was already on his feet.

"Now, if you'll excuse me, I have a showing to get to. As I'm sure I've told you, properties in this market don't last long."

Chapter 31

It was much too cold out for a human to go about with bare hands, and so Clara grew alarmed when her person pulled off one of the fluffy red mittens and tucked it into her pocket as she walked. The calico's own paws were much more resilient, and even she felt the cold of the sidewalk through her leather pads, a chill that even the tufts of fur between her toes couldn't guard against. As Becca approached the Charles, Clara shivered. Bad enough the bridge was exposed, with no place to shelter from the gusting wind. The fact of all that water moving underneath would unnerve any cat.

"Hey, Ande. Glad I caught you." Becca hunched over as she walked, a diehard jogger in MIT sweats the only other pedestrian on the exposed walkway. "No, I haven't had a chance to look at the material you dropped off. But I'm thinking there might be another approach."

She paused, listening to her friend, before responding. "No, I really can't ask my mom. And I'm thinking that buying might not be the answer. I just had a very interesting conversation with the real estate manager. He was evasive, but from various things I've heard, I think that my neighbor is buying up properties as an investment. No, it's not great for the neighborhood. But, Ande? I was thinking. Maybe, he'd be interested in buying mine and keeping me on as a tenant."

A longer pause and Becca switched hands, shoving her bare hand into her pocket. "Well, for starters, I am a good tenant. I mean, usually." Maybe it was the cold making Becca a bit defensive. As she switched hands once more, after pulling the mitten back on, she thawed. "Also, I was wondering, maybe if he bought through me, he could get it at the tenant discount. I was wondering if you knew anything about how these sales work. I mean, the goal is to help long-term tenants stay in their apartments, right?"

By then, Becca had reached the Boston shore. Looking up at a street sign, her breath formed a white puff of condensation. "It would be a partnership of some sort. Wouldn't it? I guess I really need to talk to him. Maybe you could help talk me through it? The problem is the realtor's spooked. He's trying to keep everything copacetic at my building, and I think he's afraid I'm going to go off on Neil. We didn't have the best introduction. I'll have to try to track him down tonight," she continued.

"No, I left early because of the storm," she explained after a pause. "I'm going to meet Ruby, the conservatory student who came into the shop. She's got a lead on a student apartment, and I told her I'd check it out with her. I'm a little concerned about the neighborhood." She read an address to her friend. "Makes me even more aware of how hard it is to find a place."

Suddenly, Becca smiled. "You would? Thanks so much, Ande. The name is Neil, Justin Neil. He's in venture capital, if that helps." Becca kept walking, and Clara almost believed she could hear her friend's fingers tapping away at the keys.

"That was fast," Becca responded moments later. "Your Interpol guy—what's his name, Singer?—should watch out. So Neil's got his own company? Maybe that's good. Maybe that will mean he'll have some more flexibility. Thanks, Ande. Would you text that to me? I'll call him now, and I'll get back to you if I can set up a meeting with him. I can't tell you how much I appreciate your help with this. And, yes, I will look at the mortgage info you dropped off this weekend. I promise."

The mitten came off again as Becca toyed with her phone, gnawing on her lip as she held it back up to her ear. "Mr. Neil?" Becca sniffed, her nose as red as that mitten. "Becca Colwin here. I have—well, it's a business proposal. I'd like to come talk with you about it. I've got a friend who might be better able to explain everything, and we'd like to speak with you as soon as possible." Another sniff. "Would you get back to me? Thanks."

Shoving the phone along with her bare hand into her pocket, Becca picked up her pace, and Clara had to trot to keep up. The sidewalks were emptier here on the Boston side of the river, the buildings less quaint. As the two passed quickly by an ultra-modern high-rise, Clara found herself thinking of her dreams. Surely, there was history here, behind the stone-and-steel facades. Surely, other cats made lives with their people in these tall and faceless buildings, but the calico found such an existence hard to imagine. As Becca turned off the avenue to a block of worn-down brick, she sensed the presence of other animals. Not friendly ones, necessarily. The calico drew closer to her person, even as she hurried on. These streets were cold in more ways than one.

"I'm sorry I'm late." The sky was fully dark by the time Becca reached Ruby's new apartment. "It was a little hard to find," she offered by way of an explanation. Clara, who had followed her, understood this to be a half-truth. She'd seen Becca walking up and down the middle of the tiny street. Tucked into an industrial area only a block from the conservatory, it felt unloved, rather than old, and Becca had plainly been more comfortable on the rutted pavement rather than passing too close to the boarded windows. She'd checked her phone several times before finally entering the rundown yellow brick building. Even then, she'd opted to climb three stories rather than trust the tiny elevator that ran alongside the staircase, its open-work cage wheezing and bumping on its way down.

"It is not as nice as your neighborhood." Ruby ducked her head in an almost cat-like acknowledgment as she ushered Becca into the small studio. "But it is furnished."

"So I see." Becca might be straining to keep her voice neutral. Clara didn't have to make the effort, instead focusing on sniffing the battered sofa that ran alongside one wall. It smelled of cigarettes and sweat, while the single bed opposite—a bare mattress on a metal frame—had a musty odor that had the calico looking up, searching for signs of a leak above. Her cursory examination of the scratched dresser at the bed's foot completed her survey of the room, and she jumped up on the ledge of the one window. The direct view looked out on the brick of the adjacent building, but leaning against the panes, Clara could see the street out front, where a figure in an overcoat had taken shelter against the wind.

She turned her attention back to the humans inside the room.

"I'm sorry I didn't bring your violin and your bag; I decided to make a stop first," her person was saying. "I was hoping to get some information about the family of Larry Rakov, the man who—well, the man you thought was your landlord. A name and a phone number at least."

Ruby nodded. "I would like that. That poor man bought my violin."

"Would you like to be the one to return it?" Becca spoke the question deliberately, and Clara could tell she was watching Ruby's face.

"Yes." The other woman nodded vigorously. "Thank you. I would like to meet them. To tell them the story of my grandfather's violin.

To—"

Whatever Ruby was about to say next was interrupted by a loud metallic knocking. "The pipes." She smiled apologetically. "The kitchen is not in such great shape."

"I think it may be coming from the hall." Becca turned toward the door.

"The elevator, then." Ruby moved to open it. "The man who arranged the rental did say he would come by with a paper for me to sign."

"Wait." Becca put out a hand to restrain her. "You haven't signed a lease yet?"

"No." Ruby turned back to her. "But it is a good deal, no?"

"No, it's not." Becca grabbed for her coat and Ruby's. "Quick, let's take the stairs. At the very least, I want to see what else is out there before you commit to this dump."

"I should leave a note." Ruby's protest was overruled as Becca threw her coat over her shoulders and pulled her out of the apartment. "He was a very kind man, and for a student, it is a saving—"

"It's not worth it if it's not safe." Becca paused on the landing to take stock. From the creak and grind of the elevator, it was clear it was still rising, and she started down the stairs. "The rental you were in before was illegal." She spoke softly, looking up to make sure Ruby was behind her and missing the sight of a large man, with one drooping eye, as the elevator passed them on its way up. "I don't think this one would be any better. There are fire hazards, safety codes… Put it down to my sensitivity, if you will. I want to talk to some people, at least."

Ruby hesitated. "And you do not want me to talk to Mr. Matt?"

"Mr.—" Becca reached for Ruby, to hurry her toward the door. "Wait. Matt? What did you say the agency was called?"

"I don't know if it is an agency." Ruby appeared preoccupied with the big buttons on her coat. "The man at the conservatory said it is for students—"

"Was the agency, or whatever it was, called Student Stay?" Becca stuck her head out the door, letting in a burst of freezing air.

"I believe so." Ruby was pulling on her cap. "Why?"

"I think I know him. There's something off—" But before Becca could explain, Ruby was stumbling backward, her eyes wide with panic.

"What is it?" Becca grabbed her shoulders, steadying her. "Are you okay?"

"That man." She stared over Becca's shoulder. "He's here."

"What man?" Becca turned. The rutted street was empty of everything but some trash, the only thing moving a paper bag caught in the wind. "The realtor?

"No, no." Ruby pulled back, breaking free. "It is that—that man."

Becca followed her gaze, even as Ruby shrunk back against the wall. She was staring at the corner of the yellow brick building, where a man was watching the street. His profile, unsoftened by the thick cap pulled low over his eyes, looked more hawk-like than human, an impression that had Clara hunkering down, especially as he turned slowly to take in the empty street with his raptor gaze.

"I've seen him before." Becca stepped back. Closing the door to all but a sliver, she kept her eye on the stranger. "Who is he? What does he want?"

"I do not know." A rising note of panic in Ruby's whisper. "He has been following me."

"Wait, what?" Becca whirled to face Ruby. "You never said—"

"I am sorry." Ruby looked up, pleading. "That is why that first day I went into your shop. To get off the street."

Becca nodded slowly, remembering. "And then you saw him go by and you ran. And he's come back."

Ruby's silence was her answer.

"Is he why you left the violin? Did this start when you took it?"

"No, I swear." She raised her hand palm outward. "He has been following me since I left home. I thought, at first, I imagined it. But everywhere I look, he is there."

"Is that why you sought my help?" Becca paused, her eyes narrowing in a very Laurel-like fashion.

"In part." Ruby dipped her head.

"And I thought, maybe, I could use my power." Becca stopped herself and, turning, looked out at the street once more. As she did, a loud *thunk* behind them caused Ruby to jump. The grinding that followed signaled the elevator making its return to the ground floor.

"Come on." Becca grabbed her hand, her eye still on the street. "I don't know what's going on. I do know we've got to get you out of here."

Taking advantage of a gust of wind, Becca pulled Ruby out the door. The flying grit had briefly sent their watcher back into the alley, and the pair ran in the opposite direction, ducking into the alley on the building's far side as Clara, unseen, followed close behind.

"In here!" Becca pulled the stumbling girl along. "This goes all the way up to Mass Ave!"

Ruby nodded, following Becca up the deserted passage, skirting the litter that swirled in the wind. Only once they emerged on the busy main drag did Becca appear to relax. Tucking the younger woman's arm under her own, she began walking quickly down the sidewalk as thick, white flakes began to fall.

"We're going to the police," she said, her voice firm.

"What? No." Ruby pulled away, darting back the way they had come before stopping short.

"What is it?" Becca ran to her and turned to follow her gaze. The heavy-browed man now stood in the mouth of the alley, his head craning in every direction, those deep-set eyes searching. In response, Becca pulled Ruby back into a recessed doorway. She ducked as she did so, as if to make herself even smaller. She needn't have bothered, Clara

219

could have told her. Both young women were shorter than most of the pedestrians who crowded by, buffeted by the wind. Becca dared a quick glance out to the street. The man was still turning back and forth, scanning the crowd through the eddies of snow. He hadn't seen them.

"That's it." Becca spoke in an urgent whisper. "The police. Now."

She pulled on the other woman's arm, but Ruby cried out.

"No, I cannot. Please," Ruby pleaded. "I came to you for help. This is why. Just please hear me out."

Clara's heart sank. Becca might not really believe she had any magical powers, but what she did have was a big heart. Her pet didn't need any of Laurel's sensitivity to know what her person was going to say next.

"Fair enough. We'll go back to my place," Becca said. "But you have to tell me the truth this time, Ruby. And if I think we should go to the police, then I'm going—with or without you."

The other woman nodded agreement, but Clara continued to feel uneasy until the two had hailed a ride, leaving their pursuer behind.

Even when they arrived at Becca's building, she didn't relax. Something was wrong, the little calico could tell. Something, or someone... Seized by a sudden fear, Clara raced ahead, spiriting herself through the front door and up the steps.

"*Relax, Clown.*" Laurel sat in the foyer, licking one front paw in a leisurely manner.

"*But I thought...*" Clara looked around. The sofa cushions were scattered on the floor, and, behind her sister, she could see that the bedcovers had been torn off Becca's bed. "*What happened?*"

"*It wasn't us.*" Harriet paraded out of the bedroom, tail high. "*Though I did rather well, if I say so myself.*"

"*Summoning a spider.*" Laurel coughed, though it might have been a furball. "*If I hadn't suggested that it was a venomous bug, it wouldn't have scared them one bit.*"

"*Scared who?*" Clara looked from one sister to another. Only just then, she heard the sound of a key in the lock, and the door opened.

"Whatever—" Becca stepped in, her eyes wide as saucers. "Kitties?"

But if Clara feared a reprimand, she was as stunned as Becca appeared to be when her person reached down to grab up both Clara and Laurel in one big hug. "Kitties! You're okay! What? Who?"

Ruby, meanwhile, had stepped into the apartment. "Oh no." She took in the disarray, which, Clara had to admit, was more severe than any cat could produce. "I should have known…"

"Should have known?" Becca wheeled to face her, as the cats kicked free. "Ruby, what's going on here?"

"*Watch it!*" Clara had landed on Harriet's tail. Any other cat would have scurried out of the way, but Harriet didn't do anything in a hurry, and Clara had been distracted.

"*Hush, please!*" Clara stared up at Becca. "*I'm listening.*"

Becca was working up a head of steam. "What's going on? What do you know?"

"*She's clueless.*" Laurel, who had landed much more gracefully several feet away, circled back to murmur softly in Clara's ear. "*She doesn't realize that Becca already moved it.*"

"*What?*" Clara spun around to face her sister.

"Your cats…" Ruby was staring down at them. "They are fighting."

"They're upset." Becca bit the word off. "As am I. I'm calling the cops."

She whipped her phone out of her bag, but as she started punching in digits, Ruby reached for it.

"No, please. Just—please, listen to me first."

Becca frowned, but she stopped dialing. "You know who did this."

Ruby's mouth opened but no words followed.

"You—wait." Becca glared. "The door wasn't forced. Did you give someone my key?"

"No, I swear." Ruby fished her copy out of her pocket.

"That doesn't mean anything." Becca lifted her phone again. "You could have made a copy. Maddy was right."

"No, please." Ruby reached out, placing her fingers on the edge of Becca's phone. "Please, I am sorry, but I do not think you were robbed."

Becca tilted her head. It was all the invitation Ruby needed. "Truly, I am sorry. I brought trouble to you. But I do not believe anything of yours has been taken."

She turned to take in the living room and the opened bedroom door. "Please, you can check. And if I am wrong, then call the police."

Becca made a distinctly cat-like growl, fixing Ruby with a glare that would do Laurel proud. But she turned, still holding the phone. "I'm keeping my thumb on enter," she said, even as she turned toward her violated bedroom.

"She shouldn't trust her." Clara followed, tail twitching in concern.

"You're right on that, Clown." Laurel marched ahead, her own tail high. Harriet, meanwhile, had moved into the living room. The pile of sofa cushions on the floor made a perfect nest, and the big marmalade was loudly purring as she kneaded her favorite tasseled pillow into submission.

"Thank you." Ruby followed Becca into the bedroom and watched as she piled the covers onto the bed and checked beneath it.

"This is not because I trust you." Becca rose and checked the closet. "I'm taking my cue from my cats. If there was anyone here, they wouldn't be so calm."

Clara looked up at that and found Ruby staring at her. The intensity of her gaze was strangely disconcerting. "Your cats?"

Clara blinked and forced herself to turn away.

"Yeah." Becca glanced over her shoulder at Ruby before looking through her bureau drawer. "They're good judges of situations. Of character too, usually."

The insult was obvious, and Clara felt herself stung. What had they missed? Why hadn't Laurel said anything? Even Ruby seemed taken aback, those long, dark lashes blinked rapidly as if holding in tears. She wasn't done though.

"It is more than that." She spoke softly, but there was an urgency in her voice that made her soft accent more pronounced. Clara flicked her ears forward. "When you let me sleep here, I thought they were talking to each other."

"Well, yeah." Becca slammed the bureau shut with more force than necessary. "They're litter mates, sisters. They talk. Maybe they were talking about you."

"Maybe they were." Clara could almost feel Ruby's gaze. It took all her will to appear oblivious. Just another animal. "But I think, maybe, it was more. In my country, we have stories…"

"Look." Becca turned on her. "I don't want to hear any more stories about your quaint ways. Okay? And whatever you have to say, leave my cats out of it."

With that, she waved, ushering Ruby into the living room. And as the dark-haired girl began retrieving and replacing the cushions on the sofa, Becca gave the rest of the main room, as well as the kitchen and the back entrance, a thorough once over, even checking the cabinets where she stored pots and pans and the cat's big bag of kibble.

"I could tell her that nothing has been taken." Laurel was working diligently on her other paw by then. *"I could implant the idea so that she thought it just came to her."*

"Please, let her do this." Clara wasn't sure, but she suspected that the fussing helped their person to process. She also had her reservations about the stranger, and anything Laurel tried threatened to expose them more. *"She can tell from us that there's no more danger here."*

"No danger." Laurel's dark-tipped ears flipped back, and she and Harriet—who had allowed her special pillow to be repositioned on

the sofa—exchanged a look. Harriet flicked her tail in response, but before Clara could question either of her siblings, Becca had returned. Flopping onto the sofa, she motioned for Ruby to join her. As soon as the other woman did, perching tentatively on the edge of a cushion, Becca turned toward her.

"Spill," she said.

Ruby looked at her hands.

"Fine." Becca pulled her phone out. "This was a courtesy, but I'm sick of being played. My home was broken into. I don't know what part you had to play in all of this, but it's pretty obvious you're involved. I'm calling the cops."

"No, please. I am sorry." Ruby looked like she might cry again, but Becca appeared unmoved. "It is complicated, and I am so, so sorry I got you involved."

"It's the violin, isn't it?" Becca shook her head. "Maddy was right all along. I trusted you. I thought I had power. I thought—I don't know, I thought I could help you."

"You did! You have!" Ruby was sobbing now. "And I do not care if now they have it."

"But they don't."

Ruby looked up, confused.

"Didn't I tell you?" Becca asked. "I was going to bring your stuff to you. I left it all at Charm and Cherish."

Chapter 32

"Becca, you are brilliant." Ruby looked like she was about to hug her companion, but Becca held her off. "We should get it now."

"I don't think so."

"I do not understand."

"This doesn't change anything." Becca looked around her, before returning to the foyer to retrieve her bag. "I'm still calling the police. You lied to me. You've been lying all along about what's going on. About that violin."

"No, that is not—"

But Becca was fed up. "Someone broke into my apartment to find it. That only makes it more likely that it had a role in the death of that poor man." She looked around and shuddered. "I'm just glad neither of us were here." She broke off, staring at her phone. "Bother…"

She ducked into her bedroom.

"Wait, please." Ruby went after her, taking Becca's arm as she emerged holding a cord.

"*I knew you shouldn't have been playing with that thing.*" Clara's nerves were getting the better of her temper. Still, she was surprised by Laurel's low growl.

"No." Becca shook her off. "Look, I'll do this for you. I'm going to call a detective I know. Just let me plug this in." She pushed past the other woman. "I'll talk to him and give him the background."

"Becca, I know—" Ruby tried again to interrupt, but Becca wasn't listening. Instead, she was staring down at the device.

"Oh, hell."

Meanwhile, Laurel's growl was ratcheting up in intensity.

"Hang on." Becca held up her hand for silence, even as she raised the phone to her ear. "Maddy? Is that you?"

A high-pitched burble on the other end had her focusing intently. The sound couldn't drone out Laurel's growl, however.

"What is it?" Clara was losing patience. *"I said I was sorry."*

"Don't be such a kitten." Harriet landed with a thud. *"This isn't about you. Can't you feel it?"*

Confused, Clara almost snapped back at her oldest sister when it hit her. A wave, almost like a cold breeze, only they were indoors. Safe.

"That's terrible." Becca's words brought her back, and she looked up to see her person scribbling on a pad. "Yes, yes. Thank you. I'll be right there."

Clara fought back her own horror at the rising wave and focused on her person.

"Ruby, I've got to go. And you...you should come with me."

The other woman stared at her in confusion.

"It's Maddy," Becca said, even as she pulled her coat back on. "She's in the hospital."

Chapter 33

Ruby resisted, but Becca wasn't having any of it. "No," she said, her tone quite definitive. "It isn't safe. You're coming with me."

Clara wasn't entirely sure that it was Ruby's safety that concerned Becca the most. It was, however, a convincing argument, especially given the disarray of the apartment. And so even though the dark-haired girl was clearly reluctant, she let herself be led out the door.

"I could go to the conservatory and wait for you there," she protested feebly as Becca led her up to Mass Ave. The storm had started in earnest, snow falling thick and fast, and the white asphalt was marked only by the tracks of a passing bus.

"Same problem," Becca protested, scanning the street. A car approached slowly, windshield wipers revealing an anxious face. Becca waved and the driver slammed on the brakes, skidding slightly before he backed up and rolled the window down.

"Becker? Becker Corwin?"

"Close enough." Clara was glad to see her person check the license plate before she ushered Maddy inside, if for no other reason than it gave the shaded calico a moment to steady herself in the car's rear window. "Mount Auburn Hospital."

The driver glanced back, his face drawn with concern. He was staring at Ruby, Clara saw. The dark-haired girl did look vaguely ill, with her pale face and dark eyes wide.

"Step on it." Becca must have caught that look. "Please."

Without another word, the driver took off so quickly that Clara had to dig her claws in to avoid being thrown back against the glass. Outside, streetlights were coming on, capturing the falling flakes. A hush seemed to have taken over the street as the two humans beside her whispered.

"I am sorry about your friend. Truly." Ruby leaned in, her voice barely audible, even to the cat. "But you do not need to take me with you."

"We'll talk about it later." Becca hissed back, all the while staring past the driver. "Up here is fine."

Becca was out of the car almost before it had fully stopped, racing toward the brightly lit door. But if Ruby thought she could remain behind, she hadn't counted on Becca's ability to multitask.

"Come on!" she urged the other woman out, pausing only to make sure she was being followed as she ran into the spacious lobby and paused, her head swiveling.

"Is this the way to the ER?" She grabbed a plump redhead in scrubs, who turned on her in surprise.

"Are you hurt? Is this an emergency?"

"No, I'm looking for a friend."

He nodded and pointed down a hallway.

"Thanks." Turning briefly to make sure Ruby was behind her, Becca set out at a brisk pace.

"I'm here to see Maddy Theribault." She was leaning over a counter by the time Clara had caught up. She'd been trotting as fast as she could, but the foot traffic had made a straight-out run inadvisable.

A mechanical buzzer startled the little cat, opening a set of doors

228

beside the counter and unleashing a wave of sounds and smells. Clara hesitated, overwhelmed by the barrage, but Becca appeared undaunted. Beckoning for Ruby to follow, she passed through the doors and into a space bustling with busy humans and the beeping of machines.

Clara dodged a white-shod foot. The rubber sole had made the oncoming tread almost soundless, and she jumped as a monitor buzzed nearby. Unable to see Becca, she started to panic, sifting through the sharp bite of rubbing alcohol and other, more cloying scents for the warm aroma of her person. A reassuring waft came from further along the passageway, and the little cat found her person peeking behind a set of white curtains that hung to the floor.

"Maddy?" Becca moved from one set of drapes to the next, then stopped with a gasp. "Oh, dear Goddess, Maddy. What happened?"

"I'm not sure." The woman lying in the bed bore little resemblance to Becca's usually perky friend. To Clara, who jumped to the wide windowsill, she seemed faded. Her pink cheeks were pale, and even her smooth, shiny hair had fallen down from its usual neat bun to hang in limp tendrils around her face.

"Maddy, are you all right?" Becca reached for her friend's hand. Even that short exchange had seemed to tire her. "Do you want me to call for the doctor?"

Maddy shook her head. "I'm just a little woozy."

She paused and her eyes closed. But as Becca rose to seek help, Maddy woke. "Someone grabbed me," she said, her voice gaining in urgency. "He threw me down to the ground and grabbed my bag. But he threw my bag down too. He didn't even take my wallet. I told the cops. I don't understand it."

As she fell silent once more, Becca couldn't resist a question. "Where did this happen?"

"Well, that's just it, Becca." Her friend blinked up. Already, it was clear from the swelling on the side of her face that she was going to have a nasty bruise. Possibly a black eye. "I was looking for you, and I'd gone over to Charm and Cherish. I wanted to tell you something."

She paused, and Becca leaned forward, her face drawn with concern.

"Something I wanted you to know right away." Maddy's voice was barely audible, but Becca nodded. "You weren't answering. I thought I'd come by. The shop was closed, I went around back and knocked. I'd just given up and was starting to walk away when it happened."

The two friends fell silent, and Clara, safely ensconced on the window ledge, turned from the snowy scene outside in concern. Neither of the humans before her had Laurel's power. She was sure of that. Neither had the power of a day-old kitten. And yet the calico could have sworn that a message was passing silently between them.

"That alley has always creeped me out," said Becca. "But the lot behind the store is usually deserted."

"I didn't see anyone," Maddy agreed. "It's like someone was waiting."

"If someone was," Becca's voice fell to a whisper, "odds are he was looking for me."

Chapter 34

The two friends fell silent, and Clara became more aware of the beeping of machinery further along the corridor.

"I'm okay, Becs." Maddy blinked her eyes open, gazing up at her friend. "Really. But all I remember is that I had something to tell you, and when I try to remember what it was, there's nothing there. I just can't get it back."

She shook her head, as if to clear it, and ended up wincing from the effort. "All I've got is that feeling."

"And the headache." Becca squeezed her hand. "I'm so sorry."

Her friend managed a wan smile. "Be careful, Becca." Maddy grasped her friend's hand. "Please don't trust anyone you don't know."

Becca glanced over her shoulder. Ruby was nowhere to be seen.

If Clara could have, she would have saved her person from the frenzy that followed. With the kind of expletive that the mild-mannered young woman did not often employ, Becca jumped to her feet, throwing open the curtain that had shielded her friend's privacy.

"Where—? Excuse me." She grabbed a passing orderly. "Did you see a woman—my age, dark hair—walk by?"

He shook his head. "I'm sorry. This is a restricted area."

"I know." Becca was already peering past him. "She came in with me. At least, I thought she did."

He smiled and shook his head. "Sorry," he said, carefully removing her hand from his arm before walking away.

"Maddy?" Becca retraced her steps. An attendant was helping her friend sit up. "Did you see when she left?"

"No. Sorry." Holding tightly to the aide's arm, Maddy grimaced as she swung her legs over the side of the bed and let him help her into a wheelchair.

The attendant looked up. "Your friend can have more visitors once she's admitted."

"Where are you taking her?" Becca blinked, recalled to the moment. "What's wrong?"

"My head." Maddy smiled weakly, motioning to the darkening bruise on her face. "They want to keep watch over me."

"Oh, Maddy! But I'm glad they're taking care of you. Let me know if you need anything." Becca backed off as the aide swung the chair around.

"You can check in on your friend with patient information tomorrow."

"Wait, Maddy!" Becca had stepped back to let them pass, and although she moved to follow them, she found her path blocked. "You didn't say—did you see her at all?" she called out over a stretcher and its two accompanying EMTs. "Was she behind me when I came in?" But they were gone.

Clara looked on in dismay as Becca wheeled back and forth, visibly torn between following her friend and backtracking to search for Ruby. Even if she could have communicated with her, the little cat wasn't sure what she could have shared. After braving the noise and odors of the ER, once Becca had found her friend, Clara had found herself nodding.

232

Not that napping is unusual for a cat, but seeing Becca's distress, the petite calico regretted her brief snooze.

"Excuse me." Becca finally had to move as another attendant pushed by, followed closely by yet another stretcher.

"You can't wait here, miss," a portly man in scrubs called from the safety of the sidelines. "You'll have to step outside."

Becca nodded, and for a moment Clara thought she was going to start explaining about Maddy and Ruby. She clearly thought the better of it, though, noting that the passage of one young woman most likely wouldn't have caught anyone's attention, and headed toward the double doors.

If Becca thought Ruby might be waiting for her, she was out of luck. Clara felt her exhale as the disappointment hit her, and when her person headed back toward the hospital entrance, the little feline scurried to follow. She had no idea where Becca was headed, but anywhere away from all the noise and scent was good for her.

A quick survey of the street revealed no sign of Ruby, but when Becca pulled her phone from her pocket, Clara sighed with relief. If all went as usual, a car would show up, and as much as the cat disliked riding in them, the temperature was dropping again as the dim twilight faded. She very much wanted to go home.

Becca's handling of the device, however, did not produce the expected results. Instead, it emitted a voice—harsh, male—that seemed to take Becca by surprise.

"We should talk." That was all Clara caught, before Becca was tapping away.

"Thanks for calling, Mr. Neil." She scanned the street as she spoke, a forced friendliness softening her voice even as she waved down a cab. "I got your message. I'd love to talk, and, yes, I will bring my friend."

"Central Square," she told the driver, sliding into the seat. "I'm going to the corner of Mass and Ipswich—a store called Charm and

Cherish."

"Got it." The driver, an older man, had a South Asian accent that gave his words a musical quality. "My daughter told me about that store. Said you have a nice Ganesh in the window."

"We do indeed," Becca chirped in response and proceeded to regale the driver with stories about the shop's inventory as Clara stared out the window, trying to concentrate on the swirling snow. Cars had their uses, she assumed, but the motion was unnatural, and the sudden appearance of a furball would undoubtedly raise questions.

As the cab pulled to the curb, however, Becca fell silent. As soon as she'd paid, she was out on the sidewalk, her cat scurrying to keep up, and pushing her way through the door.

"Careful!" Margaret barked from behind the counter, her usual sour look in place. "If that glass breaks again, it's coming out of your pay."

"Margaret!" Becca stopped short. "I didn't know… Elizabeth said she was going to come in and do some inventory."

"She also said you were selling candles," she said, scowling. "Until you decided to run off to play in the snow. It's not even six o'clock—"

"I'm sorry, really." Becca craned toward the back room. "Did a dark-haired woman come in? Ruby?"

"Of course. Bitsy passed your message along to me."

"I didn't…" Becca paused. "What message?"

"That some cousin of yours was going to come by." Margaret shrugged. "Though why we should be catering to your visiting relatives when I'm the one who's trying to—"

"Cousin?" Becca interrupted her boss. "She said that?" Without waiting for an answer, Becca ran into the back, and Clara scrambled to follow. Margaret did too, though by the time she had extracted herself from behind the counter, Becca was simply standing there, staring at the empty slot on the shelf.

"What are you doing?" For a moment, it almost sounded like Margaret had forgotten her pique.

"It's gone," Becca declared before turning to face her boss. "What did she mean by cousin?"

"I assume she meant a relation of some sort. Your grandmother's other daughter or the like." Margaret pulled herself up to her full five-two, attempting to regain her dignity. "But just because you work here doesn't mean you can use my shop as a public space."

"That's it!" Becca's cry startled her boss and her cat equally. "Thank you, Margaret," she called out as she opened the door with care and stepped out to the street. "And, and I'm sorry! I'll explain everything as soon as I can."

Chapter 35

Becca started down the street and then caught herself, stepping off the curb and waving one red mitten furiously. Clara braced; she'd been outside enough to know that this was rush hour, and that meant danger. But Becca hadn't been the only one to take off early, apparently. Traffic was light, and the few vehicles making their way through the snow were moving slowly. Within moments, a cab pulled up to the curb and Becca jumped in, her shaded cat close behind.

"Massachusetts Conservatory." Becca was leaning forward, over the driver's seat, as if she were about to grab the wheel.

"The Mass Ave entrance?" The driver glanced up at the sky, rubbing his steamy windshield for a better view.

"No, hang on." Some toying with her phone brought Becca the answer. "The practice rooms are at 385 Hemenway."

"By Fenway, got it." Clara dug her claws in as the driver pulled into traffic. The old cab swayed as it made its way over the bridge, and the wind that came whistling off the river sounding a little too much like the howl of a hungry beast for her to be quite at ease. Turning from the leaky window, the little cat sought comfort from Becca, who was once again engrossed with her phone. "Elizabeth? What's up? I was just at the shop—" Her uncertainty must have been caused by the connection, because after a moment, she spoke again. "I'm sorry. I don't understand."

Another pause as she pointed out a turn to the cabbie. "Cut down here."

Clara's sharp ears perked up. The voice on the phone was increasing in pitch and volume.

"Margaret told me that that girl, the violinist, came by," Becca broke in, her eyes still on the road ahead. "She said that you told her she was my cousin?"

The cab pulled over beside a parked car, and the cabbie looked back over his shoulder. "Here, miss?"

But Becca was focused on her phone. "Hang on, Elizabeth. You're breaking up. Trust? Trust myself? Or—"

She was interrupted by a loud honk. Behind the cab, a driver was gesticulating wildly. "Miss?"

"I'm sorry, Elizabeth. I've got to go."

With that, Becca hung up and dug into her bag for her wallet. As she handed a ten to the driver, she paused, taking in the street. "I'm sorry, but would you mind driving around the block? I think I'd rather go in the back."

With a shrug, the cabbie pulled out, quickly enough so that Becca was thrown back against the seat. Clara scrambled to avoid falling on top of her. The sudden weight of a cat she couldn't see would not be reassuring in this situation.

She needn't have worried. Even as she sat up, Becca stiffened. Transfixed, Clara realized, by the sudden appearance of a stooped figure, his head swiveling back and forth nervously as he scanned the crowded city street with dark eyes under heavy brows.

"Here. This is fine." As the cabbie turned the corner, Becca was already shoving another bill at him. Out on the street, she peered around, surveying the quiet back street. Clara wished she could reassure her. While she had missed the scent of the small man from inside the vehicle, out here, where she could pick up both smells and the slightest sounds, she felt confident that the stranger was not yet near. Still, she appreciated the care Becca took as she walked, hanging close to the wall until she reached a recessed door decorated with the conservatory's logo.

"ID?" The voice came from a glass-fronted cubicle to her right. Inside, a stout bearded man, his face as round as an owl's, looked up from a book, one plump hand open on the counter before him.

"Excuse me?" Becca had been looking back through the glass door. Now she turned to take in the gatekeeper, who formed a small hillock in his blue hoodie.

"Conservatory ID?" He blinked up at her, clearly wanting to return to his reading.

"I'm here to see Ruby Grozny." Becca managed a smile. "I believe she's in her practice space."

"Can you call her?" He tilted his head, shifting the beard enough to reveal the conservatory logo. It was a badge of entry, like an ID. The smile wasn't working, and Clara, who had followed Becca into the claustrophobic entryway, knew she had to think fast. Maybe what Laurel had said was true, and they all shared the same powers to some extent. With that in mind, she focused on Becca's friendliness. Her inherent decency. That was easy, and if she could only get the man in the cubicle to believe her...

"She left her cell at my place." Becca shook her head at her friend's imagined oversight. Clara sensed a movement beneath the beard. Was that, perhaps, a smile? "I wouldn't ask, but it's a family matter," Becca leaned in.

The note of confidence in her voice must have paid off, if not Clara's concentrated efforts. Or maybe the gatekeeper simply wanted to get back to his book. Nodding to indicate he'd made a decision, he reached under his desk. A click and a buzz, and Becca was in, with Clara slipping through the door behind her.

"Miss?" The back of his cubicle opened onto the hallway, and that bearded head poked out.

"Yes?" Clara could feel Becca tense and she pulled back, preparing to jump. She wasn't sure what exactly she could do if this fat man came after her person, but shaded as she was, she'd at least have the element of surprise in her favor.

"Ruby's in number eight," he said, waving at some point further down. "Keep going and then turn right. Can't miss it."

Becca's broad smile may have sprung more from relief than gratitude, but it brought an answering grin from the gatekeeper anyway.

"Tell her we're glad she's with us," he called, raising one broad hand in salute.

"I will."

Becca set out with a jaunty step that took her to the turn in the hallway. Then, out of sight of the big man, she slowed, pausing to peer down the hall and, Clara observed, to listen. The cat couldn't be sure what her person could hear. She picked up a strange reedy rise and fall—a musician practicing scales, Clara realized, though where she got that idea she could not tell—and another counting softly to herself, all from within the series of closed doors that lined the hall.

Finally, as she accompanied Becca down to the end of the passage, another sound announced the presence of the violinist within. One note, soft, plaintive almost, grew in volume and intensity, before giving way to a cascade of tones in rapid succession. The effect was strangely soothing, and Clara felt herself being lulled into an answering purr. Then suddenly, it wasn't, and Clara started. Becca didn't seem to notice.

Her person was standing by the door, leaning against the frame with a dreamy expression on her face. But to Clara, the change was jarring. The vibration—she lacked the words to describe it more fully—was simply off.

But if Becca didn't hear the strange flatness in the sound, the sudden cessation of the music caught her attention. That and what sounded like a sob had her tapping softly on the door.

"Ruby? Are you there?" She leaned in and kept her voice low. "It's me, Becca. Please let me in."

Silence. Becca tried again. "I know you're in there, Ruby. Please, we have to talk."

Becca held her breath, but Clara could hear the rustle of movement within. Moments later, when the door inched open, Becca glanced over her shoulder and down the hall.

"Let me in, Ruby. I'm worried."

With a nod, the other woman backed up, and once Clara was convinced that nobody was waiting to pounce, she followed her person inside. The practice room was small, the size of a cubicle with white-painted walls and an overhead light fixture that played up the pallor of Ruby's face. As Becca stepped in, the dark-haired girl moved back, bumping into the portable music stand. Behind her, on the room's one chair, lay the case, open to reveal the dark wood of the violin.

"I heard you playing," Becca started gently, as if trying to calm a spooked animal. "It was beautiful."

"No, it was not." Ruby looked mournfully at the instrument.

"I'm sorry." Becca took in the girl, her sadness obvious. "Was it more damaged than you thought? You said something about the bridge?"

"No, that was not bad." She shook her head. "It is me. I cannot—I *should* not be playing it."

"I understand." Becca stared at the girl but didn't approach her. She was intentionally blocking the door, her cat realized. Ruby had already bolted once. "All the more reason to talk to the authorities."

Ruby sighed and her shoulders drooped, as if all the air had been let out of her. "I know. I am sorry. I was hoping…"

"You were hoping that you could keep your grandfather's violin?" Becca's voice was gentle.

The faintest nod in response. "How is your friend?"

"She'll be okay." Becca mustered a smile, even as an urgency crept into her voice. "Though I'm thinking that she was attacked for the same reason that my apartment was broken into. And that this violin is in the center of what's going on." She stopped, momentarily lost in thought. "Ruby, you didn't tell anyone else you were coming here. Did you?"

"Me? No."

"We'll have to take our chances." Becca looked around the small space. "They must have figured it out, the same as I did."

"They? Did you see someone?" Ruby's eyes grew wide, and Clara could hear her heart begin to race.

Becca nodded. "I think so. That wiry guy? The one with the nose."

Ruby whirled around, as if the man might have suddenly appeared behind her. "He cannot—we cannot let him find us."

"I don't plan to wait for him." Becca watched as Ruby began gathering up her music. "But, Ruby? Who is he? What is going on? I've trusted you thus far. You've got to trust me now. The whole story this time."

Ruby turned to her, a silent plea on her face. But Becca had leaned back on the door, her arms crossed, and so, as she slipped the sheets of music into their compartment, Ruby began to talk.

"This violin," she said with reverence, her fingers stroking the burnished wood as she set it back in its velvet bed. "Much of what I have said is true. My mother did try to pawn it. Not sell, for we hoped to get it back. But in our town, well, there is not much money. And nobody wants something that has been used." She turned, a crooked smile on her face, even as she zipped up the case.

"After that, she tried the luthier. He always worked on it when I needed a new bridge, for example. He was not interested either. But he did call her back that night, as I said. He told her that he might have a buyer, a local businessman who had been inquiring about violins. He did not even want to play it, we were told. He was simply a collector, looking to buy.

"We did not want to sell. We hoped we would get it back. But the deal we were offered was better than we could have hoped. Too good, perhaps."

Becca nodded, urging her to go on. Clara could feel her growing anxiety. They had already spent too long in the little room. Ruby had draped her coat over the back of the chair, and as she donned it, she continued to talk.

"A man came to our house. No, not that one, a man we knew, but he was only bringing a message. That was when we knew who wanted it—a man with power wanted my grandfather's violin. But only for a while."

She paused. Memories, rather than the duffle coat's oversized leather buttons, seemed to be troubling her. "Nobody thought we would say no, and, in truth, we did not feel like we had a choice. We—my mother and I—gave him my grandfather's violin."

She sighed but steeled herself to continue. "The next morning, he brought the case, with the other violin, the student one, to our house, along with money to travel. He had made arrangements. The flights, the place to stay." She peeked up at Becca, waiting for her to acknowledge her earlier obfuscation. "I was to come here and then, once I had won my place at the conservatory, I would get my grandfather's violin back."

"That makes no sense."

"I know." Ruby was staring at the floor. "My mother would have said no if she had dared. But I...I said yes. I did not feel we had a choice."

A silence fell then, as if Ruby could feel the mix of pity and scorn in Becca's gaze. "I knew it was wrong," Ruby confessed at last. "But when I arrived at the apartment, the man—I thought he was my landlord—said a note was waiting for me, a note and a package. The note wished me luck with my audition. The package contained my grandfather's violin in a brand new Bam France case, the best there is."

"A new case?"

Ruby nodded energetically. "When they returned my old case, they had put in a hygrometer and given me a canvas traveling cover, you know, to make it nicer. But this new case? It maintains the humidity, the temperature. Everything. It was too much, and I knew something was not right. I accepted it, of course. I did not want to offend this man, or the one who had made it all possible. It is—it was—a rich gift, worth more, perhaps, than my violin. But it felt wrong. It was, I knew, wrong.

"In the morning, when I left for the audition, I could not resist—I took my grandfather's violin. Just to borrow, like I told you. But I put it in its old case. I did not want any more from those people. And then..." She broke off.

"So the violin had been given back to you?" After a few moments, Becca filled the silence. "I'm just trying to get the facts straight."

Another nod. "I knew something was wrong. I knew I should not have taken the money or the violin, no matter what the note said. But when I saw it again, my grandfather's instrument... When I picked it up... It is also why I knew that poor man was not killed for my grandfather's violin. After all, he was told to give it to me. But my fear remains. What happened. The money I took. The violin—my violin—is somehow cursed."

"I don't know if a musical instrument can be evil." Becca considered.

"People though… Did you ever meet the man who bought the violin?"

Ruby took a breath. "No," she conceded. "But I know who he is."

"And?"

Ruby eyed the windowless wall, as if longing for escape. "He is big in my city." A pause so weighty Clara could have clawed it. "Not a music lover. It would serve me right if my violin—my grandfather's violin—had been damaged."

"If only it had been the violin." Becca reached out for her. "Let's go, Ruby. I'm not sure what's going on with that instrument, but the more I hear about the people involved in this, the more I know I don't want them to find us here."

Nodding, Ruby shouldered the case and followed Becca out the door.

"Come on," Becca urged her along. But as they approached the turn in the hall, she stopped short, motioning with quick gestures for Ruby to stay behind her.

"Let me guess. You're family too." The gatekeeper's voice rang out. "Anyway, you're too late. Her cousin already came for her. I'm guessing they went out the front."

Chapter 36

Becca froze, unsure of whether to bolt for the front entrance or wait to see what the man did. Then, suddenly, it was too late.

"Hold on! You can't—" The gatekeeper's voice was cut off with a gasp.

"This way!" Ruby grabbed Becca's hand and turned, as if to run back to the practice room.

"We can't go back there." Becca resisted, pulling back from the other woman's grasp so hard she stumbled and fell hard against the wall. Pulling herself up, she shook her head in a vehement refusal. "No," she said. "We'll be trapped."

A clattering noise interrupted Ruby's response. A soft cry and a thud had her reaching for Becca's hand again. "The basement."

With a curt nod, Becca signaled her willingness to follow, and Ruby turned and sped down the way they had come. For a fateful moment, Becca paused, one hand still on the wall. Was she ill? Clara felt her whiskers droop in panic before it hit her—Becca had heard that cry and held back out of concern for the big man at the door. But when Ruby hissed at her—"Hurry!"—she raced to catch up as Ruby passed the entrance to her practice room and pushed open a fire door at the passage's end.

"Down here," Ruby called over her shoulder as she descended a flight of stairs. Easing the door back into place with only the slightest *snick*, Becca made haste to catch up, finding the other woman at the bottom, where she held another door ajar.

"In here." A soft glow illuminated a passageway lined with pipes. "Follow me." Ruby was whispering.

"No." Becca stood firm, even as she eyed the door. "This is crazy. We're calling the police."

Ruby started to protest, but Becca raised her hand, palm out. "I'm sorry, Ruby, but I'm not hiding. This has already gone too far."

The other woman visibly deflated, her shoulders sinking even as she nodded agreement. "I understand." Even her voice had gone flat, as if the adrenaline roused by their escape had finally run out. No longer trying to flee, she stood there, face gone slack, and waited as Becca pulled out her phone.

"My battery's dead." Becca spun around, her color high. "I never fully recharged it. Ruby, please let me use yours."

"I do not..." The other woman shook her head, her energy still depleted. "It is in my bag."

"Of course." Becca fell back against the wall with a laugh that sounded almost like a sob. "That was the lie I told to get past the guard. Now we're being hunted by some creep, and we're trapped here in the basement of a conservatory practice space."

"Not trapped." Ruby's voice seemed to gain some strength back. There was even the hint of a smile playing over her pale face. "I did not come down here to hide. There is a door, where the cleaners go. It opens onto Hemenway Street."

A quick, whispered consult and Ruby led the way down the passage and up a metal staircase, pushing open a door onto a wide space dimly lit. Off in the distance, voices could be heard. A radio, Clara thought, talking about a "special weather alert," the remainder drowned out by the ringing of an old-fashioned land line.

The two women beside her paused, Becca's face lighting up. And as the ringing went on, peal after peal, with no one to answer, she seemed to be weighing her course of action.

"A phone, Ruby." She had started toward the sound, when they both heard it: a thud from the stairs below. And so, dashing across the space with Ruby close behind, Becca pushed open the exit. Leaning out the door and into the blowing snow, Becca peered around like a cautious owl. The street was dark but quiet, except for the wind. "I think we're good to go," she whispered. "But, please, let's stick to the plan."

"If anything happens, go straight to the police." Ruby didn't sound enthusiastic, but Becca nodded. "But what if—if that man…"

"If you can't get to the police?" Becca paused, thinking. "Go to Charm and Cherish. You know, the store where we met. If I'm not there, you can always talk to Elizabeth." Becca must have heard Ruby's reluctance as well. "She's a wise woman in every sense, Ruby. You can tell her everything, and she'll know what to do."

With that, Becca pushed the door all the way open, letting in a blast of air and a swirl of snow that stung Clara's nose. Becca winced as well, blinking away the cold wet as, with a glance back at the woman behind her, she stepped out into the storm.

Maybe it was the alley they exited onto, the high walls creating a wind tunnel effect. Maybe the storm had picked up in the brief time Becca and Clara had been inside. Whatever the reason, the passage up to the street felt endless—ice blasting into their faces as the two humans crept, careful as cats, toward the sidewalk. Clara, whose fur provided some protection, fretted about her human, even as she followed, hugging the wall by her feet.

The constant pelting of ice—the snow having turned to sleet— eased off for a moment as the two reached the end of the alley, only to pick up again with a howl.

"This is crazy," Becca yelled, trying to be heard over the wind. "Change of plans. Follow me."

Ruby nodded. Her nose and cheeks glowed bright red in stark contrast to her pale face, and as her grip on the violin case tightened, her bare knuckles went from red to white from the pressure. *She must be freezing*, Clara thought. But she trusted Becca, and that, thought the cat, was good. The wind whirled, first propelling them forward, then shifting with a ferocity that had them both turning toward the building they had just left, hoping for relief as the wet snow began to pile up. Already it formed a layer of white on both the humans' shoulders, frosting their hats and the cloth of the case.

For Clara, the combination of cold and wet was growing painful. But as much as she wanted to pause and clean the ice out from between her toes, she knew she didn't dare risk losing sight of Becca. At least her person served to block the wind, although the little cat still struggled to keep her footing. She didn't want Becca distracted by the sudden pressure of an unseen feline against her shin.

"In here." Becca's relief could be heard in her voice as they came up to a huge white building set back from the street. She pointed up the marble steps, roiled by waves of blowing snow. Above them, the giant pillars of the portico appeared frosted, the heavy, wet flakes plastered to their street-side faces by the earlier sleet. "They're open 'til eight."

Motioning to Ruby to follow, Becca started up the steps just as a fresh gust blasted down at them, whistling. "Wait!" Ruby called, slipping on the icy stone. Reaching back, Becca caught her outstretched hand, and the two battled the wind to reach the top, where Becca grabbed the oversized brass handle of one of two matching doors. And pulled. Only to find it stuck fast.

"It should be open." Becca pushed the wet hair from her face and tried the adjacent door. Nothing. Ruby blinked at her, her lashes frosted with ice. "The dean said he's always here…" Becca pounded on the metal frame with the flat of her fist. "Let us in! We're freezing."

Pressing her face to the glass, she searched for signs of life. Clara, huddled at her feet, tried to block any thoughts of passing through to the warmth inside. If she could not save Becca, she would brave the storm with her, even if it meant her death.

"Oh my goodness!" A creak and a sudden pressure roused the freezing cat, and she jumped out of the way as an older woman in a knee-length skirt pushed a side door, smaller and hidden behind one of the oversized pillars, open. "We're closing early—this weather! I never imagined… Please come in."

Clara longed to lean against her herringbone stockings but forced herself to merely tag along as Becca and Ruby stepped clear of the door, assuming the water dripping from her fur could not be differentiated from the growing puddle on the floor.

"Thanks so much." Becca was wiping her face, talking to the woman who had let them in. We have, well, kind of an emergency. Is Dean Brustein still here?"

"I don't know." Concern creased her face, blue eyes big behind her glasses. "They cancelled evening classes an hour ago."

"The dean's still here." A deep voice caused them both to turn. A tall man in a black parka as slick as his blue-black hair was coming down the hall.

"Mr. Neil." The kindly woman's voice wavered between surprised and deferential. "I didn't realize your meeting was still going on."

"We're just finishing up." He smiled at Becca. "And Ms. Colwin and I have been planning on having a chat. Ms. Colwin and her friend, too."

"Mr. Neil, I never thought I'd run into you here." Becca tagged along as Neil strode down the hall. "I mean, I'm glad. I was hoping to catch you. But this isn't the friend I meant."

"You're not Ruby Grozny?" He turned, raising a questioning brow.

Ruby had gone silent. The cold, Clara figured. Also, Neil was walking fast. "At any rate, I'm glad you found me."

"We were actually looking for Dean Brustein." Becca was jogging to keep up when Neil turned a corner and pointed down the short passage. A door with frosted glass was illuminated from inside, setting off the gold lettering painted on its pebbled surface.

"That's his office." Neil pointed. "I've got to see to something, but I'll be right along."

"Thanks. Thanks so much." Becca gushed with relief as she watched him go off. Then, brushing her wet hair back from her face, she started toward the door.

Ruby pulled her back. "Wait, Becca." Her face was tight. "What are we going to tell this dean? He thinks I stole my violin."

"Well, that is what you told me." Becca almost smiled, but seeing the other woman's distress, she added quickly, "We'll tell him the truth. That you're a student, and we're both in danger. He's an officious little man, but he's got to help us. At the very least, he can call the police. It's funny that Justin Neil knows him, though. Isn't it?"

Ruby nodded, her mouth set in resignation as she followed Becca down the hall. But just as Becca was about to knock, hand raised to rap on that pebbled glass, she hesitated.

"It is funny," she said softly, as if to herself. "Unless…"

Whatever she was about to say was interrupted by voices from inside the office. Whispering, rather than shouting, they carried a sense of urgency. An argument, heated but private.

"You stupid fool. You were supposed to handle this." The voice was familiar, as was the way the last word dissolved into a snakelike hiss. "If you hadn't been trying to squeeze every last cent out of this…this situation…"

"You're one to talk." Another voice that Clara knew, only the last time she had heard it, it had been friendly. Cajoling. "You knew. You got your share."

Clara was almost flattened against the wall as Becca stepped back, pushing Ruby behind her.

"That's the dean," she said. "He's talking to Wargill."

"Wargill?"

"The real estate manager—the realtor. You know him as Matt." Behind the frosted door, a third voice joined the conversation.

"Shut up, both of you." A command: deeper and less hesitant. "I'll clean this up, too, but the boss is not going to be happy."

Becca and Ruby turned to each other, eyes wide, and then Becca was pulling Ruby back around the corner. There, they froze at the unmistakable sound of a door opening. The voices suddenly grew louder.

"I know that man." Ruby leaned past Becca to peek around the corner. Her voice, barely more than a whisper, was tight with dread as she grabbed Becca's arm. "He is the one who took my violin. The one who told me what to do."

"That's impossible." Becca shook off her companion's hand. "There has to be some kind of misunderstanding. The dean is a respected academic at the conservatory that you came over here to join."

"Not the man in the suit." Ruby pointed, her finger still wet and bone white from the cold. "The big man."

Becca turned to look as Ruby began to tremble. At the end of the hall, the rotund dean had bent to lock his office door. Waiting by his side were Matthew Wargill and a large, square-built figure whose face was obscured. At that moment, a drop of melt dripped from Ruby's finger, splashing on the linoleum, and the men paused. Three faces turned to take in the cold and sodden women standing there. The dean, the realtor—and a large man with a scar on his brow, one that drew his eye down.

"Well, isn't this convenient," said a voice behind them, and Becca

251

spun around to see her new neighbor, Justin Neil. In one hand, he held a small revolver, its steel the same blue-black as his hair. "I see you've met."

Chapter 37

"Come on!"

Skidding on the wet floor, Becca and Ruby turned and ran. Neil grabbed for Becca as she dashed by him, but she pulled free, leaving only the mitten in his clasp. With that he braced, legs apart, raising the revolver with both hands—and yelped in surprise at the sudden pain of a bitten ankle. Down at the hall's end, the woman who had let them in was zipping up a full-length puffy coat.

"Put that away, you fool." The dean's whisper hissed. "Stop them!" he called out, waving his arms. "Thieves!"

"Oh!" She looked up, too late. Becca went barreling past her, with Ruby close behind.

"Come on," Becca urged. Slamming into the door, they tumbled out into the storm. "This way." Grabbing Ruby's hand, she pulled her to the side of the portico, where the giant pillars provided a bit of shelter, the lights from the building making their shadow an even deeper black.

"Which way did they go?" Wargill was the first out, nearly tumbling down the slick steps. The big man followed, running halfway down the stairs before he stopped to scan the street. Behind him, the dean and

Neil stood, right by the door, and from where she crouched by Becca's feet, Clara could see Neil's glower as he cradled his bleeding ankle, peering through the blowing snow to the puddles of light below. The storm's fury should have cleared the streets, but a handful of pedestrians soldiered on, bundled into anonymity in the blowing white.

"Is that them?" The dean pointed at a couple who had emerged from a shadow to skid toward a waiting bus. The big man took off.

"No, wait." Brustein stepped out into the storm. The heavy snow was already blanketing the stone steps, obscuring any prints. Obscuring the sleet that had fallen earlier as well, and as the round administrator strained forward, Clara could see his leather shoes begin to slip. Flailing on the treacherous footing, the dean reached backward, grabbing for something or someone to right himself. But Wargill was too far away, having taken shelter deeper under the portico, and Neil simply stepped back, watching as Brustein came down hard.

"You may as well break you own back," he said as the dean scrambled to his feet, his round face a mask of pain. The scar-faced man had disappeared down the street after the bus. "You've made a mess of everything. If you two weren't so busy trying to eke out a few extra dollars, that girl would never have been here. She never would have caught on and stolen the case back."

Clara felt Becca stiffen. Behind her, Ruby had begun to shiver.

"I've got it under control." The dean was brushing himself off. "Don't forget who I am."

"What's that supposed to mean?" Neil glared. He was leaning against the pillar now, his bitten ankle in his hand.

"I'm a dean at the Massachusetts Conservatory." Brustein appeared to puff himself up once more. With the lights of the building behind him, his round features looked sunken and dark. "If I call the police and tell them a student has stolen a valuable instrument, I'm sure they'll give me the benefit of the doubt."

Neil looked askance at the little man.

"Especially if I explain that the student is disturbed," Brustein continued. "That she has delusions of persecution and was last seen running around in a blizzard with some soon-to-be-homeless misfit. A clear danger to self, I'd say." He paused to look down at the darkening leather of his shoes. "Let's go back inside and I'll make the call. If I act quickly enough, I might be able to save these Ferragamos."

Another blast of wind settled it, and the three retreated back into the light and the warmth, leaving Becca and Ruby, along with the shaded Clara, on the portico. But the pillar that hid them provided little protection from the worsening storm. Ruby, hugging herself, looked to her companion.

"What should we do?" Her lips were turning blue.

"I don't know." Becca appeared so lost in thought that she was oblivious of the cold. Still, Clara could see how she clenched her jaw to keep her teeth from chattering. "I'd like to think that the police could be trusted, but..."

She shifted to look at her companion, her face unbearably sad.

"What about this Elizabeth?" Ruby's shivering made her words nearly unintelligible. "You said I could trust her."

"So I did." As if woken from a trance, Becca reached forward and wrapped her arm around the freezing student. "We'll go to Charm and Cherish. If she's not there, I can call her. The store has a land line, and we can get out of this storm."

Picking their way with care down the stone steps, Becca and Ruby made their way to the street. Clara, who had to leap over what were, to her, chest-high, drifts, hung back. Although she had been careful to keep herself shaded, she could not control the cat-sized pockmarks she left behind each time she jumped.

"Too much awareness increases their risk." Her sisters' lesson echoed

as she looked back. Perhaps with her tail, but, no. Spurred on by the cold, Becca and Ruby were practically running as they left behind the conservatory and headed for the corner, passing the long stone face of the conservatory. Trusting fate, she raced to catch up, abandoning caution as she turned the corner after them.

And found the two young women standing in front of a metal gate. "Closed?" Becca was yelling, a note of fear mixed in with the anger. "How can the T be closed?"

"How else may we get there?" Ruby looked around. "I do not see another bus."

"I don't think we can wait." Becca, cradling her bare hand, scanned the empty street. Under the waves of snow blowing in, each one thicker than the last, even the tracks had begun to disappear, their muddy gray turning to white.

"Maybe the police would not be so bad." Ruby's voice seemed to startle Becca out of a reverie, and she turned. The woman beside her was shivering uncontrollably now, the tip of her nose had turned an angry red. "I do not know…"

"No." Becca, strained to the limit. "If I had my phone…" She looked around once more, her face white with the cold. "If I could only summon…"

Clara, at her feet, looked up in despair. Her fur was soaked through, her paw pads spiked with ice. They no longer hurt—either from the sharp crystals or the cold—but a strange stiffness had begun to set in. A desire for rest, for sleep.

"What's that?" A police cruiser had turned the corner, and Ruby, with a cry, stepped forward, raising her arm.

"No!" Becca pulled Ruby back, nearly tripping over Clara, and rousing the little calico from her stupor. As she did, Clara felt a surge. She meant to jump, to throw herself between her person and the street, the police. Danger. Only this felt different, as if a hidden source of heat had blasted open, just when it was most needed.

"Look!" As Ruby stumbled back, clumsy from the cold, Becca pointed. The cruiser had passed by, but turning the corner was a lone yellow cab, its wipers working furiously as it fishtailed to a halt.

"Ladies." The driver rolled down his window. "What are you doing out in this weather?"

"It's a long story." Becca fumbled at the door with frozen hands. "Can you take us to Central Square?"

"I was heading home, but there's no way I'm leaving you out in this." He popped the lock. "Climb in."

Chapter 38

Clara had fully cleaned her toes by the time the cab reached Charm and Cherish, the cab's noisy heater helping to melt the last stubborn crystals. Her coat would take longer, the soft underlayer was drenched through, but as the two women consulted in whispers she had managed to give herself a thorough tongue bath, making sure those all-important guard hairs were back in place. As she groomed, the calico thought back to that strange burst of warmth. Had it been an illusion? The appearance of this taxi a happy coincidence?

The cab came to a halt before she'd reached any resolution.

"No charge." The cabbie waved away Becca's damp twenty. "You two just stay safe," he said, and drove away, disappearing into the dark as the snow continued to fall.

Becca's frozen fingers fumbled with the lock, but soon the two were inside. Ruby, who had begun to revive in the overheated cab, began to brush down the violin even before the bells on the door stopped jingling, knocking the accumulated ice and melting snow off its canvas cover with her red, chapped hands.

"Here, let me." Becca reached for the instrument and placed it on the counter, pushing aside the dish of colored stones. "I have a dust cloth here someplace. As soon as I call Elizabeth, I'll find it."

"No matter." Ruby had opened the case and sighed with relief. Although the edges of the velvet were darkened with moisture and the crystal of the hygrometer was misty, the violin itself was dry and intact, showing no more wear than it had the day before. Unbuttoning her coat, she rubbed her hands back to life against her sweater, and then lifted the instrument from its worn bed, holding it away from her dripping hair and clothes.

Becca, meanwhile, had picked up the phone behind the register. "Elizabeth? I know it's late. I'm sorry. I'm—we're downstairs." She was staring at the violin case. "We need your help."

The woman upstairs must have had questions. Not even she could have foreseen what had happened, but Becca had already hung up, focusing intently on the empty case in front of her.

"What did Neil mean, Ruby?" Her voice sounded distant. Preoccupied. "She never would have stolen the case back from us?"

"What?" Ruby looked up, a healthy pink returning to her cheeks. "I don't understand."

"No, maybe you didn't." Becca pulled the case toward her, her hands running over the velvet. "You said the violin has been messed with."

"Yes." Ruby looked down at the instrument in her hands. "The bridge had been moved, and there are scratches."

"But otherwise it's fine, right? There isn't anything rattling around inside it or anything?"

"What? No."

Becca nodded, as if this made sense, and Clara, curious, jumped silently up to the counter. Once again, she found herself drawn to the pretty stones, feeling the warmth that emanated in waves from their rich colors. But, stepping daintily by the shallow dish, she realized she was sensing something stronger, stranger, from the old velvet case. Still cold, still wet, she longed to snuggle down into the cavity that had held the violin. To sprawl, as Laurel had, along its plush lining.

No wonder Becca was running her hand over the lining. Could she be sensing this warmth? They had all been so cold only minutes before.

Becca paused, her fingers playing with a patch that had been sewn in place. "Do you remember this?"

Her question sounded out of place, but Ruby answered. "Yes. My mother sewed that for her father. A music stand, I believe, had fallen…"

Becca's fingers moved on, resting on the dial of the hygrometer. "This was new though. Yes?"

"Yes." Ruby nodded. "Many of the new cases have them."

But Becca wasn't listening. Looking around frantically—for what, Clara didn't know—she finally gave up and started grabbing at the edge of the tiny dial with her fingernails.

"What are you doing?" Ruby reached to stop her, transferring the violin to her other hand.

"I don't think this was to make the case better." Becca dug in, and Clara itched to help her. Her own claws, after all, would be much more efficient at tearing into that soft fabric. Delving for the source of that heat. "This was to hide the prize they wanted you to smuggle."

"What? No." Ruby shook her head. "Becca, you make no sense."

Becca didn't answer, so intent was she on grasping the rim of the hygrometer until finally, with a small pop, the metal cylinder came free. Tossing it on the counter, she reached inside the cavity. "Then what do you make of this?" She held up a stone as big as a grape and as red as fire. Smooth and round, it caught the light and shot it forth like flame, flickering as the bells on the shop door rang out as if in response.

"You caught on." A man, his face stern and lined, a snow-covered cap pulled low over his heavy brow. "I was wondering when I would finally see that."

Chapter 39

Becca acted as quickly as a cat, tossing the ruby into the dish with the other colored stones.

"I don't know what you're talking about," she said, standing tall. "And for the record, we're closed."

He chuckled and shook his head as he pointed to the collection of colored stones, even as the bells jingled once more. Elizabeth quickly sized up the situation.

"Becca, thank you for coming in." She glanced sideways at the man. "I've already alerted the authorities."

The man laughed again, softly, as if at a private joke. "No, you haven't."

He slipped one hand inside his jacket, and the women stepped back, Becca reaching to draw Ruby close. Clara braced. But all the man pulled out was a billfold, which opened to reveal a photo ID.

"But I have, now that there's little chance they can mess up my investigation. Paul Sanglier," he said by way of explanation, showing the opened billfold to Elizabeth before stepping forward to present it to Ruby and Becca. "Interpol."

"Interpol?" Elizabeth's brows went up in surprise. "I wasn't aware there was a red notice out."

Sanglier frowned. "This is not about an individual." He spoke as if he were reading from a script. "We are assisting the Hungarian authorities in the retrieval of an object of cultural significance."

"The Vér ruby, of course," Elizabeth said, nodding. To Clara's amazement, she didn't seem surprised.

"And the counterfeits it has spawned, which are spawning their own wave of illegal activity." He eyed the dish of colored stones. "I'll take those."

"You can't do that." Margaret appeared in the doorway, shaking the snow from an umbrella. "They're my best sellers."

"Margaret, we have a box of them in back," Elizabeth uttered, exasperated.

"I don't care." The little woman crossed her arms. "This is my shop. I'll sue. Get a warrant."

Sanglier nodded. "I can do that. We do prefer to work through the local authorities once our investigation is no longer at risk of being compromised. Of course, I would then need to take these young women into custody as well. They can join the four men my colleagues in the Boston police have already picked up. There may also be a question about a student visa for this young woman here. If it was obtained under false pretenses…"

"I said, I don't care." Margaret widened her stance as Ruby turned toward Becca, a panicked look on her face. "Becca, those men…"

Elizabeth frowned, settling her gaze on a spot on the counter. "Clara?" One word, so soft as to be barely audible.

"What did you say?" Becca started.

"You have power." Elizabeth raised her voice a fraction. "Use it."

"Well, I…" Becca looked down at the counter, her cheeks reddening once more.

What do I do? Great Bast. Clara sat there frozen, aware of the disconcerting gaze of the older woman. Aware, as well, that all eyes were on her person, her beloved Becca. *"Laurel? Harriet?"*

"Your prime duty is to aid your person." The response like an echo in the close air.

Becca's hand was hovering over the dish. Surely, she could feel the glow given off by the stones. The pulse of the tiger eye. The pure and steady heat from that ruby. She reached down, her finger going toward a garnet, the one Marcia had so admired only a few days before. A red stone, but the wrong one.

"This is nonsense." The Interpol man stepped forward. "I'm not leaving without that stone. You'll get your paperwork—"

Margaret stepped forward to block him. "You do that—"

A nudge, that was all. With a flick of her paw, Clara pushed the ruby from the pile and watched as the round, bright gem slid over the others into Becca's outstretched hand.

"It's this one." Becca lifted it for all to see. "Here's your ruby, Mr. Sanglier."

The man took it, squinting down at the stone. "So it appears, but…"

Clara concentrated, her green eyes boring in on the man, but her thoughts on her sister, Laurel, with her power of suggestion. On Harriet, and all she had taught her. On all the cats who had come before and the people they served…

The warmth from the stone welled up, and the little cat felt a surge. The man before her appeared to have felt it too. He tilted his head, his lower lip jutting forward as if he were considering its source.

"Then again, we have our suspects, and my team is well equipped…" He pulled a handkerchief from his pocket and wrapped the stone in it. "I may as well take this to be tested."

With a nod, he turned and walked back out into the storm, without another word.

"How did you do that?" Ruby was breathless with awe.

"I'm not sure." Becca spoke slowly as she tried to work out what had happened. "I was trying to feel if there was any difference, and that stone just came to me." A pause, as an unreadable expression crossed her face. "I hope it was the right one."

"It was." Elizabeth's voice rang with certainty. "You have a gift."

"I knew it." Ruby, beaming, threw herself at Becca, clasping her in an enthusiastic embrace.

Elizabeth, meanwhile, looked down at the counter where Clara sat, still stunned by her own actions, and, with a sly smile, winked.

Chapter 40

By the time the storm had passed, it had dumped fourteen inches of snow on the city, a load that the ferocious winds had kicked up into drifts too high for any cat to jump over. Clara, therefore, had to tag close behind Becca as her person made her way past the industrious shovelers and city plows to visit her friend Maddy. The detour to pick up dinner at Zoe's had made the trip take nearly twice as long. But with the shop and nearly everything else in the city, except for the friends' favorite restaurant, closed, Becca seemed to be enjoying the walk.

"Ta-da!" She lifted the bag in triumph when Maddy came to the door. Her friend looked the worse for wear, pale except for the purple bruising that extended beyond the bandage on her forehead, her fine hair hanging free of its usual neat bun. She managed a smile, however, as she ushered her friend inside.

"More of your magic?" Leaving Becca to shed her snowy outerwear, Maddy took the bag into the apartment.

"Don't laugh." Becca hopped as she pulled off a boot. Clara, by her side, had set to work cleaning the ice from her paws. "I swear by the goddess that I felt which stone was real."

"Or you actually saw where it had landed." Maddy returned with bowls and retreated once more into the kitchen. "Or you've stared at that display for so long you have the fake stones memorized."

"They don't last long enough for that." Becca propped her mittens—the spare green pair—and her hat on the radiator. "Margaret was right. They are our bestsellers. And they're not fake."

"I know, they're real semi-precious stones." Maddy emerged holding two beers. "I'm not supposed to drink for seven days," she said. "But this is a special occasion, right?"

Becca's mouth opened, but it didn't take any power of Clara's to keep her from responding out loud.

"So, as far as we can tell, they probably tried hiding the gem in the violin itself." The friends had moved on from the dumplings to the noodles as Becca recounted the revelations of the previous days. "That was probably the original plan, the reason for buying the violin. Ruby did say they'd knocked the bridge out of whack.

"When they realized that wouldn't work, they put it in the case. The lining was so patched up already, nobody noticed, and it was the perfect distraction. Someone might be looking for an antique instrument, but who thinks about the case? And Ruby made the perfect mule. She had no idea she was smuggling contraband, so she didn't act frightened. And if she was caught, well, she was completely expendable."

Maddy shivered, even though her apartment was toasty. "Do you think that poor guy—the one you met—knew?"

Becca, who had just inhaled a mouthful of noodles, chewed thoughtfully. "I don't know. I don't want to think so. He seemed nice." She sipped her beer. "I think Wargill initially installed him as part of his side hustle—offering illegal sublets for the students Brustein referred. This city is so expensive, who would question it? And then, when they needed a place for the exchange, the apartment must have seemed like a natural."

She picked up a piece of bok choy with her chopsticks and stared at it. "On the other hand, he knew Ruby was going to bring a violin to his place, and that he was supposed to give her the new case." She ate the green. "I guess he was expendable too."

The friends ate silently for a while, and Clara, coiled at their feet, began to nod off.

"Do you really think they were going to let her keep the violin?" Maddy sounded desperate for some good news. "It sounds like they set up the hand-off, but…"

"I don't know. I guess it's a question of whether they thought they'd be safer buying her silence or shutting her up for good." Becca shook her head at the thought. "Anyway, she's safe now. As safe as Interpol can keep her. That inspector, Sanglier, has put her up at the agency's expense, and the conservatory board is working on her visa. They certainly owe her."

Maddy was wrestling with her next question. Even half-asleep Clara could see that, and so Becca kept talking. "You were right about my being so trusting of her, Maddy. But so was I. She knew something was up, but she didn't know the extent of it. Also, she was worried about her mother. As she told me, she didn't have a choice—she really was hoping for some kind of magic to help her out."

"Some magic." Maddy wasn't going to let her have the last word. "If it weren't for your faith in her."

"It wasn't me, Maddy. It was my cats."

Chapter 41

Those words haunted Clara, carrying with them the memory of smoke and of pain.

"Is there more?" She pressed her sisters the next morning as Becca got ready for work. The city was digging out, and she'd promised Margaret and Elizabeth she'd find a way to open the shop. *"Please."* Clara debated staying home. The snow made everything so difficult. *"Please teach me."*

"There's always more," said Laurel as she eyed her tail. It looked perfectly clean to her younger sister, but Clara knew better than to comment. *"And don't you think about it. You have a job to do—and we have time."*

Harriet, meanwhile, was silent, her head drooping into sleep until a cough woke her and she sat up, licking her chops. Clara turned toward her older sister in alarm. She hadn't picked up on anything amiss in her sisters, or herself. Then again, she was learning, there was much she didn't know.

"Oh, Harriet, you're doing it again." For example, she hadn't even realized that Becca was standing in the doorway. "I've not been a good caregiver."

But if Clara expected her person to come into the bedroom to comfort her cat, or even to remove the hiccupping feline from the bedspread to the floor, she was mistaken. Becca had instead walked into the living room, and so the calico followed in time to see her pick up her phone.

"Cambridge Cat? This is Becca Colwin, returning Dr. Keller's call." Anxiety tightened her voice to a thin pitch. "Yes, I'll hold."

"So much more to learn…" Laurel's voice, or the memory of it, soothed Clara, even as she strained to listen. *"So much more."*

A minute, or maybe ten, and Clara started, aware that she had begun to doze just as her person might have needed her. Adding to her confusion were her sisters, Harriet and Laurel, both regarding her with calm, if concentrated, stares, lulling her once more back to sleep.

"I am sorry," the cat says, her head hanging low. In her deepest sorrow she sees those basalt eyes glistening. Hears the deep rumbling, at once both purr and growl, and she waits for the blow. The bite.

"Fear not, little one. It is not I who am offended. It is they who cannot conceive of the truth. They are unable to accept our power."

There is truth in this. The goddess does not lie.

Still… "I did wrong," said the cat. "I should be punished."

"No, but you will accept this burden." The voice of command, deep and strong. "Each generation you will find a person and you will serve her as you serve me. Silently and well. Your sisters will aid you in this, but the burden falls hardest on you, little one. For you know well what it is to fail the one you love.

Clara woke with a gasp, Becca's voice ringing out from the other room.

"Maddy, you'll never believe this," she was saying. "I'm sorry, I mean, how are you? Are you feeling better?" A brief pause. "Good, good. I'm so glad. I just spoke with the vet. Yup, the new one from Cambridge Cat. I thought Harriet had been acting odd and so I took all three of them in. He did some tests and left a message. But with everything going on, I hadn't gotten back to him."

Clara looked at her sisters. They both appeared oddly content, although Laurel's tail twitched once. "The tests were fine, he said. My cats are in great shape. Maddy, he'd been trying to reach me because he knew I was worried." In the pause that followed, Harriet and Laurel exchanged a glance, sharing a communication that Clara was not party to. "But also because he wanted to ask me out. Maddy, Dr. Keller—Jerry—and I are going to dinner on Friday."

Clara didn't need Laurel's powers to decipher the squawk that followed, or Harriet's sense of history to understand the nature of what had just happened.

"You're all dug out." That night, Marcia, as usual, had arrived first, stamping the snow off her boots before she stepped into the apartment.

"I guess that's one advantage of the building going condo." Becca reached for her hat and scarf, laying them on the radiator to dry. "A team came over with a snow blower yesterday morning."

"Condo fees." Marcia handed over her coat, leaning against the doorframe to pull off a boot. "Man, I miss my sneakers. Do you want to close the door while I do this? I don't want your cats getting out."

"They're smart enough to stay inside." Behind Becca's back, Laurel swatted at Clara, catching the smaller cat by surprise and making her jump. Becca looked down at the two felines. "At least, I think so."

"I was thinking more of your neighbor." Marcia punctuated her explanation with a meaningful glance toward the stairwell.

"Deb Miles?" Becca closed the door behind her. "We're never going to be best of friends, but after all that's happened she owes me."

A questioning glance as the doorbell sounded, and Becca buzzed Ande in as she explained about Wargill. "I think he kept encouraging me to buy because he knew I'd need money. He'd be able to use my place as another illegal rental."

"Not anymore." Ande came clumping up the stairs, beaming.

"Becca, I've run the numbers and you're in!"

Marcia looked over at her host. "You can buy?"

Ande answered for her. "I know the reward money hasn't come through yet, but I think I can get you a great rate. You'll still have money in the bank."

"I *knew* something was going to come together for you." Marcia looked from one to the other. "So, tell, what did I miss?"

"You mean, besides Ande meeting her hero? Tea first." Becca waved her guests in. "The kettle's boiling."

An hour later, the circle had been convened. After the events of the week, the three focused on invocations for protection and, at Becca's request, healing. She spoke of Maddy, but both the humans and the felines present heard her concern for Ruby in her voice as well. "Peace on all who seek their way and their art," she concluded, before the circle was opened once again.

"Speaking of peace, how are your cats doing?" Ande reached for the tea. "Are they still wreaking havoc?"

"No." Becca peered over at Laurel, who lay stretched out on the sofa's back. "I think they've gotten used to my schedule."

"Maybe they knew something was up with your neighbor," offered Marcia, who was pretty openly sneaking pieces of a butter cookie to Harriet. "Cats can be sensitive to these things. Maybe more sensitive than we are. Speaking of," she broke another cookie against the plate, "I still don't understand how you found the ruby."

"I'm not sure I can explain." Becca sipped her tea. "I'd like to say it's because my cats were paying special attention to the case. Laurel, in particular, had grown fond of lying in it when it was open. I guess it's a good thing that Ruby isn't allergic. And sometimes, I swear, Clara looks at me like she's worried I'm going to run off without her or get in trouble."

Clara, who had been seated at Becca's feet, rose in alarm, turning toward Laurel, who had perked up at the sound of her own name and now perched sphynx-like on the sofa's spine.

"But in truth, I think it was just process of elimination," said Becca, reaching to stroke the calico cat at her feet. "Good old logic, and not magic at all." Behind her back, Laurel winked, as, beneath the table, Harriet began to purr.

Acknowledgments

I began writing this book before the pandemic shut everything down and decided to continue with it set in the open world we once knew. This is, after all, a cozy, and it's good to remember when we could circulate and gather without fear. However, the restrictions and unrest and general horror of this year have made me appreciate my friends, readers, and supporters all the more. You are too many to list here, but shoutouts to Karen Schlosberg, Brett Milano, Marlene Silva, Chris Mesarch, Erin Mitchell, Caroline Leavitt, Vicki Croke, Ted Drozdowski, Laurie Hoffma, Alan Brickman, Colleen Mohyde, Betsy Pollock, Frank Garelick, Lisa Jones, and Jennifer Ellwood, and with great love to the memory of my dear mother-in-law, Sophie Garelick. A big virtual hug to my book world buddies Dru Ann Love, Lesa Holstine, Joanna Schaffhausen, and Julie Hennrikus, among so many others—including Jason Pinter, of course, who gives the witch cats wings. Finally, Jon Garelick, who has kept me more or less sane: thank you, love. I can't imagine a better reader or anyone I'd rather quarantine with. I hope to see all of you again soon!

About the Author

A former journalist and music critic, Clea Simon wrote three nonfiction books, including the Boston Globe bestseller *Th e Fe line Mystique*, before turning to a life of crime (fiction). Her more than two dozen mysteries usually involve cats or rock and roll, or some combination thereof, including *A Spell of Murder* and *An Incantation of Cats*, the first two Witch Cats of Cambridge mysteries.

A native of New York, she moved to Massachusetts to attend Harvard and now lives nearby in Somerville. Visit her at www.CleaSimon.com or at @Clea_Simon.